THE WEEKEND

L. H. STACEY

Boldwood

First published in Great Britain in 2022 by Boldwood Books Ltd. This paperback edition first published in 2023.

I

Cover Design by 12 Orchards Ltd.

Cover Photography: Shutterstock

A CIP catalogue record for this book is available from the British Library.

Paperback ISBN: 978-1-83518-809-5

Hardback ISBN: 978-1-80162-597-5

Ebook ISBN: 978-1-80162-600-2

Kindle ISBN: 978-1-80162-601-9

Audio CD ISBN: 978-1-80162-592-0

MP3 CD ISBN: 978-1-80162-593-7

Digital audio download ISBN: 978-1-80162-596-8

Large Print ISBN: 978-1-80162-599-9

Boldwood Books Ltd.

23 Bowerdean Street, London, SW6 3TN

www.boldwoodbooks.com

For Aunty Kay, my godmother.
You've always been there, looking out for me and steering me in
the right direction.
Thank you x

PROLOGUE
LIZZIE

Ten Years Before

As I look up, I notice just one or two tiny stars. They're shining at me like diamonds, poking through a grey and overcast sky. One where clouds float erratically across the moon, giving the sky an eeriness all of its own.

Staring intently, I realise that the sporadic sound of music can still be heard from within the grand hall of Kirkwood Manor and that the double doors have been flung wide open to allow the air to circulate around large, stuffy rooms.

Spotting the vocalist, I watch the way he walks to the doors and pokes his head through them in a meagre attempt to gauge how many are actually listening. Turning to the other two musicians, a keyboard player, and a guitarist, he seems to begin a debate. One about whether they should continue or whether they should pack up their instruments and call it a night. ... after a few whispered words, the odd nod, and a smile, they continue to play, even though the house has now emptied of over a hundred or so inebriated people. Most of whom had recently graduated and in a last flourish, had spilled out and into the grounds or dissipated into the night with only the left-over litter, the empty bottles of both wine and champagne that had been left scattered all over the grounds, the last reminder that they'd been there at all. Whereas, my few remaining friends had begun a number of sordid, hedonistic parties. None of which looked as though they'd be ending any time soon.

Smiling, and imperiously, I swim though putrid smelling water, until I'm central to the lake. The chill of it has seeped deep into my naked body and through dazed, intoxicated eyes I try to focus on the fire baskets that are scattered around the gardens. I watch the sparks that shoot wildly upwards in colours of bright orange and red and I stare at the musicians through the inferno of fire, all the time imagining their music bouncing across the water towards me like huge, animated characters, and in my mind's eye they've taken on the form of quavers and crochets. Inflated like the biggest of helium balloons. All different in size. And while laughing at how ridiculous it all seems, I take wide eyed pleasure in the eerie reflections of an overhanging willow tree which reaches out and over the lake. It has long, spindly branches that droop downward, until they dip themselves into the water, in a place where the leaves keep falling, to create a dangerous and boggy edge to the lake.

'Thomas... where are you?' I shout as loud as I can. I can't understand where he's gone, why he doesn't answer, or why I'm alone. But quickly, I disregard the thought, throw my head backwards euphorically and immediately I feel the coldness of the water against my scalp, only to feel something flutter past me. It makes me jump nervously and with my mind in overdrive, I desperately try to imagine what it might have been. I try to remember what fish I've seen in the past, as opposed to the more dangerous ones I've heard the boys constantly joke about.

'Watch out for the bottom-biting pike.' Henry had once joked, 'You don't want him grabbing your arse, now do you?'

The thoughts flash repeatedly through my mind, as the bright, well-strung tree lights that were scattered around the garden's perimeter suddenly begin to dim. It's as though they're being switched off in a strict rotational order and as I watch it happen, a deep sadness overtakes my thoughts. The lights had been pretty, and although it was still the middle of summer, it was now past midnight and since darkness fell, they'd been blinking repeatedly, giving the whole garden a look of Christmas and now I can't do anything but watch despairingly while all the time using my arms and legs against the water to spin myself around, as one string after the other goes dim and then dark.

Sighing, I battle with the pond weed that's begun to tangle itself around my ankle. Deciding that it's time I got out of the water, I kick it away and move tentatively towards the embankment, all the time using the house as a bearing I slide my feet against the thick silt that covers the bottom of the lake. It's a feeling I don't like, and I worry about what I'll stand on. What lies deep beneath the surface? I think back, remember all the things that had been carelessly tossed into the water over the summer. All the things we purposely wanted to lose.

Holding out cautious fingers, I reach for the old wooden diving platform, but quickly turn away as I spot partially naked bodies lying between the reeds. They're illuminated by the fire baskets, prone, all curled up together in a tangled mass of arms and legs and I try to decipher who is who. Certain parts of the lake are gloomier than others, and most of the couples have moved into the well-known shadows. Their bodies are masked by overgrown plants and weeds and the only other real movement I can make out is that of another couple, scrambling around on hands and knees, and I surmise they're looking for their clothes, the ones they'd recklessly abandoned earlier.

'Thomas, where the hell are you?' I shout his name and once again, I listen for a response that doesn't come. 'Thomas, this isn't funny any more. You're scaring me.' My voice doesn't sound like my own and the overwhelming internal glow that had been radiating within me has begun to diminish. And like Thomas, the feeling of being free and unrestrained has disappeared.

Grabbing at the rushes and sedges that grow around the lake, I use them to pull myself towards the deep furrows we'd carved into the embankment. It had been a teenage attempt to create a set of steps. A transitory foothold. One we knew wouldn't last, but for as long as they did, they'd become a simple way of climbing in and out of the water during one or more of our many follies.

Standing close to the edge, I turn in circles, and squint in a frugal attempt to focus on the darkness. Slowly, as I hear familiar voices, I begin to search one side of the lake at a time. I'm fully expecting Thomas to leap out from behind one of the overgrown bushes or to be wandering down from the house, his arms full of champagne and a wicker basket full to the brim of warm, floury bread or left-over buffet.

While listening and searching, I spot the familiar shape of Lucy. She's a young, naked woman who's creeping around on her tiptoes along the embankment, her arm held protectively across her breasts. Until she notices me watching and with a look of mischief, she sweeps a hand through her hair, which she tosses seductively over her shoulder before standing upright, with a hand on each hip.

'Lucy,' I shout, 'have you seen Thomas? I... well, I seem to have lost him.' I try to ignore her nudity and allow my lip to protrude like that of a petulant child and in my temper, I fall forward and into the water. I kick my feet out behind me, float towards her, and watch the puzzlement on her face as Lucy scans the lake behind me.

'Darling, isn't he with you?' Her upper-class voice carries across the water, and nonchalantly, she shrugs her shoulders, 'He's always with you. Isn't he?' She pauses, laughs. 'What's more darling, with the noise you two were making earlier, I'd have thought he'd be permanently attached to you for the next two weeks.' Lucy's voice quivers as she shouts. She's obviously cold. Shivering. Which isn't surprising after a whole group of us had spontaneously jumped into the water right after midnight in another rapacious, and uninhibited sex session. That along with the added influence of drink and drugs had caused us all to have a feeling of licentiousness and a wild abandonment that had lasted for hours.

'My clothes have gone... vamoose... disappeared.' Lucy begins to crawl on her hands and knees until she reaches the edge of the water, where what looks like a giant rhubarb plant blocks her way. Reaching underneath, she pulls out an old, damp shirt, gives it a suspicious sniff and annoyed she points a finger, wand-like at the floor. 'My dress, the red one. I left it here and it should still be here.' Pulling the damp shirt over her shoulders, she turns back to the lake.

'Where's Jessica?' I shout. I look for her partner and wonder if like Thomas, she's disappeared too and what the chances are of them being together.

'Oh, I don't know.' Her pointed finger aims at the house. 'I think she went to get food, oh... and champagne. We'd run out of champagne. All this sex, it makes you hungry darling, doesn't it?' Spinning on the spot, she lifts her face to the moonlight and for a moment, I appreciate the shape of her perfect body, and the way the shirt now drapes over her pert, naked breasts. 'And when you find Thomas, ask him what he did with our clothes. It'd be just like him to be buggering about, hiding them from us.' She laughs and seductively runs her tongue over her lips, 'He probably thinks we'll end up walking back to the house, naked. Give old man Kirkwood an eye full. But personally, I doubt his ticker would take it.' Her words were swallowed in a gasp, as flood lights suddenly illuminate her pale, ivory skin tone against the darkness of the embankment. It's as though the house has come back to life, and quickly, she buttons the wet, clinging shirt before continuing her search for the lost and discarded dress.

Laying back, I scull at the water. Disappointment sweeps over me, and I wonder if Thomas has gone back to the house, whether he's trying to surprise me and collecting the bags ready for our escape. It's a thought that makes my mind dance in time with the music. I'm swaying dreamily at the thought of our being together and that at this time tomorrow, it'll be just the two of us.

With a delighted squeal, I look up, hold my breath, feel myself squinting at stars that seem much brighter. They've now fought their way through the clouds and are so intense, I can barely look at them. Then unexpectedly, a rush of colour begins to speed its way towards me and while changing both colour and shape, I watch the auras as they explode dramatically before my eyes. It's my very own firework display, one that makes me giggle relentlessly. It's one hallucination too many and even though I'm having a ball, I know it's time I got out of the water. Sighing, I move slowly to the side, excitedly decide that I want to dance and for a moment, I imagine myself doing pirouettes all the way around the lake, like the ballerina I could have been.

I close my eyes, allow my hands to sensuously travel across my body, across my stomach where they hover hopefully. I can still feel Thomas's touch. His passion. And I lean my head against the slope of the embankment, lift my feet and allow myself to drift aimlessly into the darkness for far too long.

Suddenly, the silence is too much, and panic overtakes my mind as a strange yowling noise cuts through the air. It's coming from the other side of the lake. And quickly, I spin in the water, until I'm sitting on the embankment where I wait and stare at the low hanging willow tree. I'm sure I can see shadows beneath it. And with my mind spinning, I try to work out if the sound I heard was a fox screaming into the night. But something tells me it wasn't, and I try to work out what else would make such a loud, guttural, and unfamiliar noise. Holding my breath, my heart begins to pound wildly. A million scenarios flick through my mind, and I watch each of them fly off, and like a flickering cinematic movie, each picture begins to race around the water's edge, and I feel as though I'm sitting central to a fairground ride, watching the pictures rotate around me.

Glancing back, I look for Lucy. I hope she's followed me. That Jessica has returned, or that one of the others heard the noise too. But when no one seems to move, I slide my feet back through the silt, edge myself closer and closer to the willow. I feel my heart skip a beat and I jump backwards as a movement catches my eye. I hear a bang. I hold my breath and watch a sporadic flurry of sparks that erupt dramatically from a nearby fire basket.

'Who's there?' Nervously, I tip my head to one side, wishing for the garden lights to come back on, for Lucy to return. For Thomas to be with me.

With the sparks from the basket still blurring my sight, I feel a violent shivering overtake me. Covering my face, I begin to rub at my eyes, in the hope that my vision clears and unwittingly, I begin to swim, slowly towards the noise.

'Lucy... did you see that?' Again, I search the embankment as I wait for a response. I soon realise that Lucy has gone. And even though one or two of the others are still entwined on the edge of the lake, there's no noise coming from them. It's more than probable they've slipped into a drug-induced sleep and the silence that surrounds me is now more than deafening. It's only now that I realise that the band has stopped playing, that the only sound that now penetrates my mind is that of the water perpetually moving around me.

'Thomas, is that you?' I know I should climb out of the water, go back to the house. But instead, I robotically move toward the willow tree. It arcs towards me, like a tumbling, oversized umbrella that I can barely see through. Reaching up. I pull on its branches. Use them to elevate my head out of the water and as I do, I think I hear the sound of footsteps. And once again, I look over my shoulder, hoping that at least one of my friends is looking out for me. But as normal, I'm alone.

'Thomas. Stop it. You're frightening me.' I put a hand to my bare chest. I feel how heavily my heart is pounding and purposely, I take in a deep breath in an attempt to slow it down. 'Thomas...' Reaching forward, I try to climb out of the water, feeling nothing but slime and blanket weed as it slips through my fingers, making me fall backwards, where I slip beneath the surface and aimlessly, I hover in a hypnotic state. And only when I feel the need to breathe, do I push myself upwards, and grasp frantically at the air. But in doing so, I swallow the water. The taste of algae hits the back of my throat, making me gag and spit, while all the time thrusting my arm in an outward direction. It's all I can do to sweep the pondweed away from my face and with a newfound effort, I make a grab for the branches of the willow, once again use them to pull myself up and free myself of the water... and immediately find myself staring into a pair of cold, transparent, and lifeless eyes.

'Thomas...?' Disbelieving, I launch myself towards him. Grab hold of his shoulders. Shake him violently, and then scream as his battered, blood covered face disappears beneath the quagmire of leaves, until eventually I can't see him at all.

1

ELIZABETH

Present Day - Friday Evening

Squinting at the dashboard clock, Elizabeth Dewhurst nervously ran a hand through her long, blonde hair, all the time trying to estimate how long the rest of her journey would take and what would be waiting for her once she got there. With at least five miles left to go, she was most probably going to be late. Something she really hadn't wanted, especially when Kirkwood Manor had been the last place on Earth she'd ever thought she'd return to. It had been a promise she'd made herself the last time she'd been here. But when Ada Kirkwood's invitation had dropped through her door, she'd seen the gold gilded card as a formal, veritable summons, with no easy option of turning it down.

Ada Kirkwood formerly requests the presence of:
 Elizabeth Dewhurst
 For the 10-year memorial of her son,

Thomas Kirkwood

Unable to bring herself to throw it in the bin, she'd simply tossed it to one side, left it on her dressing table, and did all she could to ignore it. But like a beacon, it had beckoned her. Invited her to pick it up, to turn it over, and over in her hand. Hoping for answers. And eventually, she'd picked it up once too often. Couldn't ignore it any longer. Knew that the only way she'd ever stop grieving for the life she'd wanted, for what she might have had, was to go back. To make her peace with the Manor and the people who still lived in it.

Especially as it had also been the first time she'd ever been officially invited. Even at Thomas's funeral, she'd simply turned up, stood in line, and listened to the million and one ways someone could express their sorrow. Which was why, ten years after his death, she'd found herself climbing into her car and heading for the Manor.

Pulling the visor down as low as she could, Elizabeth sat forward and upright. The sun was unusually low for the time of year, and even though she wore sunglasses to protect her eyes, she still found herself squinting at burgundy clouds that were streaked with colours of orange and gold, making it almost impossible to see the long, winding lane that stretched out ahead.

Ironically, they were lanes she used to know well, lanes she'd driven along a hundred times before. But also ones she'd never thought she'd travel down again and with her mind going into automatic pilot, she glided along in a hypnotic state, only broken by the bleep of her mobile.

Hope you're okay. House is quiet without you. xx

Smiling, she slowed the car to a stop, couldn't resist responding to her father, who for the first time in years, had the house to himself for four whole days.

I'm almost there. Don't worry. xx ps: Aunt Peggy will look in on you. Phone if you need me. I'll be home Tuesday x

Watching the dots immediately pulsate across the screen, she knew a response would come straight back and while smiling tenderly at the screen, she kept her foot on the brake, wound down the window, and took in a deep breath of fresh country air.

I can't say I'm happy about you going. Can't help but think that house is cursed 😕. But stay safe. I'll see you Tuesday x

Blowing a kiss at the phone, she wished she'd stayed at home, taken him down to the local for their Friday night ritual of fish and chips, followed by a pub quiz, surrounded by friends. Flicking at the screen, she sent her response.

Please don't worry. I'm fine xx love you loads xx

He wasn't normally so protective, didn't normally mind what she did. But she knew how unhappy he'd been at the thought of her going back to the Manor, especially after what had happened before.

'I know you love him, my girl,' he'd once said to her, 'But I really don't like him and mark my words, no good will come of you mixing with his sort.'

Her father had always been a straight talker, had always had her best interests at heart, especially after her mother had died, and for many years, it had been down to him to make sure she'd got to school, that her homework had been done, and that he earned enough money to put food on the table. And now, ten years later, she wished she'd have listened to his good advice. Especially after working out just how cruel Thomas Kirkwood could be.

Sighing, she looked through the window and took pleasure in the way the countryside always felt a little different, how the fields went on for miles. A clear reminder of her time at the Manor, a place she'd initially seen as a peaceful sanctuary, a peace that had quickly been broken the moment their friends had arrived.

Then, as though someone had picked her up and thrown her back in time, she could vividly see the police, the funeral, followed by numerous images of Thomas slipping beneath the water, along with a dark and oppressive eeriness that crept into her mind at times she didn't expect it.

Gasping, she realised how long it had been since she'd suffered from flashbacks, how bad they'd been during the days following Thomas's death. They'd been the days when she'd vowed she'd never return to Kirkwood Manor. A promise she'd made to both herself and to her father. A promise she'd always intended to keep. That was until the invitation had dropped through the door and her sudden desire to return had been more than overwhelming.

Manoeuvring the car along the lane, she felt the intermittent waves of nausea begin to rise and fall, along with a sharp spasm of nerves that hit her like a thunderbolt. Without warning, she felt the acrid taste of acid sear the back of her throat as she turned into the last road that stood between herself and the Manor.

Taking deep, inward breaths, she did all she could to calm herself down. A little over enthusiastically her foot hit the brakes and painfully, she felt the seatbelt tighten around her. It pulled against her shoulder, constricted her breathing, and suddenly, it was as though she was back in the lake, but this time it was her that was sinking beneath the surface, drowning. Grabbing at breath.

Looking down, she realised how forcefully her fingers had twisted themselves tighter and tighter around the car's leather steering wheel, until they'd gone white with the pressure. Forcibly, she counted to ten, prised her fingers from the wheel, and with annoyance, she rubbed them down her pale denim, ripped up jeans while fretfully looking through the windscreen, forcing herself to breathe.

Taking a moment for herself, she lifted her gaze, stared at the tarmac, and followed the edge of the driveway as it coiled into the distance. Feeling as though she were concentrating just a little too hard, Elizabeth realised she could have literally counted each and every pebble. Each stone looking as though it had been positioned just for effect, nothing like the ramshackle way it all used to be. Taking in a deep breath, she slowly lifted her eyes upwards to see Kirkwood Manor magically emerge.

'You're different,' she whispered. It was a feeble attempt at making peace with the house. A way of bridging the gap between then and now. 'I know I left. But I had to. I... I couldn't stay.' She paused, questioned her thoughts, felt almost too afraid to say the words out loud. 'And if I'm honest,' she glanced at her phone, could still see her father's words, the worry he felt. 'I made him a promise I thought I'd keep. I shouldn't be here.' She slumped back in her seat, staring up at the house, and with a determined effort, she pushed the car into gear and held her breath as it inched closer to the cast iron gates, where right beside them stood the new hotel signage. It was a sign that didn't belong. Not in her opinion. Not outside this house. Not ever.

'Kirkwood Manor. Luxury Country Hotel.' She whispered the words. Closed her eyes for a beat, tried to picture how the house used to be. How old and practically derelict it had looked. And above all that, how homely it had felt. With a half-smile, through rose-tinted spectacles, and while driving along it, she could still see the pot-holed driveway, the keepers' cottages, the broken stained-glass windows, and the way Thomas's father, Dominic Kirkwood, had reluctantly boarded them up after each and every golf ball had gone severely off course. Smiling, Elizabeth could still hear all manner of swear words comically falling from his mouth, each one a true English profanity, all shouted at a time when he'd been attached to a ladder, like a giant limpet. Desperate to hang on.

Moving uncomfortably in her seat, she slowed the car, felt a sense of unease. Looking at the way it was now, everything had changed. It was as though its history had been permanently eradicated, cleaned up, and wiped out. Even the stone jamb and mullion windows had been newly pointed. The stone scrubbed clean. Perfect, stained-glass panes sparkled within the large, multi-panelled window frames, with not a single board in sight. It was a sight that made her both happy and sad in equal measures, and now she wished for the way it used to be. Her mind wandered along dark and eerie corridors which led to each of the rooms, where old Victorian furniture had stood lining the walls, along with the attic space, where she'd often gone to escape the crowd. A place where shadows had lurked in every corner, giving the whole house a ghostly and haunted feel.

Jumping out of the car, she closed the door firmly behind her, and for a moment she looked down, stared at the newly laid gravel beneath her feet, and felt the need to bide her time. To take a breath before looking up and seeing the lake where she'd been told that a monument now stood. It was a monument she didn't really want to see; she couldn't bear the thought of reading the words. With a hand shielding her eyes from the stormy looking sky, she winced and looked back towards the Manor through painful, narrowed eyes.

So many memories had begun and ended here and desperately, she tried to conjure up the good ones. But seemingly only the bad ones remained. And for a moment, all she could see were the images she wanted to erase from her mind and extinguish forever.

Desperately, she tried to forget the past, forced her eyes wide open, and cast them intentionally over her shoulder to squint at the lake. Gasping, she held a hand to her brow, shielded her eyes from the light and watched the bright, reflective ripples bounce across the water's surface, until they reached the other side, where a newly erected monument to Thomas Kirkwood now stood.

2

WILLIAM

Present Day - Friday Evening

Standing by the kitchen window, William Kirkwood repeatedly slid his knife up and down the steel. Took pleasure in the sound of metal against metal as it sharpened, and with a calculated half smile, he lifted the blade, turned it from side to side and watched it glint back at him as the early evening sunlight reflected against it through the window.

'Can't remember sharpening knives like that in my time.' The former housekeeper, Mrs McCulloch, was sat at the kitchen counter, happily chopping mint on a board. 'What do you say, Bobby. Can you remember me doing that?' She looked across at where the gardener stood, just inside the doorway of the kitchen. A place he'd stood drinking tea two or three times a day for the past thirty years.

'Not a chance.' Bobby laughed and gave her a playful wink. 'But you don't think they all sharpened themselves, do you? If you hadn't gone and retired, I'd still be sneaking them back to my garage and sharpening them all for you.' Pushing his empty mug along the worktop, he tipped his flat cap. Took a step outside and pushed his feet back into mud covered wellingtons. 'Right. I'll get back to work.'

'I feel as though I've always watched you chop mint.' William kept his eye on the spit, where a whole lamb had been roasting for a good few hours. 'It's a memory I'll always have.'

'So it should be. I used to give you mint with all the meats,' she responded, 'You kids, you wouldn't eat your dinner without it.' It was true: chopping the mint was something she'd always done. And even though she'd now retired, it was something she still considered to be her job, each and every time she dropped into the kitchen.

'Oh Cookie, you did look after us, didn't you?' Using their pet name for her, William gave her a genuine, loving smile. 'I remember you sitting in that exact spot. Making our sauce. But I never knew old Bobby was sneaking off to sharpen your knives, without you even knowing.' Leaning back on the counter, William crossed his arms. Felt proud that she'd headed straight for the kitchen, giving them some time together, rather than joining in with other guests, who were now sat in the grand hall, drinking the family champagne.

'Well, if he thinks I didn't know, he's kidding himself.' She winked, cast her gaze around the room, pushed her spectacles further up her nose, sniffed for effect. 'And I didn't sit in exactly this spot. My table was closer to the window. Right over there.' She pointed. Pulled at her long, tweed skirt, shuffled in her seat, and lay her knife down on the chopping board. Rummaged around in her bag for a tissue. 'I used to love my kitchen; it was always warm. Always welcoming and my old range, it made the best bread you ever tasted, it did.' She wiped her eyes, pointed to the place where the shiny new cooker stood, with its numerous zones on top that gave William more than enough space to juggle multiple dishes, all at once.

'Oh, Cookie. You cursed it every time it wouldn't light. I clearly remember the oven door being slammed. The pans being dropped on top, the bang they used to make.' Walking across the kitchen, William put his arms around her, pulled her into a hug. 'And even with all those memories, I still miss you being in the kitchen, telling me off.' He gave her a cheeky smile, stepped away. 'I'd love it if you'd come to the Manor more often; maybe I could convince you to move into one of the estate cottages.'

With a wry smile, she stood up, washed her hands, then returned to the chopping board, where she picked up the knife, waved it around in the air. 'Oh. I live close enough. I'm only a couple of miles away, but I have to admit, I miss being here too. Although, I don't miss scrubbing these floors.' She rubbed at her knees. 'Don't think my old knees would take it now.'

'Get away with you. You're not that old.' He threw her the compliment as a loud bang outside caught his attention. 'What the hell?' It was a sound that made him take a step closer to the stone and mullion windows, where he rested a hand on the ledge.

Studying the kitchen gardens, he looked around, tried to work out where the noise had come from. Saw Bobby's wheelbarrow lying on its side, the front wheel old and wonky, with Bobby crawling around on his hands and knees, angrily shaking his head, picking up the multiple plastic flowerpots that had fallen out.

Proudly, William gazed across at the rows upon rows of freshly grown fruit, the vegetables, and edible flowers that with Bobby's help, he'd planted. Together, they'd made a plan: a rotating seasonal menu, where home-grown produce had been specifically grown to complement each of the meals he cooked in this kitchen. And now, looking out, he knew his decision to become a chef had been a good one. Even though travelling to London and staying away from home hadn't gone down too well with his mother.

But in London, he'd come to life and learned a trade. And only after his father had died, following a fall from a set of step ladders he should have never been climbing, had William reluctantly returning to find that surprisingly he'd inherited the entire Manor. A dinosaur of a building that lost money by the minute and a project he hadn't really known what to do with. Eventually, and with a business plan in mind, he'd refurbished the property, turned it into the hotel it was now, and by doing so, he'd saved the family from bankruptcy, along with all the shame and another scandal, which would have been the last thing the family needed, especially after Thomas's death.

Keeping his attention on what was happening outside. He watched his assistant, Anna, who was taking slow, deliberate footsteps through the old Victorian glasshouse. It was the only part of the house he had left to restore and he didn't like anyone walking through it. Made a mental note to ask her not to do it again. Not at least until the rest of the restoration could be safely completed.

Reaching up, William watched as Anna pulled fruit from the vines. Each piece was carefully taken and placed in her basket which was already bulging with baby courgettes, shallots, new potatoes, and at Mrs McCulloch's request, even more of their freshly grown mint.

'You're learning...' The comment had been intended as much for himself as it were for Anna. A comment that made him smile, knowing that each of the vegetables were perfect to roast and, appreciative of how fresh they'd taste, he'd decided that a ratatouille with crushed new potatoes would be the perfect complement to the lamb.

Looking across the room, he caught sight of the six security screens that were attached to the wall. It was an old system he'd bought second hand in a cost saving exercise. But liked the peace of mind it gave him, along with the way he could see everything going on outside, all at once.

But today he felt himself bristle as one after the other, familiar faces from his past had arrived in force. Taking in a deep breath, he clenched his jaw as he watched each of the guests hug and kiss his mother with the love and affection she deserved. After all, she'd been the one who'd given them all a place to be during their early vicenarian years, welcomed them all repeatedly, just because Thomas had wanted her to. Even though the family could barely afford his lavish and outlandish expectations.

Rubbing his hands down his chef's whites, William rolled his jaw, as angrily he remembered the way he'd resented his brother. How fuelled with fury he'd been that Thomas would inherit the Manor along with the estate cottages that stood in the grounds. And with another look through the window, William tried to imagine how life would have been if Thomas had lived. Whether or not the house would have been sold. Or demolished to build a housing estate, a devastating action that would have meant that men like Bobby would have lost their homes, only to line Thomas's greedy pockets.

But with Thomas's death, everything had changed. William now owned it all and the last people he'd ever wanted to see or entertain here were his dead brother's so-called-friends. Not now. Not ever. Yet, at one of his mother's many bequests, here they all were. And he had a sudden urge to wipe the smug, self-centred looks from all their faces, as he watched them passing their over-sized luggage to the young concierge before making their way into the grand hall, where he knew they'd be taking full advantage of the free food and wine. Just as they had as twenty-year olds.

In an attempt to change his mood, he walked around the kitchen, tapped the knife decisively against the palm of his hand.

Gave a half-smile at his reflection in the shiny stainless-steel pans, worktops, and backplates. 'It is a little different, isn't it?' He directed the question at Cookie, who'd stopped chopping the mint and had made her way to stare wistfully out of the window. Raising a hand, she made a show of waving to Bobby, as her shoulders moved up and down, in rhythm. A clear sign that coming back here for a memorial had been harder for her than she'd have ever admitted.

'I think I'll pop outside.' She eventually said, 'Bobby looks like he could use a cold drink.' She pulled open the fridge, poured a glass of fresh lemonade from a jug, and visibly swallowed as she turned to the door, pulled it open.

Sighing, William closed his eyes. It was good that she was here and with a thousand memories flashing through his mind at once, he thought back to the days when it had been her kitchen, with its polished Victorian tiles, and the large wooden table that had stood in the middle. A table where he used to sit, for so many hours, learning to cook. A kitchen he'd loved and the only room in the whole house that had actually felt like a home.

And now he'd seen how difficult being here had been for her, he wished he'd kept the kitchen how it had been, rather than replacing it with the new and modern alternative.

Leaving Cookie and Bobby to catch up, William paced back and forth, his eyes constantly on the screens and without knowing why, he felt his heart accelerate as Lizzie's car pulled through the gates. He couldn't work out if he felt happy or sad to see her. She'd been the only one of Thomas's friends he'd actually liked. The only one who'd ever been kind and he found himself tipping his head to one side and carefully studying the way she now looked.

Holding his breath in anticipation, he watched her jump from the car, where nervously but defiantly she held a hand up to her eyes and gave her attention to the lake. To the memorial that stood there. And even though she still looked as beautiful now as she had back then, she still stared at the house with eyes so wide, so very fearful that she reminded him of a startled rabbit, caught in the headlights. It was a look he'd seen before. One he'd never managed to forget.

3

WILLIAM

Ten years before

With pain exploding in his knees, William rolled onto the cellar floor and suppressed a scream. He closed his eyes as tightly as he could as the cellar door slammed to a close behind him. Once again, he realised that for the second time that week, he'd become a prisoner and that whether he liked it or not, it was going to be a long, cold night.

Catching his breath, he groaned, pushed himself up, tried to get his bearings. Then cautiously and with one hand on the wall, he used it for support, and tentatively put weight on one leg first, and then on the other. His normal smile was gone and in its place was an angry, twisted sneer. Limping, he gritted his teeth, and began to slide his feet gingerly across the floor as he made his way across the dark and over filled cellar. He knew that at any moment he could collide with a Christmas tree or a rack of wine. Or worse, he could fall into the fuel store, which in winter would be full of coal. But now, in the middle of summer, it was practically empty. An expensive luxury the family could live without. Leaving a deep and dangerous void that in the dark would be perilous if fallen into.

Shivering, William crouched down. Curled his arms tightly around his seventeen-year-old self and shuffled, slowly, to navigate his way through the gauntlet until he found a warm, dry area of the cellar. Every movement was calculated. Every inch of floor a possible hazard, during which he fully expected something to fall, or to land on or around him, knowing that once one thing had moved, the whole cellar was likely to collapse, like a giant deck of cards, all stood on their ends, all ready to topple, all at once.

Staring, he focused on the tiny strip of light that surrounded the badly fitting door. It was his only indication as to whether it were night or day. And with deep inward breaths, he felt a new and more powerful rage tear right through him. A scream that began in his toes and travelled upwards with force. But before it could burst out of his mouth, he decided that screaming was not the way forward and instead, he needed to devise a plan, a way of making Thomas pay. Once and for all.

With his eyes adjusting to the light, William realised that he'd been in the cellar more times than he could remember. First, it had been just one of the punishments handed out by his so-called-father and recently, something his older brother Thomas had begun to copy. Especially on nights like tonight, when all the friends Thomas had begun university with were at the Manor. Drink and drugs were free flowing and the beautiful women were everywhere. All of them wanted to grab themselves a Kirkwood and with Thomas's controlling ways, getting William out of his way was always high on his agenda.

'I don't want you round these kinds of women, they're only out for one thing and that's to trap you into a lifetime of misery... into you getting them pregnant, marrying them. And this family doesn't need a scandal. Mother would be furious. Don't you get that?' Thomas had shouted just moments after catching William kissing one of the house maids. 'And what's more, I don't want you getting pissed, not at your age.'

'I'm almost eighteen, you can't tell me what to do.' William had thrown back, 'And if I want to get pissed, I will.'

'Not if I have anything to do with it...' had come the retort, before Thomas and his friends had ironically thrown William into the cellar which was a prison full of alcohol, where box upon box of Champagne stood next to racks of wine and spirits. The amount of alcohol down there had always surprised him, seeing as the family had barely a penny left at the end of each year and yet for some reason his father wouldn't allow the cellar to run dry and more often than not sold items of furniture, in order that he might replenish his stocks.

Leaning against the wall, William rested a hand against a box of champagne. Considered opening it and drinking the contents, just to prove a point. But instead, he took slow, deep breaths. Tried to ignore the chill that surrounded him, the sound of small rodents he could hear scurrying around in the far and distant corners.

'William...' The soft, whisper cut through his thoughts and into his dream. And for a short second or two, he shook his head, and gave himself a satisfied smile before remembering where he was and what Thomas had done. 'William, are you in there?' Once again, the voice echoed softly through the cellar.

Stirring, William yawned, sat up and listened intently. He tried to decipher what he'd heard. Then, for a third time he heard Lizzie's voice, as it sang out almost musically in the darkness, like a soft, calm melody coming over a radio. 'William... it's me, it's Lizzie.'

'I... I'm here...' He knelt up and winced at the pain that

remained in his knees, and through narrowed eyes he stared at the light behind the door, hoped for it to open, for Lizzie to be stood there. 'Lizzie, don't let him catch you...' he yelled as loudly as he could. And with eyes that searched the darkness, he prayed for release. Knew how much trouble Lizzie would be in if his brother knew she'd helped him. Deep inside, he wanted to shout, to tell her to go, to keep herself safe. But selfishly, he listened, waited, hoped she'd hurry. He stood with his back to the door, listened to her footsteps, the rattling of a chain that was followed by a loud bang, as what sounded like a lock was lifted and dropped. Each rattle was followed by another of Lizzie's exasperated sighs, a signal to him that his release wasn't going to happen anytime soon.

'William, I can't do it. It's... God damn him, he's put a really heavy bar across the door and... well, there's a chain and a padlock.' Sighing she stamped her foot. 'Do you think it would make a loud noise if I hit it. Just once with a hammer. I... I could get a mallet from Cookie's kitchen?'

'Lizzie, don't. I've made a bed down here. Seriously... it's really comfortable. I'm fine.' He lied, 'Go back to bed.' Knuckle rubbing his eyes, he felt the moisture within, grew angry inside and not because he was hurt, but because Lizzie was being kind. She was trying to help him when no one else would, putting herself at risk. Determined not to show any emotion, he bit down on his lip. 'He always does this. So, I threw a sleeping bag down here earlier today. It's really comfortable, honest.' Pausing, he considered his words, didn't like to lie, wanted to finish on a truth. 'And besides, he'll let me out before breakfast, before mother finds out, you know he will.'

Hearing Lizzie's feet shuffling across the stone floor and her voice drifting away, William resigned himself to a long, cold night and slunk back down the wall until he sat leaning against it. He felt both frustrated and humiliated. And now he'd said it, he realised that maybe he really should have thrown a sleeping bag into the cellar, but on second thoughts, he knew how many mice were down there. How many would make it their home before he did. His thoughts fuelled his anger, and while sitting there wishing for the night to end, he considered revenge. Tried to imagine a way where for just one night Thomas would sleep in a place like this, feel the humiliation, along with the pain he happily bestowed on others.

Then, at the far side of the cellar, a loud grating noise caught his attention. The sound of metal upon metal, until moonlight filled the cellar and he saw Lizzie peering at him through the fuel chute with eyes as big as saucers, her fear more than obvious.

'I knew there was a way in and out of this damn cellar and just so you know, I would have come sooner. But your brother is furious and made it very clear that no one should help you.' She paused, nervously looked over her shoulder. Pushed her head further through the hole. 'So, I had to wait until he fell to sleep.' She stared through the darkness, 'And I thought you said you had a sleeping bag.' She pushed her head through the hole, tried to look around the corners. 'Where is it?'

'Lizzie, listen to me.' He took in a deep breath, held her gaze. 'I'm fine.' Looking down, he scratched at the floor with his boot. 'And you, you need to go back to bed before Thomas realises you're missing.'

'But...'

'No buts... now please.' Giving her a half smile, he fixed his eyes on hers. 'Go back to bed, Lizzie. Trust me, it's for the best.'

'You... you could climb out this way.' She peered over the edge of the hole, saw the drop beneath. 'Or maybe not.'

Despondently, he took a step backwards, wanted nothing more than for Lizzie to go, to be safe and to be warm in her bed. Even if he hated the fact that her bed was the one she shared with his brother. 'Lizzie, I won't forget this.' He held her gaze for a moment too long, wished she were someone else's girl and not his brother's or that he'd have met her first.

'William...' With fear crossing her face, Lizzie spun on the spot, her hand reaching for the coal chute. 'Someone's coming.' Suddenly, she was gone and from inside the cellar he could hear her running. A run that unexpectedly became halted.

Staring upwards, he imagined her crouching. Hiding in the undergrowth. It was a thought that made his heart pound, his mouth grow dry. Terrified of what his brother would do, he had no choice but to create a distraction, to give her the time to get away and without any thought to what would happen to him, he pounded his fists against the door. Kicked at the frame. Screamed as loudly as he could. Until rattling could be heard, and the door sprung open to show Thomas stood in the doorway. His broad shoulders filled the frame, almost touched each side of the architrave and with a menacing look, he stepped through the door into the cellar and twisted his mouth in a cruel and suspicious way.

'You need to be quiet, you little shit.' Reaching for a shelf high above his head, Thomas grabbed at a baseball bat he'd obviously hidden earlier, began to slap it precariously against his palm. Then immediately, his eyes shot to the coal chute. 'Who are you protecting?'

'Why the hell would I be protecting anyone?'

'William...' Again, the bat hit the palm of his hand, then the wall. 'You wouldn't normally scream and shout. I know you so much better than that. It isn't your style. So, before I beat the living crap out of you... you're going to tell me what's going on.'

'Do what you like.' Defiantly, William stood his ground, glared, and waited for Thomas to take a single step. As soon as he did, and with the rage of a bull, he lowered his shoulder, ran towards him, and heard Thomas groan as he fell to the ground. With a wry smile, William dodged past him and slammed the door. For a moment, he thought he'd got his wish. That Thomas would have to spend the rest of the night in the cellar, but as he spun around to lock the door, he cursed. The lock was missing and with no time to look for it, he angrily made a dash out of the back hallway and towards the stairs.

'You'll pay for this.' He heard Thomas's voice yell out, as the cellar door flew open. A single look over his shoulder showed him an angry Thomas, who stood there, the baseball bat still in his hand. 'If I find out who was helping you, I swear to God...' The bat bounced off of the door surround. 'I'll be locking them in there too. Is that what you want?'

Shaking his head, William couldn't bear the thought that Lizzie would be locked in the cellar. Knew he had to protect her, and that even Thomas would quickly realise that it could have been her. And only by way of protecting her further did he suppress his anger, along with the overwhelming urge to take the baseball bat out of Thomas's hands and hit him with it.

4

WILLIAM

Present Day - Friday Evening

'William...' Bursting through the back door, Anna screamed, dropped the basket of vegetables, and launched herself towards him as the courgette and tomato became scattered all over the floor. 'What the hell have you done?'

In a daze, William felt his heart leap in his chest. His stomach contracted and, in his confusion, his eyes shot to the cooker and he began to reach out, twisting at knobs.

'Your hand. What did you do to it?' Anna grabbed the knife, tossed it to one side and watched in horror as it landed with a crash next to Cookie's chopping board. Snatching at a tea towel, she twisted it around, wrapped it around his blood-soaked fingers. Held it tightly.

'The blade, it's gone and cut you, so it has.' Yelling through the door, she shouted out loud, 'Mrs McCulloch, please... get Bobby, we need to phone for an ambulance.' Her normally soft Irish accent had gone up a whole octave, her face pale, almost white with shock as she exchanged a worried glance with the much older woman.

'Anna, please, don't be dramatic. The knife, it just slipped...' he lied, but kept hold of his own hand just a little too hard as he stemmed the flow of blood.

'I'll do it,' Mrs McCulloch said, 'Bobby's already gone for the day.' She stood on the step, raised herself onto her tiptoes, 'Unless I can catch him.'

'Cookie. Seriously. Don't bother Bobby. I'm fine. Honestly.' Annoyed, he closed his eyes, could still hear the two women chatting erratically. It was a noise he desperately wanted to block out; and with slow intakes of breath, he tried to go back to the visions he'd had, to the memories of when his brother was still alive, and to a time when a single event could have changed everything that followed.

Feeling the nausea begin, William walked to the sink, held onto its side. And for a moment he wished his brother were still alive. Life would be so much easier if he were here to organise the hall, to take over the responsibility, to either sell or demolish it as he wished. It would have given William the opportunity to stay in London, to follow his career. To leave the past behind and to fall in love.

But then, his mind went back to the way Thomas had been and clearly, he could still see Lizzie's face, the morning after she'd been leant through the coal chute. How she'd unusually looked down and away, wouldn't meet his eye and the way she held a hand protectively over one side of her face, in an impossible attempt to hide the bruise that clearly stained the side of her cheek.

'Anna. Please...' Annoyed that Anna had taken it upon herself to become his nurse, he angrily pulled his hand away, hoped she'd take the hint. Being a chef, he'd cut himself more times than he could remember and knew that before he was done, he'd do it again. It was a part of life when knives were the thing you handled the most and after dropping the blood-soaked t-towel into the sink, he began to slowly assess the damage, which thankfully didn't look anywhere near as bad as he'd thought.

'William, show me. I'll make it better.' Once again, Anna moved towards him, grabbed at his hand.

'No.' Shaking his head, William pulled a first aid box out of the cupboard, began pulling at the rolls of bandages, dressings, and steri-strips. 'I'm fine, now please... let it be.'

'William, you're not fine. You've gone as white as a sheet.' Her hand rested on his shoulder, where her fingers squeezed protectively. 'Let's get you sat down, where I can take a better look at that for you.' She moved slowly in front of him, caught his eye for a moment too long, gave him a slight, but definite smile.

'Anna... if the boy says to leave him alone, then it's probably best you just do that.' Mrs McCulloch studied the scene, furrowed her eyebrows in question. It was a scene she'd watched so many times in the past. A teenage crush that one of them had got over, and the other one hadn't. 'You should know by now he doesn't like us fussing.' Moving the knife from where it'd been thrown, she stowed it in the dishwasher and slammed the door closed.

Giving her a distant but grateful smile, William pushed his way past Anna and turned his attention back to the security cameras. His eyes flicked anxiously from screen to screen. But Lizzie was gone. Her car no longer on the drive. Which could only mean one of two things. Either she'd changed her mind and left. Or finally, ten years after the last time she'd been here, Lizzie was back. The question was: how long would she stay?

5

ELIZABETH

Present Day - Friday Evening

'Lizzie, you came. I... I wasn't sure that you would.' Almost afraid to turn, Elizabeth heard the voice of Ada Kirkwood come from somewhere above. Her staccato voice sounded tired, breathless, and almost a little too distant.

Taking a moment, Elizabeth held onto the car, counted to five and then forcibly, she turned around, looked up, and saw the vast oak door already swinging backwards. It was almost played out in slow motion and the shadow that had been Ada Kirkwood emerged from within.

Seeing her stood there was a moment of both pleasure and pain. A moment of stark realisation. Ada was no longer the strong, capable woman she used to be. The years had taken their toll and to see her in such a frail and vulnerable state was a sight that made Elizabeth lean against the car. She hoped her legs would hold her and while blinking repeatedly, she did all she could to try and hold onto the tiny scrap of composure she had left, all the time praying that the look of shock on her face wouldn't give her away. Nervously, she rubbed each of her sweaty palms down the front of her jeans, took deep, inward breaths, and forced herself to give what she hoped would look like an open and affable smile.

With her heart pounding rapidly, Elizabeth imagined the way Ada Kirkwood would have previously glided towards her. She'd been graceful and eloquent and in the first ten seconds she'd have given off more energy than anyone else Elizabeth ever known. Whereas now, Ada was a middle-aged woman, struggling to walk. She was holding tightly to a walking frame and sadly, she could barely take more than a step at a time. And rather than the chic, stylish clothes of the past, she now wore oversized, dark, dowdy colours, one's that veiled her body in a cloak she'd obviously chosen to hide beneath.

'Don't just stand there.' Ada shouted, her voice broken, 'Come up here. Let me look at you properly.' Unexpectedly, Ada let go of the frame, limped towards the newly built ramp, and leaned against the stone balustrade and with arms outstretched, she waved them around, gave Elizabeth the warmest, most startling smile. 'Now then... come and see what we did with the place.' She paused, caught her breath. 'It's changed... changed so much since you were last here.' Turning, she looked up at the shiny, stained-glass windows. 'Not all for the good, I might add. I doubt you're going to recognise it at all.'

With her fingers still gripping the car door, Elizabeth noticed the deep, furrowed lines that were clearly etched across Ada's face. And with an overwhelming sadness, she realised just how much the years had changed her. How much had obviously happened in her absence and how, after a catastrophic chain of events, this woman's whole life had fallen apart. Feeling an overwhelming sense of culpability, Elizabeth wished she could turn back time, spare the family some pain by doing things differently. If she could have just altered one occurrence or outcome, she knew how differently things might have been and that ultimately, Thomas might have lived and so much pain would have been avoided.

Having had no reason to come back, Elizabeth knew she'd turned her back on both the Manor and on the family. Ada hadn't wanted her here while Thomas had been alive, and she'd had no reason to believe she'd have ever wanted her to return. Instead, life had moved on. She'd gone home, settled into a daily existence where family had come first and her ambition to overtake the world of architecture had been set to one side; instead of designing houses for the rich and famous, she'd taken a position with a local builder, created the three-bedroomed semis that sold en mass. She took the occasional private commission, an odd extension here and there, and more recently, a beautiful barn conversion, with its open living spaces, accordion doors, and a ground floor bedroom. It was the kind of home she could only dream about, but the truth was she felt too afraid to move and had no wish to face the nightmares alone. Staying at home with her dad had always been the safer option. And it had worked for them both; her dad had always loved the company and she liked to know that someone was there to talk to or was sleeping, in the next room.

'Mrs Kirkwood, thank you so much for inviting me. It's...' With one hand still shielding her eyes, she held the other out. Allowed it to hover limply in the air.

'Mrs Kirkwood?' Ada snapped. 'I've known you for years... you, you practically grew up in this house, were almost a part of the family and now I'm Mrs Kirkwood?'

Feeling the blood drain from her face, Elizabeth sheepishly stared at the floor, 'I... oh my God, Ada. I... I'm so sorry. I really didn't mean to offend. It's just... it's been... well it's been so long and...' she gave an apprehensive, half smile, wished she could take back the words. 'It really is lovely to be back. I was really pleased when I got the invitation.' She lied through gritted teeth, cautiously leaned into the familiarity of Ada's hold, felt her arms fold themselves around her and did her best not to stiffen.

With a sob leaving her throat, Elizabeth pressed her lips tightly together and felt a tidal wave of emotion sweep over her. With a distant gaze, she looked over Ada's shoulder and kept her eyes fixed on the lake. On the monument. And finally, on the old drooping willow tree, that now looked much smaller than she remembered. But even with its current height and breadth, it still arched over the water like a formidable giant umbrella, billowing in the breeze, shielding its secrets.

'You should go over, pay Thomas a visit.' Ada suddenly whispered as she leaned back and stared deep into Elizabeth's eyes. 'When it was first erected, I used to take flowers every Saturday before breakfast, but...' The words caught in her throat, and she pointed to the walking frame, 'It's much too difficult now... and the ground, it's much too soft and Bobby, you remember Bobby, don't you?' She paused, wafted a hand in the air, then continued without waiting for an answer. 'He put me a path all the way around the lake. I think he thought I'd be able to keep up my visits. To take a walk every now and then. But I can't. It's much too easy to fall...' She stared wistfully at the memorial; the longing in her eyes clear to see.

'Maybe I'll go a little later...' Picking up her bag, Elizabeth looked between Ada and the memorial. It was a visit she wasn't keen to take, knowing that once she did, she'd be scrutinised and watched. Just as she had been before.

'Why don't you give me your car keys,' Ada finally said, 'I'll get one of the staff to move the car?' She paused, smiled. 'I'll get them to take your bags up to the room, too. I've put you in the room that used to be Thomas's. Thought the familiarity would be nice for you, and then... then you can go and see the others. They're all in the grand hall, waiting for you.' Holding out her hand insistently, she took the car keys, passed them to a concierge who'd conveniently appeared behind her.

'Others?' The word fell from Elizabeth's mouth. Her mind spun violently as she realised what that meant and a number of faces flashed up and into her mind, faces she hadn't seen since Thomas had been murdered. Quickly, she tried to work out who might have already arrived and with a sickly feeling in the bottom of her stomach, she stared across the deserted driveway, realised that all the other cars must have been moved, leaving the driveway clear and picture perfect. Cautiously, she followed Ada through the front door and into the old, familiar hallway where she took a deep breath in and felt the house surround her. Just as it always had, like a blanket shrouding her shoulders.

The smell of roast lamb drifted towards her and unexpectedly her stomach growled with hunger as she contemplated the evening meal. It was a meal she presumed they'd all be sharing and once again, she pondered how it would feel after so many years. Tried to work out who would be sat at the table. After all, Ada had said *they* were already here. Already waiting, within these walls. Nervously, she stared around the hallway, knew exactly which door led to the grand hallway and anxiously, she began to go through all the reasons why she'd stayed away. And suddenly, she couldn't understand why she'd agreed to come back.

For the past ten years, she'd purposely distanced herself from just about every person she'd previously known. They'd all hurt her in one way or another. Which had made her wary of new people. She'd often refused to make new friends or allow anyone to get close. Yet today, she'd gone against everything she'd previously believed. She'd returned to the Manor. And now, she had no choice but to face each and every one of them. The idea of a quiet and intimate weekend dissipated into the distance, like a giant ball of tumbleweed, disappearing across the grounds and into the depths of the lake.

'I didn't realise the others would be coming... who, who else is here?' Her voice sounded distant. It had turned into a terrified whisper, almost too afraid to be heard. But the reality was, she didn't really need to ask the question. She had a good idea who 'the others' would be. And now she struggled to catch her breath. Held it for a moment too long. Immediately realised her mistake and felt the hallway spin violently around her.

'Of course the others are here. It wouldn't be a real or proper memorial without all of Thomas's friends. Now, would it?' Ada emphasised the word *all*, turned, and flicked an imaginary particle of dust from a dark oak table. Her soft warm smile had disappeared and instead, she stared through the air with steel-grey eyes that could have easily pierced metal. 'I've organised everything. We're going to have a lovely few days. We're going to remember my son, Thomas. And you, my darling. You're going to help me figure out which one of his friends is his killer.'

6

LIZZIE

Ten years before

With rain beginning to fall, unknown footsteps approaching, and shadows looming around every corner, I give William an apologetic look. 'I have to go. Someone's coming,' I whisper the words, drop the coal chute carefully back into position, and with my stomach churning, I look over my shoulder, squint in an attempt to see through the moonlit darkness.

Trembling, I creep barefoot. Step in and out of flowerbeds. Use each of the trees and bushes to hide behind. Then finally, and with much negotiation of the overgrown garden, I run to the great oak, and with every inch of my body trembling, I crouch down behind it. Looking up at Thomas's bedroom window, I watch, wait, hope he isn't awake. I don't see a light. Not a single one, and fearfully, I look from window to window, then down at the solid oak door of Kirkwood Manor.

'Please...' I whisper, 'Please don't be locked.' Using the tree to hide me, I use the moonlight to study my feet, and in an attempt to rid them of the dirt, I rub at them frantically on the grass while cursing my stupidity, as I realise just how dirty they are. Wish that for once I'd had the foresight to wear a pair of shoes. But rummaging around for them in the darkness and disturbing Thomas was something I hadn't wanted to risk.

After sitting in my hiding place for far too long, I decide to make a move, and inch as slowly as I can towards the door. Nervously, I glance backwards, over my shoulder, listen for movement, for the faintest footstep. For a sign that someone has followed me and only when I'm sure that I'm truly alone do I make my way across the lawn and feel the roughness of the old, gravel steps against my bare toes. Reaching the top, I hold my breath, push tentatively at the door, and with a sense of relief, I step into the familiarity of the hallway and crouch in the entrance. Leaning against the wood panelled wall, I once again try to rub the dirt from my feet. Wriggle around. Stand up a little too quickly and accidentally, I catch my head on one of the antique pictures. Only once I'm sure it won't fall, I resort to wiping my feet on a rug that has been laid for so long, I can imagine the plumes of dust that will be jumping up and into the room with each and every movement I'm making.

Aware that Thomas could be close behind, I know I should make my way up the stairs and with the precision of an SAS soldier, I step slowly across the hallway, from floorboard to floorboard. Make sure my feet only touch the ones that don't creak and I begin to feel grateful for all the hours I've spent creeping around in this house from room to room without Thomas's parents being aware. I knew that tonight, it was imperative that I didn't make a noise, that no one was disturbed and while manoeuvring between pieces of antique furniture, I make my way to the bottom of the staircase, and immediately, I freeze as I hear footsteps approaching.

With lightening reactions, I duck behind an ox-blood chesterfield and stretch out behind it. I feel sure that the settee will act as my shield, and I hold my breath as I wait patiently for the footsteps to pass. Peeping around its edge, I see William making his way up the staircase. His young, solid frame looks lost and defeated. His shoulders are slumped, and even though he looks sad, I breathe a sigh of relief that he's found a way to get out of the cellar. That he's no longer a prisoner. And that now, he can sleep in his bed for a good few hours before his day begins.

Crawling on my hands and knees, I watch him climb the staircase. He quickly disappears through a door at the top and once again, I wait and listen. But before I can move, I hear more footsteps and with the anticipation of who it might be, I curl up and into a small but necessary ball.

The footsteps are masked by the sound of my heart. And in an attempt to stop the sound which is audibly booming in my head like a bass drummer making his mark during trooping the colour, I close my eyes for a beat, then fearfully I open them as wide as I can, as the footsteps get closer.

'Thomas. Why are you sneaking around in the darkness?' Ada's voice growls and I look upwards to see her gliding down the staircase. Her long, white dressing gown billows out behind her, giving her the look of an angel guarding the household. And while admiring her elegance from my hiding place, I can hear Thomas's feet tapping nervously back and forth, like those of a naughty schoolboy, waiting to be scolded.

'I... I needed some water.' He lies, the tell-tale way he looks away as he speaks gives him away and from where I'm hidden, I can clearly see the way he nervously runs a hand through his overgrown mop of bright auburn hair.

'So?' Ada questioned, 'Where is it?'

'Where's what?'

'The water.'

A long, uncomfortable silence fills the room. There's more shuffling of feet, followed by a long, drawn-out sigh. 'Okay. Okay. I was looking for Lizzie. She's disappeared. I don't know where she's gone, and I went looking for her.'

Closing my eyes, I feel the nausea turn in my stomach. He knows I'm missing, and a trembling begins within me, until it begins to shake every inch of my body. Uneasily I stretch my leg, fear that I'm about to get cramp and while taking short, sharp breaths, I clench my teeth tightly together, and feel the pressure within my jaw, wait patiently for the feeling to pass.

'Darling. What have I told you about that girl?' She pauses, adjusts her dressing gown, and ties the belt tightly around her. 'You just have to realise. She isn't one of us. She comes from a completely different kind of family to ours and the lord knows, she has no idea how to act in polite company.' She rested a hand on his shoulder. 'Seriously darling, I'm amazed it's lasted this long. Or that we still have the family silver.' The words fell from Ada's mouth like venom. 'I've told you before, she's completely feral. Looking out for herself. Mark my words, she's simply trapping herself a Kirkwood.' She lifts a hand up to Thomas's face, pats his cheek. 'Now do as you've been told. Get rid of her. Before it's too late and we're dealing with a scandal.'

Holding back a sob, I close my eyes and slowly, I shake my head. I hadn't realised how evil Ada could be and I try to think back, try to understand what I ever did wrong or why she dislikes me so very much. Of course, there had been the times when she'd rolled her eyes at something I'd done, the odd comment here or there about inappropriate behaviour. But she loved her son and had been the one who'd encouraged us to share a room. To do things as a couple. And on one or two occasions, she'd even invited me to family events. Loaned me the most exquisite of evening dresses, with jewellery to match, introduced me as, 'Thomas's wonderful girlfriend'. They'd been the nights I'd loved the most. The nights when I'd almost felt accepted. Yet now, hearing those words fall from her mouth, I feel as though I've been punched in the gut and like a wounded animal, I want to crawl to my bed, curl up in a ball, stay there for hours. But then, as though being attacked for a second time, I realise that I don't have a bed, not here, not in this house. What I have is Thomas's bed. The one we share.

'Mother. I know you're right. But where Lizzie's concerned, nothing is easy. In fact, I've found it all really difficult...' he pauses, begins to pace, takes a step closer to my hiding place, until his foot is almost touching my hand. 'She depends on me.' He walks across the room, sits on the oak pew that stands by the door, and leans forward with his face in his hands. For a moment I think he'll cry. 'I didn't want to say anything,' he finally says. 'But Lizzie, she's a little bit crazy. God only knows what she'll do when it's over and...' Nervously, I watch as he twists his hands together; it's like he's wringing out a cloth, determined to get all the water out in one final squeeze. '...Well, I still have finals to do and Lizzie, she's still at uni. She mixes with all the same friends as I do and ending it would make things awkward, so for now I'd rather not stir the pot, not till I've graduated, and then it won't be a problem, will it? I'll be home, fully trained and ready to go out into the big wide world and earn myself a living, just like you wanted me to,' he says, proudly. 'Then I'll make new friends, have work colleagues. I won't need any of the uni friends and that'd be the time to cut the ties, don't you think?'

Disbelievingly, I shake my head. Play his words over and over in my mind like a reel on repeat. Then cautiously, I realise that he didn't make a promise. He did say that I depend on him, and I do. But I feel reassured by the fact that he didn't mention my name directly. What he had said was that after graduation he wouldn't need his uni friends; it was true, he didn't. But I wasn't just a uni friend. I was so much more. And smugly, I sneak a peek around the edge of the chesterfield and glare as he dutifully stands up, steps towards his mother, puts an arm around her shoulder, and with the act of a perfect son, kisses her gently on the forehead.

'Darling.' Ada turns her face, to look her son directly in the eye. 'The last time you got yourself into trouble, it cost me a lot of money to get you out of it. Just imagine how much it would cost me if you did get this girl pregnant.' She paused, then gave a soft cough for effect before carrying on. 'So, you need to promise me you'll end it with Lizzie before it's too late. You will, won't you?'

Thomas gives her one of his most perfect smiles but once again, he looks away as he speaks. 'Mother. I've always done whatever you've asked. Haven't I?'

The words cut deep. I know he's being pushed into a corner. But I feel hurt and betrayed. I know he looked away as he spoke, that once again, he didn't actually promise. But now, I doubt myself. I doubt the love we've shared and deep down, I begin to wonder if he's telling the truth. If he'd really end our relationship, just because his mother had demanded it.

It's a thought that breaks my heart; before meeting Thomas, I'd never really had too many friends. After my mother had died, I'd grown up in a small, terraced house where I'd lived with my father. It had been all I'd ever known. And although it had been a place where I'd felt much love, and where most of the neighbours were relations, all of which chose to live closely together, being here was different. I'd experienced a new kind of life. One where there were fields, trees, and lakes to swim in and wishfully, as the walls begin to close themselves in around me, I close my eyes and breathe in, as though every breath is my last.

'Thomas...' Ada's voice trails off. Something disturbs her and I open my eyes to see the way she's stood just a few feet from me. Inquisitively, she tips her head to one side. I'm sure she stares straight at me. She knows that I'm there. And with my eyes wide open, I stare straight back. Not daring to move, or breathe, I see a twisted and malicious smile cross her face before she moves in the direction of the kitchen and beckons her son.

'Darling, come with me. I'll make us some hot chocolate. Like we used to do.' She pokes him in the ribs playfully and laughs. 'We'll leave the dirty pan in the sink for Cookie to wash. She'll be furious. Especially when she sees all the mess we've made.' She pauses, laughs. 'Do you think she'll have some of those scrummy marshmallows, the ones she keeps in the cupboard?'

As they leave. I realise that Ada has done me a favour. She's given me the opportunity to move. To make my escape. Without Thomas knowing I'd been listening. And with a final look at the door, at the escape route out of here, I jump up from my hiding place, turn towards the stairs. Feel the pain erupt in my cheek as I collide with the sideboard and watch as the lamp wobbles precariously on top. Holding it tightly in my hands, I wait. Hope that Thomas hasn't heard the noise, that his mother keeps him penned up in the kitchen. With a sob, I lift a hand to the side of my face, hold it there, knowing that by the morning there's going to be a bruise, one I'll have no way of explaining.

7

ELIZABETH

Present Day - Friday Evening

Swallowing hard, Elizabeth moved back to the door. She considered leaving. Wondered how she would do that without offending Ada. Whether she'd really care if she did. Most of all, she felt the need to run before she came face to face with the others.

The silence in the room became uncomfortable. It was more than obvious that Ada had said just about as much as she wanted to say and slowly, she inched across the room with her walking frame, past the ox-blood chesterfield that still stood there and with a slight tug, she eased the door to the Grand Hall ajar, just enough for Elizabeth to hear the sound of the voices and joviality beyond.

'Are you just a tiny bit nervous about being here?' The woman's voice was followed by a nervous laugh, a chair scraped against wooden floors, the clink of a glass as it touched another.

'Sure I am.' Another woman responded, 'Feels like there's a bit more to this weekend than meets the eye. I mean, look at all the champagne. It all feels a bit like a celebration and with dinner in less than an hour, a dinner we're all to dress casually for. It's all just a bit weird. I mean, who doesn't dress for dinner?' The woman paused, listened as all the others laughed, before she continued. 'And, I don't know about you, but I can't understand why they're doing it now. It doesn't seem right to do it after all this time. I mean... it's been ten whole years?'

'And Ada? Did you see her? She looks so frail, doesn't she?' Another voice chipped in. 'Not surprisingly though; a lot's happened over the years. First the way Thomas died, then poor Dominic. So soon after. And Lizzie, what ever happened to Lizzie? Do you think she'll turn up?'

'She just disappeared, didn't she? Someone said she'd gone to London.' The first woman said. 'I heard she went back to look after her dad, turned into a bit of a recluse.'

'He was an alcoholic, wasn't he?'

'That's right, he depended on Lizzie all the time. I've no idea how she got away with her constant weekends at the Manor. He moaned every time she went back to uni.'

'Well, from what I heard, she was committed... sent to an institution for the mentally insane,' a man bellowed, 'Thomas being killed right in front of her. It probably sent her over the edge.' A whistling noise left his lips, followed by a bang and nervous laughter as he'd obviously made an act out of how she'd have hypothetically fallen, in one big swoop from the edge of a cliff. The sound of mumbling travelled rapidly around the room. Then, an uncomfortable pause was followed by a nervous cough.

Moving away from the door, Ada nodded. 'See, your friends. They're already here. They're already deciding as to what did and didn't happen,' she whispered. 'They're settling in nicely, don't you think?' She ignored the personal comments, wafted a hand through the air. 'And what's more, they've already worked out that this weekend isn't a simple memorial, haven't they? They're not stupid. Memorials don't normally last for four whole days.' She scoffed, 'I planned it this way because I needed the time, you see. I needed to observe them all. To see how they interact. How coming back here affects them and how they try to cover up what one of them did.' She paused, tapped the side of her nose with a long, spindly finger, raised both eyebrows. 'I honestly believe in the saying that a killer always returns to the scene of a crime. And someone in this house,' she nodded decisively, 'they got away with murdering my boy. They're as guilty as hell.' She gave Elizabeth an inquisitive look. 'I've tried to let it go, to come to terms with it all, but I can't. I was a barrister in my day. I was good at what I did. Never failed to work out who the bad guy was. Until the bad guy killed my boy.' She lifted a hand, wiped away a tear. 'And it kills me that I couldn't solve this one.' She shook her head, stared at the chesterfield. 'Everyone in this house had secrets. Most for good reason and scandal, it had to be avoided at all cost.' She released a sob, held a hand to her mouth. 'But my boy's murder is one secret too many. I need to know what happened and...' she paused, turned her attention to the oak floorboards, as though checking them for imperfections. 'I'm running out of time, Lizzie. I'm dying and I won't... no, I can't rest. Not until I know what really happened...'

Swallowing hard, Elizabeth felt a surge of panic. She wasn't sure how she should feel. After all, this woman had been both cruel and kind to her in equal measures. But for Ada to die would mean the end of an era. And even though she hadn't been back since Thomas's death, she'd always known that Ada being here had given her that link to the Manor.

Once again, the room began to move slowly around her. Reaching out, she took Ada's hand in her own. Realised how frail she really was. 'You can't be... I mean, do you need to sit down...' Looking around, Elizabeth manoeuvred Ada towards the chesterfield. 'There has to be something they can do. Surely.'

With a shake of her head, Ada gave Elizabeth a half smile, one that was meant to cover the look of pain within. 'I don't want to sit down.' She grabbed the walking frame, pulled it into position. Stood upright. 'It won't be long before I'm lying down permanently. So, there's no time for that now. Is there?' Determinedly, she pushed the door to the grand hall closed, cut off the sound of the others who were still questioning the weekend. 'No one knows. Although if anyone paid any attention to me at all, you'd think it would be more than obvious.' She lifted a hand, wiped away a tear that dripped down her face.

'That's why you're having the memorial now?' Elizabeth held onto Ada's hand, saw the transparency of her skin, an obvious effect of the illness.

'Things would have been so different if he'd lived, you see.' She sighed. 'Thomas, he would have never let this house become a hotel. But William, he has a mind of his own. He's very different to the rest of us and God only knows how, but he's in charge now... and...' She waved a hand around in the air. It was as though she were trying to point to all the antiques all at once and even though she'd continued to speak, Elizabeth didn't hear. The sound of William's name made her catch her breath, the memories came flooding back, and she tried to concentrate far too hard on the highly polished sideboard, the oversized lamp that still stood on top.

'Was it William that changed everything?'

'Of course, he did. Who else would have done it all?' Ada gave her a knowing smile, and a roll of her eyes that said so much more than words. 'But Lizzie, this weekend isn't about William, is it? It's all about Thomas.' She nodded hopefully, allowed herself to look through the window. 'That lake. This house. His friends. They all know what happened to my boy. I know they do. And you... you have to help me find the truth.'

8

ELIZABETH

Present Day - Friday Evening

Pulling at the door to the Grand Hall, Ada once again left it ajar, gave Elizabeth a mischievous smile. 'Now. Go to your friends,' Ada taunted, 'I've told you before, they're waiting.'

'I can't. I have to get changed first. I have to...' Elizabeth looked between the door and the staircase. She tried to think of an excuse. The last place she wanted to go was into the grand hall but equally, she couldn't bear the thought of going up to the room she'd shared with Thomas. Going in either direction was a terrifying thought, and she wanted to delay doing both for as long as she possibly could.

'There's no need. As you heard, everyone is staying casual tonight. That way, they'll feel more relaxed, act more naturally.' She pointed to the door, began to move one step at a time along the corridor, and with a cynical smile, she disappeared in the direction of the library.

Feeling the need to sit back down, Elizabeth made her way across the floorboards, habitually stood on all the ones that didn't make a noise, until she reached an old Victorian pew that stood by the door and with shaking fingers she reached out, held onto the old worn, weathered arm where the last of the sun still warmed it through the window. It was a heat that now travelled through her hand and with a need to feel that warmth on the rest of her body, she eased herself into the seat, sat listening to voices that drifted from the grand hall. Each one piercing her mind with a memory she'd rather forget.

From where she sat, she could hear the sound of forced conversation and over exaggerated, fake laughter that could only come from a group of people who were trying much too hard to be nice.

'Why would you be nervous?' A man's voice growled. He emphasised the word *you* in a way that Elizabeth recognised his voice. Immediately an image of Jordan filled her mind. She could see the young, arrogant student as he used to be and right now, she could imagine him stood in the room, finger pointed. 'It's a weekend away. One I wouldn't normally be able to afford and the Kirkwoods want to remember their son. They're paying. What more could we ask for?' His voice was deep, and for a moment, Elizabeth closed her eyes. He was the last person she wanted to see and anxiously, she felt her stomach turn with nerves.

'Saying that... Lucy's right. There has to be a reason why we're all here. It is the first time since the funeral we've all been here together. There were around a hundred of us at the party that night, so why did they just invite us and none of the others? It's all a bit odd, isn't it?' Another man said, then cleared his throat. 'Although, I guess we were the ones that were here most often, but still... it did take me a bit by surprise, when the invitation dropped through the post. If they were going to have a memorial, surely they would have had it before now, don't you think? Yet here we all are. Present and correct. Even though none of us really want to be here.'

'Speak for yourself... I wanted to be here.' A man with a softly spoken Scottish accent filled the air and with her brow furrowed, Elizabeth tried to think back to university, to the days when they'd had nothing to do but drink and party and to a time when there had only been two Scottish men in their year group. One had been Timothy. The other, her former high school boyfriend, Henry. And with a sense of disappointment, she realised that she'd have recognised Henry's voice anywhere, meaning the mystery voice must belong to Timothy.

'Lucy, I'm just saying what everyone else is thinking.' Timothy's voice rang out again, 'I saw it in the Yorkshire magazine, a full article all about the hotel's restoration and if I'm honest, I was quite excited when the invitation dropped through the door. Couldn't wait to get back here.'

'You were excited. About a memorial?'

'Sure, I was. I came out of curiosity. I wanted to see what they'd done with the place, you know, with my own eyes.' He laughed. 'The thought of this place being a hotel now, it intrigued me. Plus, I wanted to see what you lot looked like these days, you know... see if you'd gone all wrinkly, bald, or started dying your hair.'

'Jesus Tim, We're thirty-three, not bloody ninety-three. And as for our hair, I doubt any of us are the same colour we were born with.' An Irish woman's voice joined in the conversation. 'Besides... as Lucy said, you speak for yourself. I wanted to come too. I really wanted to see Ada. I just wish Dominic was still with us. He was always so lovely to us, even if he was a bit eccentric, climbing ladders all the time. There's no wonder he eventually fell off one.' She paused, thoughtfully. 'And quite honestly, if the family want a memorial, it's only polite that we turn up, be respectful, and give them one.'

'Freya, it's a hotel. What they need are paying guests... not us lot leeching off of them... not again. I seem to remember that we did enough of that as teenagers.' Timothy paused. 'We were here so often, drinking the contents of their wine cellar, eating them out of house and home and if I'm honest, I have no idea how we got away with it. We must have cost the Kirkwoods a small fortune. And what our parents thought to it all, I have no idea. We hardly ever went home, not unless our laundry needed doing.'

'Well, Patty and I... we really needed the break.' Henry's soft Scottish voice joined in the conversation, making Elizabeth's eyes shoot to the door. She swallowed hard. Felt her heartrate accelerate, then plummet all at once. 'With work and all that, we didn't get a honeymoon, did we darling?' Henry paused, laughed. 'We're hoping we get the room with that big four-poster bed. I saw it on the adverts, looked so big.'

A woman's affirmation was followed by a loud, shrill giggle that made every nerve in Elizabeth's body go on high alert. This was the same Henry she'd had a teenage fling with, the same Henry who'd tossed her aside and ironically, the same Henry who'd been Thomas's long-time friend, another person who'd tried to convince Thomas to end it with her.

Turning to the window, she held a hand to her mouth. Did all she could to drag the air into her body. *What did you expect: a memorial without any other people?* She once again questioned her decision to come, wondered how easy it would be to slip away, down the steps, climb back into her car, and disappear without trace.

Disappearing had been something she and Thomas had found easy to do back in the day and had spent most of their time making fires in the woods, lying beside them. They'd been the days she'd loved the most. The days when it had just been the two of them. A time when neither his family nor friends could influence his decisions and once again, her eyes went to the chesterfield, to the memory of the night she'd hidden behind it. 'Don't get all stary eyed. It wasn't all good, or perfect,' she whispered to the room, and knew that hiding or keeping a low profile in a house full of so many people and memories would be close to impossible. 'I'm sure there was a time when he loved me.' She tried to convince herself and nervously, she blew out through puffed up cheeks, tried to think about the others.

So, Henry. What kind of woman did you eventually marry? The words automatically filled her thoughts as she tried to imagine what sort of woman she'd be and whether or not Henry had the perfect life he'd always craved. She'd often overheard him telling Thomas how much he wanted the perfect marriage, the perfect family. The two point four children. A life, envied by others. And now, she wondered if he'd got his wish or whether like her, his life hadn't quite turned out to be quite the way he'd expected.

9

ELIZABETH

Present Day - Friday Evening

Rubbing her hands down her jeans, Elizabeth flicked away a thread of cotton, wished she'd gone to her room and changed. She'd brought a beautiful Karen Millen dress with her. One she'd bought earlier in the year. But instead, and because Ada had insisted, she had no option but to walk into the room wearing her 'go to' high street top, her jeans that had been washed a million times and her old, worn out plimsoles that used to be white.

Pulling at the hem of her top, she remembered doing exactly the same thing years before to a charity shop purchase she'd once worn at the Manor and at a time when everything she'd worn had made her feel as though she hadn't belonged.

Why the hell did you come? The thought spun around her mind repeatedly and she closed her eyes, bit down on her lip. It was all she could do to control her emotions and with one eye on the door, on her escape route, she took a moment to glance in a mirror, ran a hand through her hair, flicking it up and backwards.

'Lizzie. Is that you?' Spinning on the spot, Elizabeth saw the door to the grand hall burst open to reveal a tall, striking woman with short, jet-black hair, carved cheek bones, and the tightest black leather trousers she'd ever seen. They were dressed up with a floral top and black stilettos, with the outfit finished off perfectly with a military style jacket that had been casually slung across her shoulders.

'Lucy...' The word stuck in her throat. She could still see Lucy stood by the water's edge, naked and brazen. She'd been the last person Elizabeth remembered seeing before she'd found Thomas. His eyes wide open. An open wound to the side of his head. The blood that had spilled into the lake. 'It's... it's good... to see you, again.' She forced a smile, took a step forward.

'Mwah, mwah... oh, darling, are we allowed to hug? Please say yes. I'm never sure what we should do nowadays. People don't always want you hugging and kissing them any more. Do they?'

Without answering, Elizabeth felt herself being pulled into an overwhelming and claustrophobic hug that went on for what felt like hours. 'Hey, everyone. Come and see. Our Lizzie's here. I told you she'd come.'

'Elizabeth.' The word abruptly dropped from her mouth and looking up and into Lucy's eyes, she saw the look of dismay cross her pale, ivory face. It was something about her that hadn't changed. In fact, if Lucy were to go back to the lake and stand naked on the embankment, Elizabeth doubted she'd look any different today, than she had on that night, ten years before.

'What was that darling?'

'No one calls me Lizzie. Not now. I'm Elizabeth.'

Raising her eyebrows, Lucy began to laugh. Placed a hand in the small of Elizabeth's back, moved her through the door. 'Everyone, are you listening, Elizabeth's here.' She pushed a tongue firmly into her cheek. 'Not Lizzie. Oh no. You all have to be good boys and girls and call her Elizabeth. She insists.'

A nervous laughter filled the room as one after the other they all stood up, held out their arms, moved towards her, and pulled her into hugs that were both unwelcome and unnecessary. It was a slight extension of how things used to be between them. A no holds barred approach to a summer of constant parties, too much champagne, drugs that seemed to appear from nowhere and the unadulterated sex that had followed. They were actions Elizabeth regretted now. A life so different from the way she'd grown up and her mind flew back to Ada's words: *She's feral, she isn't one of us.* Realising now how cruel she'd been, it occurred to Elizabeth how desperate she'd been to belong to this group. How much she'd wanted Thomas to love her. But just because she'd grown up in a mining village, in a house that would have fit into a single room at the Manor, it didn't make her feral. And now, with all she knew, she wished she hadn't met Thomas at all. Wished she'd walked away with her head held high the moment she'd heard Ada demand that he ended it with her. Maybe then, things would have turned out differently. Maybe then, Thomas would still be alive.

Looking up, she caught Henry's eye. He'd been slinking around in the background. An arm protectively wrapped around his new wife, Patty. A woman who looked exactly as Elizabeth had expected. She had the perfect hair, the perfect figure, and the most beautifully manicured nails that Elizabeth had ever seen. Her dress was long, black, and more suited to a black-tie event than a casual dinner and with a poised smile, Patty held tightly onto Henry's hand. Obviously defending what was hers.

Shaking her off, Henry took a step forward. 'Lizzie...' he nodded at her, obviously nervous, 'You... well, you look really well.'

He slowly looked her up and down, gently kissed her on the cheek, allowed his hand to linger on her shoulder. 'It's good to see you.'

Swallowing hard, Elizabeth forced a smile. 'Elizabeth,' she whispered, feeling determined to make a point. 'I said earlier, it's Elizabeth now.' She shuffled from foot to foot. Breathed in the scent of his soft musky aftershave and caught herself blinking back one memory after the other, like when in high school he'd held her hand and treated her with a tenderness she'd never known. A typical teenage crush that had dwindled into friendship, and while staring deep into his eyes, she wondered what had gone so very wrong between them. They'd attended the same school, acquired the same friends, and kept their schoolyard promise of going to the same university. It was a memory too far, one that caused her much sadness and through glazed over eyes, she smiled at the others as she tried to forget.

Feeling a glass of champagne being pushed into her hand, she lifted it up in an embarrassed salute, felt him lean forward and towards her. 'Do you know what? You'll always be Lizzie to me,' he rubbed the top of her arm, fondly, 'no matter how much you wish you were someone else.' Holding her gaze, he winked, then turned back to where Patty pulled at her dress, flicked her hair with a hand, and gave Elizabeth a long and disapproving look.

Nervously, Elizabeth sipped at the champagne, noticed where both Jordan and Patrick sat to one side of the room and inched her way in the opposite direction. Watching from a distance, she noticed the measured but heated discussion. The way each of them had puffed out their chest and commanded the others attention with a series of hand signals, that went back and forth, like a tennis court rally that had no end.

'No way, Tim. You... and Rowena Cooper? Really.' Lucy made a point of standing up, pouring more champagne, waving the bottle around in salute. 'I mean, come on. You were polar opposites. How the hell did you two get together? Did you hear that everyone, Timothy and Rowena Cooper, married, three kids later.'

A general consensus of opinion about Tim's marriage went around the room, with everyone then talking at once about who they did, or didn't marry. Who they'd have liked to marry, and which relationships had been doomed from the beginning. It was a subject she didn't want to get into and found herself scouring the room, hoping for a distraction.

Feeling the breeze coming in from through French doors, Elizabeth made her way to them and stepped out and onto the patio where she took a seat on a bench, beside a large, rotund woman. She was sat singing a lullaby, her soft Irish accent beautifully calming the baby who lay in the pram that she pushed back and forth.

Sighing, Elizabeth kept her eye on the lake, on the monument beside it. And wistfully, her eyes followed the way the river snaked past it, until it disappeared beyond the edge of the distant treeline to where an old and unusually slow spaniel plodded by the embankment with a familiar looking woman.

'Well, it's not quite the welcome I'd thought I'd get from you.' Peering into the pram as she spoke, the woman turned her face to one side, gave Elizabeth a huge, but welcoming smile.

'Freya...?' Recognising the voice, Elizabeth beamed a smile back. But felt a sense of unease travel through her. Furrowing her brow, she tried to dispel a rush of feelings that flooded through her as she looked Freya up and down but barely recognised her. Before, she'd been a tiny slip of a woman, her figure more like that of a boy than a woman, and her hair had been short and spiky. Pure white, with a purple tinge. Whereas now, she had big, beautiful curves. Breasts that would be the envy of a supermodel and long, brunette hair that reached down to her waist. 'You've... wow, you've changed.'

'Of course I've changed. Giving birth changes you in ways you'd never imagine.' She placed a hand on each breast, laughed. 'Three kids I've got now, and these just get bigger and bigger. You should have seen the size of them after I'd had the twins.' Returning her hold on the pram, she continued the rocking. Flicked her head backwards and towards the room. 'Do you feel as awkward as I do?' She rutted her brow in question. 'We were all so close. Too close most days. Yet now, I don't feel as though I know them at all.' She smiled awkwardly. 'Although, young William. He's looking really good. Wish I'd have taken more notice of him in my younger days, so I do.'

Turning, Elizabeth looked back towards the Grand Hall, caught sight of where William now stood beside a serving table, where a huge piece of lamb had been lay on a long silver platter. Watching she felt herself mesmerised by the way he ran a knife up and down a steel, and the large blue dressing that covered his thumb. Catching her breath, she took in the way he looked, the way he'd grown into a man. 'That's William?' She raised her eyebrows in question, moved slowly to the door, cast her gaze across his broad, muscular frame, the short, trimmed beard and the attractive smile that gave him an aristocratic look. He was the duplicate of Thomas, both in stature and looks. 'He certainly looks every bit the lord of the Manor now, doesn't he?' she said, wistfully.

'He certainly did grow up, didn't he?' Freya laughed, bit down on her lip, and blushed. 'And I'd say he looks just a bit like Thomas did. Like seeing a ghost, if you know what I mean.' Lifting the baby from her pram, Freya placed her carefully onto her shoulder, allowed the baby's head to nestle under her chin. 'Do you remember the way he used to follow us around and the way Thomas used to hate him for it?'

Shaking her head, Elizabeth sighed. 'That's because Thomas had a side to him that was cruel. He'd always make out that he didn't want William going with all the wrong girls, getting one of them into trouble, but in truth, he was simply being a bully. Nothing more. Nothing less.' She turned, paid attention to the baby, lifted a finger to stroke her cheek. 'And William, well... if I'm honest, I liked him hanging around.' It was true. Elizabeth had enjoyed his company. Especially in the days following Thomas's death, it had been a time when they'd both been young, a time when sticking together had been better than being alone.

And now, she watched William proudly. Admired the way he was dressed in the chef whites he'd always wanted to wear. Just watching him carve made her smile with delight. It was more than obvious he'd followed his dreams. Gone into the world and done exactly what he'd wanted to do. 'Good for you, William,' she whispered as she watched him place the meat on a hot plate beside him.

'Freya. We'd best go in. They're bringing out the starters.' Elizabeth took hold of the pram, pushed it towards the door, could hear Freya soothing the baby that nestled against her shoulder. She stopped in her tracks and felt her breath catch in her throat. 'That woman...' she said, 'The waitress stood near William.' She paused, closed her eyes for a beat. Tried to remember. 'Didn't she work here before?'

'Who, Anna? Of course, she did. You remember her, don't you?' Freya stepped forward, placed the baby in the pram. 'She always had a sweet spot for William; she was the one Thomas didn't approve of.' Freya replied. 'In fact, don't you remember the day we were sunbathing by the lake. The day Thomas threw William in the water...'

10

LIZZIE

Ten Years before

With my pale freckled face turned into the heat of the sun, I feel a welcome breeze sweeping in from the fields. The whole of Kirkwood Manor is surrounded by vast acres of farmland and from where I lie, I can literally see for miles, hear nothing but the sound of the river, the laughter of friends, and the birdsong that surrounds us as the overgrown meadow grass continually tickles my partially naked skin.

Lifting a hand to shield my eyes, I turn my head to one side, and while squinting through narrowed eyes, I study the tiny soft, white and yellow flowers. They grow randomly in the grass around me, and I suddenly realise that the meadow where I now lie had once been a manicured lawn, and what I'd thought to be random trees and bushes had actually been part of the landscape, all positioned according to a plan. A plan it seems that had been long since abandoned. Looking across to the trees, I see Bobby working hard with the loppers. He was the only gardener employed by the family, the only one who maintained the grounds, all alone. Which was a near to impossible task, giving the garden little to no chance of resurrection.

Sighing, I close my eyes, watch the red and yellow images ripple at speed across my eyelids, and take pleasure in the way they dance in a wild and uninhibited way across them. It's like watching a fast-burning flame, one that's completely out of control and reminds me of the bonfire we'd built just the week before. It had been a time when I'd been happy, when Thomas and I had lay with our bodies twisted together, as we'd dreamily watched the flames dance beside us until the last of the embers had disappeared. Then, Thomas had kissed me. Tenderly at first, but then with a passion to match the heat of the fire, and even though the others had been heckling, he'd taken my hand and led me back to the house, where we'd continued our love making for most of the night.

It's a memory I want to hold onto. And subconsciously, I lift my arm to create a barrier between myself and the sun. It causes too much of a contrast, and my eyes are immediately thrust into a deep, and sudden darkness. Visually, I'm back in the hallway, hiding behind the settee, listening to the words he'd shared with his mother. It's a conversation I'd rather forget. Especially after I'd spent most of the night wishing I hadn't heard it at all and as I try to erase the words from my mind, my fingers touch the bruise that now covers one side of my cheek. Knowing he'd noticed both the bruise and my dirty feet, I try to work out what he might or might not say. Or whether he'll simply ignore it. Sitting up, I realise that his mother was most probably right, that I am feral. But for me, to run around barefoot is much more preferable to shoes. It's the way I am and living wild amongst the trees would be much nicer for me than living with people, who don't want me around.

Propping myself up against the trunk of a tree, I take my frustration out on the hem of my top. It's a top I'd bought just a few days before and suddenly, I begin to question the charity shop purchase. It's much too big and hangs loosely from my shoulders. But the bright yellow sunflowers had brought a smile to my face. And because I'd desperately wanted to be a part of the crowd, I'd used my last two pounds to make the purchase. A decision which meant I'd had a long and arduous walk ahead of me, rather than my normal bus trip home.

'Freya… are you asleep?' I find amusement in the way my friend jumps at the sound of my voice, the way she curls up on her side, pushes a hand beneath her face by way of a pillow. 'Freya…' I wait for her to move. 'This top?' Again, I pull at the hem, 'Is it okay? Is it something the others would wear?' I pause, consider everyone around me, and as always, I feel like an imposter amongst my peers.

'If you don't like what you're wearing, you should just take it off, so you should.' Freya finally snapped, her Irish drawl filtering through. 'And as for everyone else, why don't you take a bit of a look around yourself. They're all practically naked for most of the day, anyhow. All of them, flaunting everything they have in the hope of catching themselves a Kirkwood. It's disgraceful.' Sitting up, she rests her hand under her chin, leans against it thoughtfully, and gives me an apologetic smile. 'There's not a single one of them who wouldn't screw Thomas right behind your back. You mark my words.' She nods, assertively.

I allow my gaze to drift back to the lake, to the small, broken dive platform, where Thomas had been just a few moments before, spade in hand, digging groves into the embankment. He'd slipped while climbing in and out of the lake once too often and had decided to dig a transitory foothold, a place where we could all climb out without trying.

'Thomas wouldn't do that and what's more, he doesn't like other girls throwing themselves at him.' I pick up my hat, waft it in front of my face, feel the colour rise to my cheeks. 'Not any more. Not now we're together.' I speak defensively, hopeful that Freya will back down, take back the words.

'Don't be naïve, Lizzie. Thomas thrives on all the attention. And you might be his "girlfriend" today, but just don't you count on being his girlfriend tomorrow, or next week.' She sits up, uses her hands to make speech marks in the sky as she says the word 'girlfriend'. Gives me a sympathetic smile. 'It wouldn't surprise me if he didn't have half a dozen different girlfriends. He probably has them all on the go, all at once. They could all be sat in various positions, all around the lake.' She used a finger to point. 'He's probably moving from one to the other, right this minute. Telling them all how special they are, how they should keep their love a secret, just like he used to do with you.' She purses her lips, pouts in my direction.

Disbelieving of Freya's words, I do my best to block them out and anxiously, I pull a daisy from the ground, begin to rhythmically pluck at its petals to throw them one by one at the grass. *He loves me. He loves me not.* Biting down on my lower lip, I keep my eyes on the water. I keep wishing that Thomas would emerge, walk across the grass, and take me in his arms. Do something to show me how he feels and to make the others see how much he loves me. But deep down, my mind is working overtime, and I begin to question everything and everyone around me.

Taking in a breath, I turn confidently to Freya. 'Don't be silly. Thomas loves me.' I emphasise the word, me. 'I sleep in his bed all the time; he wouldn't have time for anyone else, would he?'

'And you don't think he has any opportunities? You're not always together. You're away at uni more often than not and he works all the hours he can, all those night shifts, weekends, overtime.'

'Freya, just because we're not together twenty-four hours a day, you can't just assume that Thomas is playing away, can you?' Even though I know that Thomas is a player. I feel as though I have no choice but to defend both him and the relationship we have. 'Me and Thomas, we've made plans.' I blink away the tears, feel the pain rise up within me as I consider what a life without Thomas would be like.

'Go on then. What do you think, is going to happen? What plans are you going to make?'

Thoughtfully, I search the flower that I hold in my hand. There's just one petal left. *He loves me not...* It wasn't the outcome I should have had from the game, and in disgust I throw the flower on the grass and quickly pluck another. 'We've already said, we're going to go travelling. Back packing across the world. Get ourselves a little married. Have half a dozen children. All of which we'll bring up right here. In this house, once he inherits it.' I nod decisively. And while frantically plucking the petals from the new flower, in the hope of a better outcome. I wish I were speaking the truth.

'Really.' She runs a hand through her short, spikey hair. 'So, if he loves you that much, what's the bruise all about? Everyone's taking bets on what you did to piss him off this time.'

Quickly, I lift a hand to my cheek. 'Oh my God. What do you mean, this time? Thomas has never hit me.' I stare, my eyes wide, disbelieving. 'This, this was my own fault, it had nothing at all to do with Thomas. Nothing at all.'

'Yeah, sure... you seem to forget, most of us know Thomas a whole lot better than you do...'

'Freya,' I snap, 'Last night, I went to the kitchen for a drink. It was dark and I didn't put a light on. It was my own fault, I was too busy watching the shadows, sneaking through the dark and I walked into the bloody sideboard.' Closing my eyes, I could still feel the pain. 'And that really big lamp that sits on top, I almost knocked it off.' In my temper, I look everywhere but at Freya. I shouldn't have to explain myself. My word should have been enough and with tears threatening to fall, I cast my gaze around the grounds, focus on four of Thomas's friends who whack a tennis ball back and forth. They're using temporary base and service lines. Each line has been roughly painted onto the broken tarmac. An old tennis court that should have been dismantled, along with a net that had long since lost its tension. Even the chain link fence that surrounds the court has bigger holes in it than doorways. Which means that a lot of the time, his friends are chasing the balls that slip through the holes, rather than actually managing to play the game.

'Go and ask them if you can play?' Freya suggests as she pulls a bottle of water from her bag, takes a long, slow slurp. 'Unless you're too posh to play. You know, now you're going to be lady of the manor?' She smirks, lies the bottle down beside her, then thinks better of it and returns it to the bag.

'I don't want to play. It's far too hot.' I move my gaze back to the lake, watch how the sun is shimmering above the water. It's created a mirrored reflection of the trees on its surface. A golden streak of sun shines down its centre. And then I see the dragonflies. They're dancing merrily around its boggy edge. 'I'd love to live here. Bring my children up here. It's so peaceful.' I add in a dreamy, wishful voice, then I begin to laugh as the peace is shattered, and a loud yell is followed by the biggest splash. 'Oh my God, I think someone just got tossed in the lake.'

'Lizzie. Everyone we know lives in a house like this.' The comment automatically falls from Freya's mouth, as she jumps up to stand on her tip toes, looks around the trees that restrict their view. 'Looks like William took a dip and Thomas. Well, it looks like Thomas threw him in.' She moves from foot to foot, stands on a tree stump to catch a better look. 'Something to do with that assistant, Anna. I have no idea why she's always hanging around him.' I watch the amusement cross Freya's face. 'Look. She's skulking back to the house, like a horse that's just been whipped.'

'He whipped her?'

'No, she just looks like she's been whipped. It's just a saying.' She gives me a look, a roll of her eyes. 'I expect Thomas has gone and caught them at it again. Fourth or fifth time this week. And now, well now she has a face as long as her arse. Look at her.'

Shrugging. I turn on my stomach. Keep my eyes on the house. 'Not me. I don't live in a house like this.' I go back to my earlier conversation, pull a pair of sunglasses from my bag, place them over my eyes and peer aimlessly across the grounds, desperate to see what's just happened. 'My house, where I live with my dad,' I pause. Almost too embarrassed to continue. It's the first time I've had to explain who I am, where I'm from and nervously, I hope that my background doesn't go against me. 'It's just a terraced house.' I close my eyes and see the paper-thin walls, the anaglypta wallpaper, the open coal fire, and the kitchen that's so small, it resembles a ship's galley. 'All the houses in our street, they're really close together. Literally joined to the next. Most days, I can hear the conversation that's happening in the house next door, and only when I'm really lucky do I get the chance to park right outside our own property. Some days, I can't even park in the same street.' I laugh, feel the colour flood my cheeks. 'Yet here.' I look at the house. My arm outstretched. 'There are no other houses for miles and at a guess, I'd say they could easily park thirty or forty cars without a problem.'

'Urgh, your house. It sounds delightful. I can almost smell the poverty.'

'Freya, don't mock.'

'You know he'll inherit it, don't you?' Freya said as she began to casually rub sun cream into her shoulders. 'Even though it's practically a bomb site… it'll be up to him to restore it. To work every single day of his life just to pay for its keep.' She pauses, holds the bottle up in the air, as though she's trying to see how much of the contents is left. 'He'll probably end up paying a shit load of inheritance tax too. Is that still a thing and more so, is that what you really want?' She flops back down onto the grass, and moves onto her knees, and perches, meerkat fashion.

Nodding, I give Freya a genuine smile. 'I'd give anything to live here.' With my architect mind jumping into full working mode, I tip my head to one side. 'Most of the work's cosmetic. It's the gardens that will take the time. But with Bobby's help, we could easily do it.' I wave a hand in dismissal but realise that Freya has already lost interest; she's moved and is now lying on the grass ready to snooze, giving me the chance to study the house. I pay close attention to the multi-faceted roof and begin to wonder why I hadn't really noticed it before and whether or not it indicates a hidden layer, another level to the property that can't be seen from the front.

'Freya, have you noticed the roofline?' Instinctively, I cock my head to one side. 'I must ask Thomas, I'm sure there's a third floor. I wonder if that's where they keep the Kirkwood family secrets.'

'Darling. If they had any secrets, don't you think they'd sell them? Hire back the gardeners and pay for repairs, rather than old man Kirkwood climbing up and down those rickety, old ladders? I swear, one of these days, those ladders, they'll be the death of him.'

I partially close one eye and focus on the roofline. 'Do you see the way the ivy grows?' I whispered. 'It's blocking out a small window near the eaves. One that even Dominic's ladders couldn't possibly reach.' I laugh, then I poke Freya in the ribs. 'Freya, pay attention?'

'Darling, do you know what, I really have no interest in a window, a third floor, or the Kirkwood's fucking secrets. What I really want is lunch. Do you think they'll feed us today, or do you reckon it's up to us to go scavenging?'

Sitting back, I watch the way she scowls. The way she shows an obvious dislike to anything Kirkwood and for a moment, I wonder if there's a hidden reason behind her disdain, something she hasn't told me.

'Freya. You and Thomas. Were you ever a couple?' I ask the question without thinking. A part of me has no idea why I've asked and I almost don't want to hear the answer.

Laughing, Freya turns on her side. Looks across the meadow to where Thomas is stood, spade resting on his shoulder. 'Darling, Thomas has done the rounds with everyone here. More than once. And mark my words, he'll most probably take another round with those who'll let him before he settles down and chooses a wife.' She rests a hand almost affectionately on my knee. 'Just don't take it personally, don't get too close, and don't get hurt. He's a player, always has been, always will be. You know that.'

Feeling betrayed, I move my knee from beneath her touch. Stand up and give Thomas a wave. 'If you don't like them, then why do you come here?' I raise my eyebrows and smile as I ask the question.

Laughing, Freya lifts both hands, palms up, shrugs her shoulders, 'Oh, I don't know. I suppose it's fun. Most of the time. Being Irish, my parents, they're quite strict, but here, there's a new party every night, Thomas's parents don't seem to care that we're all as high as bloody kites, or that we take over their house for our own enjoyment. And I could ask you the same question. Who wouldn't want to be here?'

11

ELIZABETH

Present Day - Friday Night

Pushing the Crème Brulé from side to side, Elizabeth lifted the last remaining spoonful to her mouth and did all she could to swallow. It was a dessert she'd have normally loved, but as the whispers circulated and the pointing began, she felt the tension in the room escalate and her appetite diminish.

Without exception, everyone was skirting around the subject of Thomas. Telling jokes that didn't strike her as funny and making comments that were laughed at with a forced hilarity. It was as though no one really wanted to acknowledge what had happened, or to talk about what really mattered and as she looked around the table, she wondered whether or not his killer really had returned to the scene, just as Ada had predicted.

Taking short, sharp breaths, she listened to the hushed tones that came from around the table from the people closest to her. Some were the friends they'd met at uni. Whereas the others were

Ada's relations, ones Elizabeth had previously met at the family parties she'd been allowed to attend and with an unnatural smile, she caught the eye of one of Thomas's aunts, then that of an uncle who uncannily had a look of Dominic. He gave her an inquisitive look that told Elizabeth he hadn't remembered her at all, not in the way she remembered him. Then, with tear filled eyes, she felt a hand drop onto her shoulder, a gentle squeeze. One that made her close her eyes with gratitude as she recognised Cookie's familiar touch.

'Keep smiling, my girl.' The words made Elizabeth lean back in her chair as she watched Cookie walk across the room where uneasily she stood by the side of the fire. Lifting her glass to her lips, she winked at Elizabeth, then quickly moved to one side as two of Thomas's aunts headed into her space, where they chatted in words that were louder than whispers. Whereas a few of the younger ones stood around, their voices speaking over each other in waves. It was a noise that was getting louder by the minute. Then there was Ada who smiled politely and, without hesitation, she invited both Cookie and Bobby to sit beside her. It was a wonderful thing to see, although at first when Bobby had walked in, Elizabeth had barely recognised him in his smart jeans and a shirt, rather than the outdoor clothes he'd always worn.

Smiling, she appreciated the way he lifted a glass in her direction. It was a gesture that made her grin and in response, she did the same before watching him tentatively pull out a chair for Ada to sit in.

Pushing the empty bowl away, Elizabeth counted the people who remained at the table, realised that out of a room of what had been around forty, only sixteen of them still sat at the dining table that had been decorated with crisp white tablecloths, nine-armed Baroque style candelabras, and white, flickering candles. There were fresh-cut flowers scattered directly onto the tablecloth, all lying randomly down its centre and interspersed with silver salt and pepper shakers that perfectly matched the antique coffee pots that were being passed around the table.

Elizabeth's attention was drawn to the door where Anna, the waitress, pushes her way through. She's pushing a hostess style trolley that's piled high with cups and saucers, which she carefully places on the table in front of those that remain. The others are taken across the room, to where both Ada and Cookie are sat in comfortable chairs, now surrounded by members of Ada's family, all who look a little over-excited to be there. With Bobby pacing back and forth, looking as though he'd rather be anywhere else in the world.

Feeling desperate to speak to Cookie again, Elizabeth inched forward in her seat but noticed how all the chairs had been grouped together to form a small and intimate gathering. A gathering she didn't feel she could join and what's more, she certainly couldn't face the agony of once again having to explain who she was and why she was here to all the people who didn't already know her.

It was only then that Elizabeth realised that Freya had disappeared. She'd somehow managed to discreetly slip from the room, along with the pram and baby Louisa. The sudden and distant hungry cry of a baby told Elizabeth that once again, Freya had gone to feed her daughter, something she'd continuously done throughout the evening. Smiling to herself, Elizabeth threw her mind back to the Freya she'd known before. She'd had a young and hedonistic attitude that had been a huge part of her personality. She'd previously thought nothing of nudity, of sitting around practically naked. A life that had far less boundaries than the ones that governed them today.

Now it was only their old school friends who remained at the table. The same people she and Thomas had begun university with. Which had been fun when they'd all been together, but once Thomas and Jordan had gone off to their placements, the group had drifted apart, only meeting on weekends or bank holidays at the Manor and only because the food and drink had been free. They'd been the people they used to call friends. Friends who were now unfamiliar, and Freya had been right: they did feel more like strangers.

With a sudden urge to make her own excuses, Elizabeth inched even further forward in her seat.

'You're not going, are you?' For what seemed like only the second time that night, Henry let go of Patty's hand and moved into the seat that Freya had vacated. 'So, what do you make of it all?' With an attentive smile, he scanned the room, focused on where Lucy and Timothy sat at the opposite side of the table. 'They've kept themselves to themselves all night, haven't they?' he whispered. Laughed. 'If I didn't know better, I'd have thought those two were a lot closer than we've been led to believe.'

Nodding, Elizabeth rubbed her hands down her jeans, accepted the coffee from the waitress, took her time over the adding of milk and stirring the contents. 'They were always as thick as thieves; back in the day, we all thought they'd be a couple.' She gazed across the table at them, saw the way they looked lovingly into one another's eyes, the sparkle within that shone through the smiles. Unexpectedly, she felt envious of their friendship, the obvious affection they shared, wished for just someone in this room to look at her in that same level of affection.

'By the looks of them, there could still be a chance, don't you think?' Furrowing his thick-set eyebrows in question, he lifted them up and down comically. They were eyebrows that spoke for him. Made suggestions Elizabeth felt sure he'd never say out loud. 'They do look close.'

'Don't be daft.' She tapped him playfully on the leg. 'I think

Lucy would prefer a date with me rather than Timothy.' Pausing, she leaned in a little closer, caught the undertones of his after-shave. Closed her eyes for a beat. 'Talking of which... where is Jessica? I thought she'd be here.'

'Ah... you don't know.' Moving uncomfortably in his seat, Henry took in a slow, deep breath. 'Jessica. She was killed in a car crash. I thought you'd have heard.'

Shaking her head, Elizabeth swallowed hard, and kept her eyes averted. 'I didn't know.' Staring at the floor, Elizabeth felt lost for words. No one had told her. But then, after Thomas had died, she'd blamed them all for his death, changed her number, deleted her social media. But had still lived with her father. Which meant that if any of them had really wanted to find her, they could have. And instead of following everything they did, she convinced herself that starting again had been the right thing to do.

For years, she'd kept away from any kind of relationship. Hadn't taken any of her casual boyfriend's home. There wouldn't have been much point, not when her father hadn't encouraged it. For him, no one was good enough for his daughter. And the thought of taking a man back to her terraced house bedroom for a night of passion hadn't appealed.

'I didn't know,' she repeated, 'But, I guess that explains things.' The whole way through the meal, Elizabeth had watched the way Timothy and Lucy had focused on each other. The way they'd chatted in whispers, giggled at private jokes, and were so engrossed in each other's company; they'd barely spoken to anyone else at the table. Unlike both Patrick and Jordan, two men who were polar opposites. Patrick had taken his time to work his way around the group, he'd commanded attention, and had constantly boasted about every achievement he'd ever had. Aggressively pushing himself forward and onto anyone who'd listen, just as he had before Thomas had died.

Then, unnervingly there was Jordan, who'd made his way across the room to sit beside her and Freya for over an hour and with piercing eyes that stared directly at Elizabeth, he'd pleaded poverty with an unwavering conviction. He'd made sure that everyone knew how difficult his life had been. How walking away from his degree had left him with no choice but to take low paid work and how some years he hadn't been able to work at all. Typically, blaming everyone but himself for how things had turned out.

'Everyone's changed so much...' she whispered to Henry, as she realised how much time had altered them all and even though Elizabeth hadn't arrived expecting anyone to look or act the same, she remembered how clean shaven they all used to be and the sudden appearance of so much body hair on all the men had taken her by surprise. The last time she'd seen most of them, had been at a time when they'd have had more pimples than whiskers. Whereas now, Timothy was twice the size he used to be. Broad, and muscular, with a mop of wild, ginger hair, and a thick, impressive beard.

Feeling claustrophobic, Elizabeth pushed her coffee cup to one side. 'Sorry Henry, it's all been lovely, but I... I can't do this... not tonight...' She began to walk away, felt a hand on her wrist.

'Lizzie. Please. If not tonight, when can I speak to you.' He lifted his eyebrows in question, searched her eyes, 'I need to speak to you about sticking together? I think we'd all be safer if we do.'

'What do you mean?' She said the words much louder than she'd intended and caught her breath as a sudden silence hit the room, as people stopped what they were doing and waited for her to continue. It was a moment that made her quickly skim her gaze from one person to the other. She began to feel uneasy, wondered if Henry felt unsafe too, whether he thought them all at danger now they were back and with suspicious eyes. She began to see why each and every one of them might have wanted Thomas dead.

Leaning forward, Elizabeth pressed her mouth close to Henry's ear. 'I don't know what the hell you're up to, or what you mean, but you're scaring me, and you need to stop, right now.' She eased away, caught his eye. 'It's hard enough being here, Henry, without you making it out to be more than it is. Besides, you don't impress me. Not any more. And I've already told you, it's Elizabeth.'

Annoyed, she shook her hand free, took note of where Ada sat in her chair, guarding the room with eyes of steel. And even though she was surrounded by her family and friends, it occurred to Elizabeth that Ada looked totally alone. *We're not that different, you and I*, Elizabeth whispered internally as she realised how much Ada's life had changed. And for a moment Elizabeth actually felt sorry for the woman. Wished she could fill the empty chairs that stood around the table, and bring everyone back who'd sat in them, including Thomas.

'I'm going to take a walk down to the monument,' she whispered over her shoulder at Ada. 'Would you like to come with me?'

Shaking her head, Ada tapped the walking frame with a finger, smiled back. 'Not tonight...' she held a hand to her chest, struggled to breathe, 'It's been a long day. An interesting day, and...' she paused, looked around the room. 'And you... you need to spend some time alone - with Thomas.'

Making her way outside, Elizabeth tried to understand why she needed time alone with Thomas. It wasn't as though he were really there, buried in the ground, beside the lake. Yet suddenly Ada seemed to be an advocate of the relationship they'd had and with her brow furrowed and confused, she could still hear the way Ada had openly encouraged Thomas to find himself a new and more eligible girlfriend. One who'd make him the perfect wife. The wife she'd always wanted him to have.

Closing her eyes for a blink, she stepped up to the balustrade, took in a deep breath, and looked up at the sky. The heat of the sun had diminished, and although the darkness wouldn't fall for another couple of hours, she knew that dusk would begin quite soon. Sighing, she took in the familiar skyline that had now filled with colours of bright orange and red, against a darker blue backdrop. It was an image she'd always loved. One that had been imprinted on her mind during the years since she'd left, as was the drooping sun that now shimmered with the heat of summer, like a mirage of warmth waiting to explode, just as soon as it touched the surface of the lake that waited below.

Leaving the patio behind, Elizabeth headed across the lawns, suddenly felt pleased she hadn't had the time to change, that her old, soft, white plimsoles were comfortable to walk in and although it had threatened to rain, it hadn't. The ground was pleasantly firm, and the meadow easy to walk on. Sighing, she walked in circles, touched every tree, ran her fingertips through each of the flower beds. It was as though she were saying hello, apologising for not being with them for such a long time, taking pleasure in the fragrance that exploded from them.

As she neared the monument, Elizabeth forced herself to stare at the large, oblong stones that stood one on top of the other. Each of them pale, cream, and just a little smaller than the one below, with ridges carved vertically into their sides, perfectly lined up to give an illusion that the monument was much taller than it was.

Standing on the newly laid path. Elizabeth realised it was the one Ada had spoken of. It circled the lake, meandered in and out of the trees and if followed, it was more than obvious that you could do a whole circuit around the gardens, and without turning around you'd end up back where you'd started.

Stopping in front of the tall, stone monument. Elizabeth swallowed hard. Felt her heart accelerate with nerves and without knowing why, she looked at the floor. No matter how much she wanted to, she couldn't bring herself to read the words. To do so would make it real. Instead, she crouched down, glanced across the surface of the lake, took in the full, mirrored effect that always happened at this time of the evening. Just one or two slight ripples formed in its centre and without trying, it spoiled the effect of glass that reflected the sun onto its surface, to throw all the colours of orange, red, gold, and blue back at her.

'Red sky at night, isn't that what they say, Thomas.' Speaking to the base of the stone, Elizabeth lifted a hand, and with her eyes tightly closed, she pressed her hand flat against it. 'Oh, I don't know why I'm talking to you, why I don't want to see the words. It's just a stone and it's not like you're really here, is it?' She opened her eyes, gave the stone a pensive smile, felt her shoulders drop as she crossed her legs and picked at the grass. 'I never wanted to be one of those women who sat by gravestones, chatting. It was never something I did after mum died and to be honest, I always thought it a bit crazy when I saw the others doing it, if you know what I mean. But such a lot has happened since... well since...' she timidly lifted her eyes towards the willow tree, saw a small white duck swimming in and out of the drooping branches, totally oblivious to the trauma that had once happened beneath it or the secrets it still held.

'We're all here for your memorial.' She shrugged her shoulders. 'Although, I have no idea what your mum has planned. It's as though she's on a final mission to catch your killer, but I have to say, she looks unbelievably frail, so very sick and well... she needs to know what happened. That night, at the lake.' Pausing, Elizabeth felt her eyes fill with tears. 'I wish I could remember; I wish I'd seen who it was.' She closed her eyes as tightly as she could, tried to remember and saw images flickering in and out of her mind. Hallucinations of a huge, dragon-like cartoon. It flew across the sky. Across the lake that was surrounded by lots of naked people. There were fire baskets, with sparks that flew up and into the air. Then, there had been Thomas's grey, battered face, slipping slowly below the water's surface and disappearing from her view.

Despairingly, Elizabeth lay down on the grass, ran a hand through the small, yellow and white flowers that still grew in the meadow, gazed across the top of the water and dreamily, she looked towards where the old, battered diving platform used to be.

'Oh Thomas... our platform, it's gone,' she gasped, held a hand to her mouth, thought of all the things that had been hidden beneath it and of how on the night Thomas had died, the others had scrambled around the lake, removing all traces of the drugs they'd got and of how Patrick had taken them to the clearing, and buried them in the ground as a final act of defiance.

12

LIZZIE

Ten years before

Being piggy backed across the lake, and with my legs straddled around Thomas's waist, I hook my arm around his shoulder, press my chest tightly against his back, and feel his heart pumping wildly within.

Sweeping the pond weed away with my arm, I grab at the reeds, take a deep breath in, kiss the back of Thomas's neck and then nervously, I bite down on my lower lip. I'm doing all I can to try and forget the conversation I'd overheard the night before, but the words keep coming back and thoughtfully, I watch the sky turn from grey to black. The bright summers evening we thought we'd have had now become dark and moody. Thick black clouds have begun to merge, and they monopolise the sky with the overbearing promise of rain.

Leaning back, I let go of his shoulder. Realise that we're the only two left at the lake. That everyone else has deserted us and have ventured up the embankment, where they're sat on the grass around the burning fire baskets, drinking, smoking weed, and making the most of the evening before the rain stops play. Stretching, I see one or two of them wandering back to the house and with the weather being on the turn, I presume they've gone in search of the warmth and hot drinks from Cookie's kitchen.

'Where's everyone going?' Thomas points to the fire basket, to the group beside it, who are now shivering, wrapped in towels. 'They're not seriously done for the night, are they?' He lifts his arm, looks at his watch. 'Hey lightweights. Don't you dare drink all the wine before we get there... we'll be there in a minute.' He shouts as loud as he can and wishfully, I hope they do go back to the house. That for once, I'd get just a couple of hours alone with Thomas without being disturbed.

Savouring what's left of the evening, I close my eyes, try to imagine how life would be if it were just the two of us. What we'll be doing ten years from now. And after last night's revelations, after what Ada had said, I wonder if we'll still be together. Or, if as Thomas promised me, we'd have been back packing around the world, before settling here and bringing up our children in this house, teaching them how to swim in this lake. And with an overzealous sense of excitement taking over my mind, I wonder how many children we might have, and what their names could be. But then I try to decide whether Ada and Dominic would allow it.

'Thomas.' I pause, not knowing how to continue. 'You do love me, don't you?' As I ask the question, I immediately feel stupid for the needy tone of my voice. Wish I simply knew the answer without having to ask. 'I mean... we are good together, aren't we?'

Turning his head, I see the sparkle in his eye as he captures my mouth with his, pulls me into a deep, loving kiss that without speaking any words, answers my question. Then, as quickly as the kiss began, it stops, and I hear myself screaming as Thomas spins me around. He's moving at speed. We're in the deepest part of the lake, the part where we can only just touch the bottom, but without a care, I hold on tight and hypnotically, I revel in the sound of his boyish laughter.

'I do love you, Thomas.' I say the words out loud, press my mouth to his neck, hope for an immediate response, for him to finally tell me how he feels.

'Hey, come on. Where's this all coming from?' He asks, before gently, and in a well-practised manoeuvre, he pulls me around until I'm straddling his waist, I'm facing him, and I can feel his arousal against me. The warmth of anticipation flows through my veins and I press myself sensuously against him, and while smiling with excitement, we move slowly back to the side of the lake where we lean against the embankment.

'Nothing... oh, I don't know... I just...' I want to ask him about the night before. About what he'd said to his mother. But for some reason, I'm scared of the truth and know that if these are my last days with Thomas, I want them to be happy, not sad. I want us both to look back on them with a fondness, rather than Thomas remembering me as being an anxious, slightly crazy, or over-bearing girlfriend. One who'd asked far too many questions.

'Thomas. Make love to me...'

'What, here in the lake?' Smiling, he doesn't need telling twice and I feel him pull at my bikini bottoms, at the ties that hold them in place, and then with a mischievous grin he lifts them up and out of the water, tosses them towards the bushes. Watching the deep sparkle of his eyes, I love the way they shine back at me through the semi-darkness of dusk. With a gasp, I once again feel his arousal, and I reach up to hold onto the wooden dive platform, use it for support.

Taking his time, Thomas teases my mouth with his tongue. His hands and fingertips gently arouse me and then, I feel my lips crushed against his. The strong muscular contours of his body shape themselves to mine and then, without warning, he thrusts himself deep inside me, making me gasp with pleasure. Moving against him and while I'm still holding tightly to the platform, we begin a fierce and powerful tempo. One that has an urgency I've never known. My heart pounds in my chest, and as Thomas's mouth leaves mine, I feel it sear a path down my neck, and as I lift my face up towards the sky, I feel the first drops of rain bounce against my skin and knowing that a downpour is about to come, I lift my mouth back to his. Savour the idea of making love in a storm.

'Jesus Lizzie, I want you so damned much.' Thomas whispers the words between kisses. His hands skim my hips as he thrusts against me. Sending a sporadic current of desire spiralling through every inch of my body and instinctively, I arch towards him, the rhythmic motion deepens and in the heat of the moment, I allow myself to scream with desire, as my whole body erupts in a volcano of pleasure.

For the next few minutes, we simply lie there, against the muddy embankment, curled up naked, in each other's arms. Listening to the sound of his breathing, I lie as still as I can. I'm too afraid to move. Too afraid to break the spell and even though I'm trembling with the cold, I close my eyes and smile, as the threatened rain now pours relentlessly around us.

'We should go back to the house.' As Thomas whispers, he breaks the spell and as he leaves my arms, I feel the coldness surround me. Standing up, he grabs his t-shirt from the embankment, begins to dress. 'Come on, the others have gone.' With his fingertips reaching for me, I curl my hand into his, allow him to pull me up until I'm stood naked beside him.

Staring into his eyes, I repeat the question I'd asked earlier.

Feel the need of his answer even more now. 'Thomas. You do love me, don't you?'

Reaching up, he cups my chin with his hand, pulls me towards him, rests a gentle kiss on my forehead. Then, with tears in his eyes, he stares into mine. 'No matter what happens. Lizzie. You know I'll always love you. You do know that, don't you?'

13

ADA

Present Day - Friday Night

Feeling exhausted, Ada sipped at the last of her whisky and allowed it to coat the surface of her lips and tongue, as though it were nectar being taken from a flower. It wasn't something she'd normally do, but tonight was different. Tonight, she was surrounded by all the people she blamed. All the people who'd been here on the night that her son died. Or at least, they were all the people she suspected of his murder. With that thought in mind, she'd wanted to look them all in the eye, savour the moment, and try to work out which one of them was guilty.

Finally, and after much deliberation, she signalled to a young waitress to bring her another drink. Then, as discreetly as she could, she excused herself from the group and with a firm grip on her walking frame, she used it to shuffle carefully across the room, and as she did, she felt everyone turn and watch and deep inside, she knew that they were all taking great delight in watching how easily the mighty could fall.

Smiling as fondly as she could at Lucy, Ada gave an involuntary sigh. Wondered how different life would have been if Thomas had met a girl like her. A girl from the right family, and with the right connections. Of course, she'd known all about Lucy's indiscretions. She hadn't been blind. But had felt sure that if she and Thomas had been a couple, Lucy would have changed. She'd have given up on her adolescent crushes towards other women and she and Thomas would have settled down, had children of their own. After all, Thomas had always wanted to fill the house with children. But her job as his mother had been to ensure he filled the house with the *right* children. Ones who would have had the right lineage, the right ancestors, and in her opinion, Kirkwood Manor would then have had the heir it had always deserved.

'Are you okay?' Mrs McCulloch had obviously noticed how the atmosphere had changed, how everyone in the room had turned and stared and protectively; she'd moved into a position behind where Ada now stood, looking frail, wounded. 'Would you like to come to the library, I could get you settled, make you a fresh pot of tea?' Carefully, she placed a hand on the walking frame, slowed Ada's pace.

'I don't like it in here. Not any more.' Ada replied, 'The whole house. It's changed now that William owns it. I'm going to go outside, to calm myself down. Take in some air.'

Nodding thoughtfully, Mrs McCulloch continued to walk with her. 'Is it so bad that William did all of this? I mean, he's a wonderful chef and the food, well, I loved every mouthful.'

Standing still, Ada turned. 'He should have been a doctor, or a barrister. Like me.' She growled. 'If that had happened, I could have turned a blind eye to it all. But it didn't. Instead, my child chooses to work in a kitchen, where he chops vegetables for a living.' Staring, she took in a breath, 'And what's more, the chances of him marrying the right kind of girl are close to non-existent. No one wants to marry a kitchen hand, do they? You should know that.' She flashed her a look, turned back to the frame. 'My Dominic, he'd be turning in his grave, when he should be here to sort things out. So in his absence, it's down to me.'

Stepping through the French doors, Ada looked over her shoulder, gave an arresting smile as the elderly cook disappeared into the distance. She knew how much home truths hurt. But now, it was time for William to learn a truth of his own, for him to do as she wanted, once and for all.

Moving across the patio, she took in a deep breath. Loved the fresh summer air and smiled as she saw that her favourite bench stood empty. It was a bench that Bobby had erected for her and was perfectly positioned to gain the best of the sunlight. A place she'd often come after her dinner each night. A secluded spot where she could look at the gardens, the lake, and the monument all at once without having to move.

With a final step, she let go of the frame, allowed her body to drop awkwardly onto the bench where she shuffled herself into position, got herself comfortable, and then as aggressively as she could, she pushed the walking frame out of sight. It was the last thing she wanted to look at. A constant reminder that her body was failing, much quicker than she'd hoped.

Holding a hand up to her eyes, Ada used it as a shade and enviously she watched the way Elizabeth moved rhythmically across the lawn. It didn't seem fair or right that somehow, she'd survived. How conveniently, she and Thomas had become separated, that he'd lost his life, and that hers had carried on as though his death had never happened. What's more, she still had so many more years left to live. Unlike herself, whose time was running out fast. Or for Thomas, who'd been taken away from her far too soon. It was a thought that left her with a bitter, acrid taste in her mouth, a need for revenge, and an undying desire that his killer be brought to justice.

With an exacting eye, she noticed every movement Elizabeth made. The way she moved in circles, took notice of every plant, every tree. The way she allowed her fingertips to brush across them all as she passed. It was as though she didn't have a care in the world, and as she reached the monument, Ada felt herself become furious with grief. A grief that became vehemently worse when she noticed the way Elizabeth kept her eyes averted, the way she failed to look up, and didn't even take the time to read the name that had been so carefully carved into the stone.

Disgusted, Ada pulled a lace handkerchief out of her bag. The air had turned humid, and she wafted the piece of lace around in an attempt to create any kind of draft she could. Then, as her anger grew, she looked back at the house, wondered where the waitress had gone. Whether her drink would ever come. It was just another thing that had changed. The staff didn't attend to her properly. Not any more. Whereas ten years before, they'd have brought the drink promptly.

Gripping the edge of the bench tightly, she watched as her fingers went white with the pressure. Then, she stared up at a sky that was streaked with a vivid violet hue and although most saw red skies for the good weather that followed, the sky tonight was a mixture of violet and blue. A sign that a storm would follow soon and she felt surprised by the birdsong that suddenly filled the air, like a choir, waiting to greet her.

Hearing hesitant footsteps shuffling up behind, Ada glanced angrily over her shoulder. Saw a young waitress approaching. The look of fear and anxiety splashed all over her face. And with a large tray, laden with drinks, she hovered expectantly.

'Finally. You took your time. Did you serve everyone else first?'

Ada spat the words, 'I'm still the lady of this house, you do know that, don't you? And you, young lady, would do well to remember.' She paused for breath. 'Just put it down.' Sitting forward, she tutted and used a pointed finger to tap on the table. 'And that needs wiping. It should always be clean.'

'Yes, Mrs Kirkwood.' With a shaking hand, the girl pulled a cloth from her pocket to clean the table, then as though an afterthought, she lifted the glass from the tray, placed it in front of Ada. 'Would... would you like me to get you some ice, or water for that, Mrs Kirkwood?'

'Water?' Scowling distastefully, Ada lifted the glass, swirled it around. 'This is a single malt whisky. You don't put water in it. Not ever.' Sipping, she rolled the fluid around her mouth, savoured the taste and, as though proving a point, she tipped the glass backwards, swallowed the drink whole, slammed it back down on the table. 'Now, bring me another,' she said with a sardonic smile, before turning her attention back to Elizabeth, who now lay on the grass, apparently sleeping. 'Oh, and while you're in there,' she snapped at the waitress, 'tell my son I want to speak to him.'

14

WILLIAM

Present Day - Friday Night

'Your mother, she's on the south patio.' With eyes full of tears, Tracey stood nervously in the entrance to the kitchen. 'She...' Taking a breath, she placed the heavy black tray down on the worktop, began taking the empty glasses from it, and while stifling a sob, she pulled one of the dishwashers open and angrily began to drop glasses onto the top tier.

At the mention of his mother's name, William stopped stirring the soup, moved the pan from the heat, and looked over his shoulder, 'Tracey... what was that about my mother?' He tipped his head to one side, gave her a puzzled look.

'Sorry. She... she wants to speak to you.' The tears that had previously threatened now dropped down her cheeks and with the back of her hand, she swiped at her face.

Turning back to the pan, William closed his eyes for a beat. He'd wanted to finish making the soup but palpitations began to race in his chest. An involuntary action that sent his blood pressure soaring, until all he could hear was the sound of his heartbeat vibrating noisily in his ears. It wasn't that he was scared or even nervous of his mother; he just knew that being summoned never ended well. And ever since being a child, he'd always dreaded confrontation. Especially the ones where demands were made. The ones where repercussions would follow, and the fallout could last for many days.

Thinking back, he could remember all the demands she'd made of Thomas. The way she'd constantly told him what to do. How to act. Where to go to school. And most of the time, he'd done exactly as she'd asked. He'd gone to the university she chose. Taken the hospital placement she'd approved of and had dated all the right girls, until he'd met Lizzie. Which had always been a relationship his mother disapproved of.

Slamming the pan to one side, William took in a deep breath, closed his eyes as a mixture of sweet potato, celery, and apples hit his senses. It was a thick, creamy soup he was making for one of his elderly aunts. A recipe he just knew that once blended, she'd absolutely love. One he now reluctantly had to leave for Anna to finish.

Wiping his hands on a paper towel, he tore off his chef's whites. Threw them down on the worktop, raked his hands through his short, auburn hair. 'What does she want?'

'I don't know.' Tracey sobbed, 'But she's drinking whisky like it's going out of fashion. So, it could be just about anything. Which reminds me.' With her hand visibly shaking, she picked up a bottle that stood to one side of the unit. Shook it in the air. 'She... she wanted another one of these, although it's almost empty; you might want to give her it all.'

Seeing Tracey's unease, he walked towards her, placed a hand on her shoulder. 'Look, take a few minutes. Compose yourself. Get a drink. Some food. God knows you deserve it.' He paused, smiled. 'Seriously, you've been a star today.' Seeing the colour rise to her cheeks, William looked towards Anna, hoped for support. Felt the relief as she walked over, placed an arm around Tracey's shoulder. Then, with the bottle in his hand, he poured the last of the twenty-three-year-old Glenfiddich into a glass.

Placing the whisky on a small tray, he walked steadily through the hotel corridor, continually checking the pictures and ornaments as he went. Took note that each was in exactly the right position and when he passed a small Lowry that wasn't, he stopped. Straightened it. Smiled. It had been a picture he'd obtained just the year before and with pride, he thought of the way he'd saved for the one thing he'd wanted for himself. A picture that depicted normal working people, living normal lives. An item he could call his own and after buying it discreetly, he'd hung it there, in a corridor where most of the time, only he would see it.

With dread, he chose his route, made his way around the outside of the house and along the back path. It was a route not frequented by the guests and a way of navigating the property without bumping into any one he didn't want to talk to.

'Mother.'

Standing up as quickly as she could, Ada reached for the walking frame she'd discarded earlier, twisted her fingers around it. 'William.'

Looking her up and down, he immediately saw the fragility in her stance. Wished she'd sit on the bench, and concerned for her safety, he moved to her side. 'Is something wrong?' He placed the glass of whisky down on the table. 'Was the lamb okay for you?'

Giving an indifferent nod, Ada pursed her lips. 'If I'm honest, it was a little rare for me.' She replied with an obvious pleasure, 'And that courgette in the ratatouille, it wasn't quite soft enough. You need to sauté it for just a little longer.'

Crossing his arms protectively, William stiffened his jaw. 'So, you didn't like it?' It was more of a statement, rather than a question. One he hadn't needed to ask. After all, she was always going to find something wrong with his food. It was her way of constantly telling him that she didn't approve of him, and that by becoming a chef, he'd gone against all she'd ever wanted.

'I'm sure the other guests would have enjoyed it, dear.'

Clenching his stiffened jaw even tighter, William leaned over the balustrade, pretended to look at the gardens. Caught sight of where Lizzie lay sleeping on the grass. The way she had one arm lifted above her head. The other rested across her stomach in an innocent, childlike fashion.

'Did you want me for anything else, mother, or was it just to berate me about the food?' He forced himself to turn, looked her in the eye. 'Because I was a bit busy. Aunty Joyce, she wanted a soup making. Something she could easily digest. Oh, and I need to go and perfect the rata-bloody-touille. Just in case I ever decide to make it again.'

'William.' Ada said sternly as she pulled herself back towards the balustrade. Standing there, she nodded decisively. 'She came.'

'Who did?'

'Lizzie.'

Stopping in his tracks. William closed his eyes, immediately knew where this was going. 'Yes. I saw her.'

'Oh. You saw her, did you?' Thrusting the walking frame forwards, Ada growled the words. 'So, what the hell are you going to do about it?'

Feeling cornered, William began to retreat, spotted some of Thomas's friends heading towards the lake and did all he could to keep himself out of their view. 'What am I going to do?' He repeated her sentence, shook his head. 'I'm doing nothing. Oh no.

This bloody circus of a memorial is all your idea. I'm not getting involved.'

Pointing to where Elizabeth still lay, Ada's eyes filled with tears. 'You want revenge for your brother, don't you? And, Lizzie, she was there that night. She knows our secrets. And I'm sure she knows what happened...' Sitting back down on the bench, she began to sob. Gut wrenching sobs that were all part of her act, the emotional blackmail she'd become quite an expert at delivering. A way of getting exactly what she wanted.

In the blink of an eye, William felt himself begin to crumble. He wasn't sure whether his armour had begun to thicken or fail. He'd always known how good his mother was at putting on an act. How she normally got exactly what she wanted. But this time, he didn't like her tone and took a step back to study her mannerisms. Watching through the corner of his eye, he noticed the sneaky way she peered over the edge of her tissue and the way she over drama- tized her actions the moment he looked in her direction.

'You don't seriously think Lizzie knows, do you?' He paused, shook his head. 'You're right. She was there. In the lake. But like the rest of them, she was as high as a kite and from what I saw, she didn't even know her own name when we found her screaming by the water's edge. She was traumatised to the point of hysterical. And I'm absolutely sure that if she'd seen the killer, she'd have said something... unless...' Disbelievingly, William once again shook his head. 'You don't really think...' He closed his eyes for a blink, clenched his teeth in anger. 'You don't really think that Lizzie had anything to do with it. Do you?'

Watching as Ada turned, he saw the look of revenge in his mother's eyes. It was a look that could have cut through ice. A look he knew meant business as she turned her back on him to glare across the meadow, where her fierce, determined look landed on the spot where Lizzie lay.

'She knows, William.' She continued to sob, to dab at her eyes. 'She knows what happened to my boy. Why else do you think I brought her here?'

Flashing an incensed glance between his mother and Lizzie, he felt the tension rise within him. Knew his mother was about to ask the impossible, that she'd have concocted a plan that would make no sense to anyone else but her and whatever her plan was, he wasn't getting tangled up in her games. Not this time and not when it involved Lizzie. She'd been his friend. Especially during the hours after Thomas had died, a time when everyone else had been so caught up in their own grief, they hadn't noticed his. Everyone, apart from Lizzie, who'd sat by his side, chatted to him for hours and held tightly to his hand. Staring across the meadow to where she lay, he felt torn in two because although she'd been there for him, she'd also left and at a time when he'd needed her the most. Whereas his mother, she was still grieving, and she needed his support. He just had to decide whether or not he could give it.

'William,' Ada finally said, 'I want revenge and you're going to help me get it.'

'Not a chance,' he spat back, 'I'm not getting involved.' He turned on the spot, began to walk away.

'William.' Ada growled like a savage dog, 'You'll do what I ask, you'll help me get my revenge because if you don't, I'll ruin you. I'll make sure you lose it all, every last brick, and you know I can do that. Don't you?'

15

ELIZABETH

Present Day - Friday Night

With screams and shouts infiltrating her mind, Elizabeth stirred from her sleep. In panic, she threw her arm outwards and grabbed at the ground. In a single second, her mind had gone from complete rest to flying fast forward; as her eyes shot open, she jumped to her feet, and found herself staring at the exact spot where Thomas's name was carved in stone.

With the realisation hitting her with the force of a jack hammer, she took a moment, leaned against the monument, took short sharp breaths. Her accelerated heartbeat boomed in her chest and in an attempt to stop herself looking back up, she sat back down on the grass, wrapped her arms around her knees as a bout of violent, involuntary shivering began to overtake her body. It was a fear she'd known would come, the reason she hadn't wanted to come here at all.

'Hey, come on sleepy.' Playfully, Timothy poked her with a toe,

'You coming for a dip?' Jogging past, he made his way to the water's edge, with Lucy and Patrick both close behind. Standing well back, they knew not to get too close. And eventually, they settled themselves onto the floor, next to where Henry and Patty leaned together lovingly against the old oak tree. 'Come on guys, it'll be like old times.' Timothy laughed, 'The water looks delightful.' Pulling a face, he ran a hand across his beard, wobbled precariously by the edge of the lake, dipped a toe in the water. Jumping backwards, with his arms and legs splaying in all directions, he squealed comically. 'Whoa, maybe it isn't as welcoming as it bloody well looks. I don't ever remember it being that cold.'

'Don't say you didn't want to go in...' A shout came from behind the tree. A sudden rush of sound was followed by Patrick flying through the air. His arms reached out, grabbed Timothy around the waist and within seconds, both had hit the water at speed and quickly, they disappeared below its surface.

With a surge of panic, Elizabeth held her breath, stared at the water. Immediate memories of Thomas flashed into her mind. His grey, lifeless face. The blood that poured from his skull. The way his body slipped out of her grasp. 'Don't... please... don't...' She reached out, fell forward, grabbed at the rushes. Waited anxiously for the two men to surface, to climb out of the water.

'Hey, come on. It's okay.' Freya knelt down beside her, threw an arm around her shoulders. Squeezed. 'Take a breath, come on, breathe, they're only messing.'

'I didn't...' She grabbed at air, 'I didn't think they'd go in, not after...' she paused, swallowed. 'Not after Thomas.' She was going to add that no one had gone in after Thomas had died, after the police had dredged the lake and after most of its sunken content had been strewn along the embankment.

'I know, I know. But you know what they're like. Grown up two-year olds. Men, acting like little boys. I doubt they'll ever change.'

She gave Elizabeth a pensive smile. 'What did you expect, old habits and all that?' She moved slowly forward until she perched by the water's edge as both men swam to the side. 'You two. come on, get out of the water.' She shouted, 'You're upsetting our Lizzie.'

'No... Freya. Please. Please don't make a fuss. I'm fine. I'd literally just woke up, it... well, it was a shock that's all.' Scanning the area behind her. Elizabeth noticed the pram. A pair of little arms waving around frantically inside. 'Freya, Louisa's awake. You want me to get her?'

'Nah. She'll be fine. By the time you get to the third, you don't get as anxious. Not unless they're screaming the place down. Until then, we're all good.' Standing up, Freya walked cautiously along the edge of the lake and in the same way that Elizabeth had done earlier, she touched each tree with fondness, ran a hand through the flowers, smiled with each memory that crossed her face. 'Feels kind of odd to be back. Don't you think?'

Sitting forward, Elizabeth focused on the reeds, on a small, white butterfly that hovered by the water's edge and for a few seconds she envied its freedom, the way it could flutter around without a care in the world and wishfully, she wanted to join it. To take off, to fly away, to leave all the others behind.

Watching, Elizabeth took note of the way Freya walked by the lake, the way she threw pebbles to skim the water, then smiled in her direction. They were all things she'd seen a thousand times before. So why did they now seem more poignant and why did she feel as though she were constantly watching the others, as though waiting for one of them to confess and weirdly, her eyes went from one to the other in a systematic fashion while wondering what she'd do if they did?

'No. It's not odd at all. I'm enjoying it. It's really nice to see everyone again,' she lied, all the time wishing she were just about anywhere else in the world.

16

WILLIAM

Present Day - Friday Night

Storming away from his mother at speed, William could feel his temper boil. He literally couldn't believe what she'd just asked, or the threats that had followed. And out of principal, he'd refused to listen, felt his breathing accelerate as he walked away.

How dare she threaten him?

In his temper, he stopped walking, caught his breath, leaned against the wall of the Manor, and furiously, he kicked backwards at the wall. Tried to understand her motives. But couldn't. None of these thoughts would have come to her overnight. In fact, they were so damning, he realised that she must have been thinking about them for a very long time. Especially when she'd followed the demand with the threat. For her to have threatened him with losing the Manor, the house he'd grown up in and to make sure he wasn't left with a single brick, was a threat he'd never thought she'd use. Not when it would involve a scandal, something she'd always tried to avoid.

He wondered if this was how it had been for Thomas. Whether she'd asked him to do the impossible too and out of all the times she'd asked, how many of her crazy ideas he'd actually gone along with, and ultimately, whether it had been down to one of her many schemes that had resulted in his death.

Thinking about everyone here, he knew that every one of them had their secrets. They'd all had reasons to both love and hate Thomas in equal measure and every person could have wanted him dead. *Including me*. The thought had passed through his mind on so many occasions and angrily, he slammed his hand repeatedly against the wall. 'Ten years, it's been ten whole years.' Yelling the words, he closed his eyes, shook his head. 'And now you want this, now you threaten me...' He considered phoning the police, telling them how crazy she'd turned. But he couldn't. Crazy or not, she was still his mother and he still respected her.

Circumnavigating the hotel, he avoided the last of the guests, the ones who'd lingered on inside the Manor. The ones who'd still be in there for the next few hours, so long as the drinks kept coming and the nightcaps were poured. These were the people he hated the most. Some of the others were down by the lake, and their screams travelled towards him at speed. It was a noise that pierced his mind, a sound he didn't want to hear. Because by hearing it, it meant that Thomas's friends were here, right now, in his home and at a memorial he hadn't wanted.

In need of fresh air, William set off across the grounds and even though he could see Patrick and Timothy climbing out of the water, with the others laughing and joking by the water's edge, he felt sure he could stay out of their sight, use the trees as camouflage, take a route down the riverbank and get past them without being noticed. It was a plan that was working out well, until he saw

Lizzie who stood in the tree line, half hidden by the bushes. She walked aimlessly in circles, in and out of the trees. Her hand periodically swiping at her face and for a moment, he wanted to hold her, comfort her, and even contemplated following her. Instead, he found himself looking upwards and through the trees in search of answers. But the more he stared at the canopy above, the more he saw nothing but the natural umbrella the trees had created, all overgrown and complicated, where each of the thicker branches extended outwards until eventually, they turned into long, thin, spindly fingers, reaching out until they intermingled with the tree next door.

Hearing the rumble of thunder and spotting the darkening of the skies, he took notice of the deep-purple hue. It was almost too dark to head into the woods but to have stayed in the house, listening to his mother's threats, would have driven him crazy and the need to escape had been all he could think of. Yet now, Lizzie was heading in the same direction, albeit she'd taken the wrong path for the clearing. He was left with a moment's indecision. Did he leave her be, allow her to get lost in the woods, or go across and send her back to the Manor? *She knows the woods almost as good as you do*. He knew it were true, and with his mother's words ringing in his ears, he knew how dangerous it would be to get too close to her.

17

ELIZABETH

Present Day - Friday Night

A soft breeze blew through the trees, to form a whistling sound that left Elizabeth with a feeling of *déjà vu*. So much had changed – the trees were thicker, the bushes more overgrown – yet everything felt so similar to how it had been before.

Biting down on her lower lip, she peered ahead and with a flickering smile, she looked for the clearing. A place where they all used to go to. It had been a small area central to the woods where they went for some privacy away from the adults. Not that the adults watching had ever seemed to matter – they'd still acted out their wildest fantasies in full view of the house – whereas the clearing had been special and quite often, it had been the place where she and Thomas had gone to make love beneath the stars or lie naked by the bonfire.

Pushing the undergrowth to one side with her foot, she trod it down. Took great care as she did and felt the sharp heat of nettles as they grazed her skin. The pain made her wince; she rested a hand against the craggy bark of a tree and checked the damage she'd done to her ankles.

Usually, the woods were noisy and full of life and even though they'd had an earlier burst of birdsong, now it was painfully quiet. Even the sound of the river seemed to have dissipated, and for a moment she wondered just how far she'd walked and in what direction. The disorientation had left her feeling lost and alone, and she spun in circles, tried to desperately find the clearing, to regain her bearings. Nervously, she stood on her tip toes, realised how easy it had been to take the wrong path and now, she found herself dangerously deep in the woods, not knowing which way she should go.

Hearing a noise in the distance. The crack of a twig. The crunch of leaves and the possible sound of a footstep, then another. Elizabeth blew out nervously, searched the area around her. Tried to work out if the noise had come from a person or an animal. And immediately, the stag she and Thomas used to see sprang into her mind. It had often ventured out of the trees to walk by the lake. But that had been before, and she had no way of knowing if ten years on, it would still be here. Although she did know that if she'd walked right by one hiding in the trees, it would have stayed still and silent, hidden, without her knowing it were there.

'Hello, who's there?' Yelling into the dusky eeriness that now surrounded her, Elizabeth waited for an answer, felt her skin crawl with anxiety. 'Seriously, come on guys, stop messing around. I've heard you. So. You know. Show yourself.'

Taking a step forward, Elizabeth peered into the shadows, her mind was back at the lake. She felt alone, scared, and without understanding why, she felt the danger around her. With short, sharp breaths of despair, she scanned the floor, tried to work out which path she was on. And with the feeling that she wasn't alone, Elizabeth stopped in her tracks, could hear a distinct booming take over her mind as the sound of another footstep made her spin on the spot. Running, she stumbled along the path, hoped it was the direction she came from and that the trodden down nettles would show her the way.

She looked from one path to the other. Then, with a feeling of frustration, she kicked out at a tree before leaning heavily against it. There had once been a time when she'd have happily walked along these paths without ever getting lost and regularly, she and Thomas would have escaped the crowd, in the dark. Made their way along them and spent whole nights by the light of a bonfire.

Again, the sound of a footstep alerted her senses. It was a definite noise that made her crouch as low as she could. Cautiously, she held her breath, wondered whether someone had followed her into the woods and whether Ada had been right. Had Thomas been killed by one of the others, one of his so-called-friends and if so, which one? Who had hated him enough to want him dead? Using both the tree and the undergrowth for cover, she listened as the footsteps neared, kept her eyes peeled, searched the floor for something she could use as a weapon. And with thoughts of Thomas now quite clear in her mind, she kept her back to the tree, hoped that no one could creep up from behind. Closing her eyes, she tried to rely on her senses but instead, all she could see was Henry's face, the warning he'd given. *Safety in numbers*. He'd tried to warn her, to keep her safe, yet here she was crawling around in the undergrowth, all alone.

Slowly, the footsteps moved further away and into the distance, until eventually she could barely hear them at all and while she kept the tree close, she turned, almost wrapped her arms around it as through narrowed eyes, she peered around its edge, could just make out the image of someone moving through the trees. They were a long way in the distance, wearing a big coat, with a hood that camouflaged their face. And if she wasn't mistaken, they were creeping up to and peering around each tree as though moving incognito. It was a sight that made her catch her breath, but unexpectedly, it wasn't a sight that frightened her. After all, it could have been just about any one of the guests. Any of them could have come out for a walk, or got lost in the trees, just as she had. Instinctively though, she took a step back and waited for what felt like an age before leaving her hiding place and tip toeing in the opposite direction.

Reaching a turning between the trees, she heard the first drops of rain. They noisily hit the canopy of trees above her and with a smile, she looked up to see the thousands of tiny drops falling through the branches like tiny diamonds, plummeting towards her.

Within minutes, what had begun as the odd spot of rain had soon turned into a storm and the woodland floor had become a slippy, formidable quagmire. Shivering, she pulled at her clothes, felt the way they clung to her, how rivulets of water ran down and into the small of her back and how her hair, that had been blow dried earlier, was now plastered to her head.

With another sound of rumbling filling the darkness, Elizabeth found herself slipping and sliding as she quickened her pace. She was desperately looking for the right path. The way back to the lake, for anything she recognised. But now, all paths looked the same and went in all directions. Each one now had trodden down nettles and it occurred to her that she'd been moving in circles. Just as she resigned herself to a cold, wet night in the woods, she turned a corner and saw the clearing open up before her like a veritable paradise, waiting to be found.

Feeling both relief and anguish all at once, she stopped in her tracks. Saw the large, wooden shed in the corner, the glimmer of light that shone from within. Someone was in there, taking refuge in the very spot where she'd wanted to be.

18

WILLIAM

Present Day - Friday Night

With the rain bouncing down on top of the wooden structure, and drips of water coming through a small hole in the roof, William lit a candle, manoeuvred his body into the furthest corner of the shed, sat down on the floor, and listened as the storm raged on outside.

Breathing in, he curled up his nose, felt a little overpowered by the smell of damp wood that had been piled up in one corner. They were trees he'd had no choice but to cut, ones he'd put in there to dry, and he laughed at the irony that he'd created a wood stock, filled the shed with all the necessary items for a night of camping. Yet during a storm, none of it helped.

Kicking himself, he focused on the flickering flame. Watched the way it wavered from side to side, dancing and shaking unsteadily as just one of the many gusts of wind repeatedly blew in through the gaps around the door. Creating an environment that was both cold and unnerving.

It was a stark reminder of his nights in the cellar and how even back then, he'd wished for a coat, a camp bed, or even a sleeping bag. But in a place where the rodents had scurried around, just like they did here, packing luxuries was an art in itself and mentally, he made a list of items he should bring to the clearing. With one eye staring out of the window, he considered building a shelter, a small cabin that had a chimney. Then, on nights like tonight, he'd have had a warm, dry place to stay where he could cook a snack or boil a kettle on the fire.

Concentrating on the sound of the forest, William closed his eyes. He could imagine how the trees were swaying back and forth in in the storm, their branches intermingled high above him and the river which had been silent earlier, now rushed past in a fast-moving torrent. Every noise was one he'd heard a hundred times before. Until he heard the sound of squealing, followed by fast-moving footsteps.

Jumping to his feet, he stared into the darkness, kept an eye on the treeline, and immediately saw Lizzie with hair so wet, she looked as though she'd been dragged from the river. Immediately, he threw the door open, saw her hurtling towards him. A look of recognition on her face, that went from terrified to relieved in just over a second.

'William, what the hell are you doing here? Thank God it's you.'

Reluctantly, William grabbed her by the shoulders, moved her into the corner, and with a hand steadying the candle from falling, he watched as a puddle of water began to form around her feet and in the same, dry corner he'd previously occupied.

'What am I doing here?' he questioned angrily, 'I was sitting out the storm until you rudely interrupted.' Pushing his hands deep into his pockets, he blew out a long breath, ran a hand over his face. Watched as she inquisitively spun around and took in her surroundings.

'So, what was all that about earlier?' She snapped, glared in his direction. 'You scared me half to death. Do you know that?'

'What?'

'Following me through the woods. I saw you.' She lifted a hand, took a swipe at his arm. 'I can't believe you'd be so childish.'

Furrowing his brow, he pulled at his shirt, 'Lizzie. Do I look like I've been out in a storm?' He paced, then decidedly, he reached into the wood pile, pulled out the machete he'd left there earlier. 'I've been right here for over an hour, used the shed as a shelter. But if someone's out there, following you, they shouldn't be.' He waved the machete around in the air, slammed his hand against the wall of the wooden structure. Turning back to the open door, he searched the tree line fully expecting his mother to appear between torrents of rain, shouting her demands on the top of her voice. But deep down, he knew how ridiculous that would be. She'd barely been able to walk between the bench and the balustrade and he could still see the way she'd stood there, watching helplessly as he'd thundered away from the Manor.

'But if it wasn't you…?' Fearfully, Lizzie shrank into the corner. Wrapped her arms protectively around herself. 'I heard their footsteps. They were really close. I saw the shape of someone in the distance with their back against a tree.' She pressed her lips tightly together, looked over his shoulder.

'Are you sure it wasn't a deer? Digging around in the woods, looking for food?' he said with a dismissive tone but saw the look of indecision, the shake of her head.

'Nope. Not unless the deer have taken to wearing coats. I'm sure it was a man.' She stared at the candle, 'Or I guess it could have been a woman. The coat had a hood.' Using her hands, she moved them up and over her head, indicated the way it had covered their face. 'I couldn't see them clearly.'

'It'll have been one of the other guests.' Once again, he bristled. He didn't want these particular guests in the hotel, or in the grounds and the fact that he'd had to take himself into the woods, to hide in a damn shed, just to get away from them all, showed just how much he hadn't wanted to see them.

'I don't think it was; they all went back to the Manor.' Elizabeth responded. 'Timothy and Patrick, they ended up in the lake, said something about getting into dry clothes and I'm sure Lucy and Jordan went with them. Henry and Patty went for an early night, sloped off hand in hand. And Louisa, Freya's baby, she needed feeding for the twentieth time in an hour. I have no idea how Freya does it.'

'Lizzie, why are you here?' He snapped, 'This memorial, it's just one of my mother's bad ideas. A bloody circus that has no meaning.' He suddenly pointed to the path, 'But hey, I've got an idea. Why don't you take that path and go back to the house. In fact, go home. Stay there. Have a wonderful life.'

'William, what the hell is wrong with you? You never used to be this horrid and if you'd looked out of the damn window in the last ten minutes, there's a bloody monsoon going on out there.' She threw him a look, 'And, what's more, I didn't imagine it. Someone is out there and I for one don't fancy running into them. Just in case they're in as bad of a mood as you are.' She paused. 'Saying that, it sounds like staying here with you could be equally as dangerous.'

Seeing the look of anguish and confusion all over her face, he took a step back, wondered how on earth he'd ended up stuck in the woods, arguing with Lizzie. Right now, he wanted to do nothing more than hug her, to sit on the floor, talk over old times, and pick up exactly where they'd left off. But that had been ten years before, a time when they'd been young, naïve. And after what his mother had just said and the threats she'd made, he knew he needed to keep a distance and control his emotions. He counted to ten, closed his eyes, and immediately saw all the times Lizzie had been nothing but kind. The times she'd tried to help him.

Shaking his head, he turned on his heel. Feeling relived that the rain had stopped, he felt the need to escape and in is temper, he flounced out of the shed, bit down on his lip, and looked over his shoulder to see the astonished, wide-eyed look that crossed Lizzie's face. It was a look of surprise, followed by shock, and if he wasn't mistaken, a little spark of fear.

'William, I... I'm sorry. I don't know what the hell I've done to upset you, but...' She'd followed him into the clearing and gasped in disbelief, '...you're being really mean.' Staring, she took in every millimetre of his face. 'You're so much like him.'

William stiffened. Looking like Thomas was something he couldn't help or alter and if he were totally honest, if Thomas had been the last man on earth, he still wouldn't have been a man he'd ever have wanted to emulate. Another reason why he hadn't wanted the memorial. He couldn't be two-faced and stand there blinded by grief. Not when the reality was that his brother had been a cruel and insensitive bully, nothing more, nothing less. And out of all the people who'd turned up at the Manor, he could probably think of numerous reasons why each of them could have wanted him dead. Including him. Yet, come Sunday, they'd all stand there by the memorial, saying practised words and pretending to care.

Nervously, she stepped forward, reached out and touched his cheek. 'Yet now I really look at you, you're so very different.' She gave him a smile. One that lit up her face, made her eyes sparkle. Hypnotised, he slowly shook his head from side to side as he fought the urge to lean forward, or to pull her into his arms, and kiss her in a way he'd wanted to so many times in the past.

'Lizzie... please. I'm telling you. You shouldn't have come here.' Pushing his hands deep in his pockets, with a determination to look everywhere but at her, he kicked out at the shed door, watched as it slammed back into place. 'This place, Lizzie. This house. You know what's it's like. I swear to God. It's evil. Nothing good will come of this memorial or of you being here. You do know that, don't you?'

'But... your mother. She...' Elizabeth looked over her shoulder, towards the edge of the woods, suspiciously. 'She wants this memorial and...'

'Lizzie, forget my mother; she wants a lot of things. More than you know. Certainly, more than either of us would ever want to give her.' He spat out the words, closed his eyes, shook his head. 'I don't really want you getting caught up in her games.' Once again, he looked up as though searching for an answer. 'So, for God's sake, Lizzie. Just do yourself a favour. Go back to the Manor, get in your car, and go... before she embroils you in something you really don't want to be a part of.'

19

LIZZIE

Ten years before

With the darkness and shadows of the Manor surrounding me, I creep barefoot down the stairs, lose my footing, and slip precariously down the last two steps to land heavily at the bottom. My whole body has landed in a crumpled, disorientated heap. I can't work out which limb to move first and in my inebriated state I try not to giggle.

Comically, I try to stand. But my legs don't want to help me. Not one single part of me feels real and precariously, I grab at the oak balustrade. My feet shoot out in every direction, and I feel more like Bambi trying to walk on ice rather than a grown woman doing her best to simply navigate a room.

Closing my eyes, I hold my position and even though we're in the middle of summer, I'm shivering relentlessly and sighing. I try to remember why I'm out of bed. Why I hadn't stayed where it was warm. But the dryness of my mouth soon reminds me that I'd desperately needed water and with a feeling of puzzlement, I wonder why I hadn't simply gone to the en-suite, rather than doing what I'd have done at home and headed for the kitchen. And now I'm here, at the bottom of the stairs, where it's easier to stay where I am, and use the step as a hard and uncomfortable pillow that's swaying like an unsteady boat, rocking beneath me. Finding it impossible to doze, I take a deep, inward breath and try to relax but the sudden sound of erratic panting fills the room, and Alfie, the Kirkwood family spaniel, runs excitedly towards me.

With great difficulty, I lift a single, wavering finger. Hold it to my lips, struggle to find them. 'Alfie. Hey... hey... shhhhush... you... you have to shhhhush.' I whisper drunkenly, feel the pain shoot through my champagne induced brain as I move my position and as carefully as I can, I try to get Alfie to lie down beside me. Inadvertently, I bang my hand against the rug, then recoil as the dust plumes from it. With my hands held up and protectively in front of my face, I giggle as Alfie thinks it's a game. He becomes even more excitable, hurriedly circumnavigates me in a ritual of nuzzling, licking, and fussing. It's his way of getting me to play or go for a walk. A ritual that normally works, but tonight it isn't going to happen, not when I can't even walk myself and with reluctance, he finally curls himself up in disgust beside me. Positions himself between myself and the red, leather chesterfield. Then, with a long sorrowful whine, he looks up at me with wounded spaniel eyes, in the hope that somehow, I'll find the enthusiasm to do what he wants.

'I wasn't coming down here to play with you, silly... I needed water, but... you know.' I'm talking to Alfie and whisper the words more loudly than I should. It then occurs to me that he isn't going to answer, and I close my eyes and feel the room begin to spin around me. It's going much faster than before and the staircase sways violently beneath me. 'Oh no, no, no... this isn't good.' I slur the words, grab hold of the step, open my eyes, and try my best to focus, to stand. I need to get to the kitchen, to the much-needed water. But my hands and legs don't want to work. Not in any kind of co-ordination. The earlier plume of dust has made my nose begin to tickle; it's a nose I want to rub, but I can no longer find it with my hand and as another giggle erupts uncontrollably from my throat along with the inability to walk, I set off to crawl awkwardly on my hands and knees, with Alfie obediently trotting beside me.

For some reason, the kitchen seems to be a very long way and as I move from hallway to corridor, then corridor to kitchen, I reach the ceramic tiles that cover the floor, and with relief, I almost throw myself through the door and slump heavily against the unit where I lay, staring at the sink. It's still a good six feet away, I pray for the antique mixer tap to magically move just a little bit closer. It's unwittingly out of my reach and I'm regretting the champagne, the way we'd simply drank it from the bottles and now, just a couple of hours later, my inability to do anything means I'm paying the price, while Thomas is happily sleeping in our bed, even though I'd done all I could to poke and prod him awake.

Using a stool, I push it until it stands in front of the sink, then use it as a ladder as slowly, I pull myself up it. Perch on its edge. Droop over the ceramic bowl like an oversized rag doll and study the tap for what seems to be a very long time.

'Jesus, Lizzie. Are you okay?'

Hearing the familiar voice, I turn and slide comically down the side of the stool, until, once again I'm sat on the floor and with a delayed reaction, I smile, lift a hand in a small and pathetic wave. 'I... needed... a drink.'

'Well, you look as though you've had enough. Come on, go back to bed?'

Feeling his strong, muscular arms surround me, I submit to the help. Fall against his body. Allow him to pull me to my feet and lovingly I cup his chin with my hand, press my face close to his. 'I knew you'd come.' Anticipating his kiss, and the passion that comes with it, I wait and hope.

'Lizzie...' His mouth hovers close. I can see the shape of his lips, smell his warm, minty breath, and feel the tenderness of his touch. The expectation makes my heart pound in my chest and even though the anticipation is killing me, I lean back, stare into his eyes and see a mixture of lust and confusion that lurks within.

'Baby.' I whisper. 'I want you so much' I allow my lips to brush against his and with a teasing flick of my tongue, I move my hand slowly downward. Capture his erection in my hand and feel his body jerk backwards with pleasure. Then, without explanation I feel myself being firmly pushed away, I'm lowered back to the floor and with a hand on each shoulder, he holds me there until I no longer have the energy to respond.

'Okay. Don't move. I... I won't be long.' Suddenly, I feel the coldness hit me. Once again, I'm shivering, and sadly, I feel lost, alone. And with a deep-seated sob, I pull my knees tightly to my chest, wrap my arms around them in a solitary hug and with my eyes still fixed angrily on the tap, I feel my lip protrude outward, like a small and vulnerable child, I hope that Thomas soon returns.

Looking around, I realise that even Alfie has given up on me. He's gone back to his bed. And I consider the idea of curling up by his side, cuddling in his basket and staying there till morning. But even that seems like too much effort and as darkness seeps into every corner of the kitchen, I sit silently, feel my eyes droop heavily until eventually the kitchen door springs opens and I see him. Two of him. Stood side by side, in the doorway.

'Lizzie, you're drunk.' Confused, I fall into the familiarity of Thomas's hold. Lean against him and feel the nausea begin as the smell of tequila wafts into my face. It's a smell I hate at the best of times, and even less when I'm feeling so drunk and with tired, blurred eyes, I look from one face to the other and hysterically, I begin to laugh and point.

'Thomas... there's two of you.'

20

ELIZABETH

Present Day - Friday Night

Feeling her feet go from beneath her, Elizabeth fell heavily against a tree, disturbed a mass of raindrops that had been clinging precariously to the tree's branches and now they dropped in rapid succession, rained down and quickly, she raised her shoulders and lifted her hands to form a small and inadequate umbrella.

With the memory of the 'almost' kiss firmly planted in her mind, Elizabeth pressed her lips tightly together, felt them tremble nervously and with a roll of her eyes, she decided that William had probably been right. Maybe it was time for her to leave the Manor and this time, maybe she should keep her word and never return.

In her temper, she pulled at her top and then wished she hadn't. It snapped back against her skin, cold, clammy, and still wet from the rain. Her jeans were clinging, rubbing, and the thought of walking back through the woods and into the Manor wasn't a thought she cherished and wholeheartedly, she wished for the warmth of Cookie's kitchen, for a bowl of hot soup, some of that warm crusty bread she used to make and right now, she'd give anything to be there, in the veritable sanctuary both she and William had run to during the days that had followed Thomas's death. A time when William had been a kind, gentle, teenager. One she'd loved spending time with. Unlike the man she saw now, who seemed full of angst and no longer seemed to like her at all.

With her bottom lip wobbling precariously, the emotion hit home. Everything had changed. The kitchen no longer belonged to Cookie and in reality, it never really had. And longingly, she looked through the trees, imagined she could see the house as it had been. The people who were gathered within, currently sat around the tables. It was a bittersweet thought that made her gasp. Determined not to cry, she wrapped her arms around herself, trembled with the cold, and watched William stride indignantly in and out of the undergrowth, his shoulders slumped, his face stern, angry, with an obvious rolling of his jaw. It was a sight she couldn't bear, not here, not in this place. And with a final look at the clearing, she tried to capture the image and fix it permanently in her memory, knowing once she left, it would be the last time she'd ever see it.

With memories flying all around, she took a moment, looked down at her feet, saw the mud that now covered her previously white pumps and she wished for the times she'd run around barefoot, sat in front of the bonfire, and warmed her mud-covered toes by the flames. It was a memory that caused her to glance back, to look at the ash that stood central to the clearing. A clear sign that someone still came here, stayed for a while, and that every now and then they lit a bonfire, sat beside it, and for a moment, she wondered if it was William and whether or not he brought anyone with him.

Looking him up and down, she saw the good-looking man he'd

become. The perfectly square jawline, broad muscular shoulders and piercing blue eyes. He had every inch of his brother's looks and more. Albeit now she looked more closely, there were a million and one little differences.

'William, what is going on?' She lifted a hand, palm up in question. 'This isn't like you. You're acting really weird... and I... well, I thought we were friends. I thought you'd be happy to see me.' Again, she nervously pulled at the rain soaked top, felt it cling uncomfortably to her.

'Lizzie, you've been away for a long time. Things change. People change.' Raking his hands through his hair, he looked up to the sky. Struggled with the words. The torment on his face more than obvious to see. 'And friends, they stay in touch.'

His words were wounding, but true. She had purposely severed all connections with the Manor, and with the people in it. A decision she'd been comfortable with at the time, especially when she'd thought it was something Ada had fully expected.

'I'm sorry. I...' There was nothing she could say that would eradicate the past ten years. But irritably, she didn't feel she should shoulder the blame. 'I didn't think you'd care. I mean it's not like you picked up the phone and called me either, is it?' She argued, 'and if you think I left without ever thinking about the Manor or the people in it, you're wrong. I thought about it every single day.' It was true. At some point in each day a random memory would explode in her mind. And now, now she was back, she could see both the good and the bad that had been here. Looking up, she caught William's eye, unnervingly held his gaze. Saw the confusion within.

'You shouldn't have come back. None of you should.' Trudging towards the shed, he picked up a torch. 'Take it.' He hurriedly passed it to her. 'It's dark, I don't want you falling,' he said as he quickly turned, began the pointless task of gathering kindling. He was doing his best to ignore her, to prove that he didn't want her at the clearing. And with only the briefest glance in her direction, she saw the look on his face, the scorn within.

Kneeling down in the middle of the clearing, and even though he'd never get it to light, William began tossing kindling into the ash. 'I didn't want this damn memorial,' he said, 'It's digging up way too many old memories. For everyone.' Standing up, he stamped back to the shed, came back with a handful of rolled up newspapers and a dozen more sticks of dry kindling. Both of which he added to a bonfire that he still hadn't lit.

Feeling battered, Elizabeth snapped. 'What, and you think it was my idea, do you?' With her heart beating wildly, she took a last remorseful look at the clearing. It used to be her happy place and now it was the place she'd last argued with William. 'I just responded to an invitation. I didn't want to come to a bloody memorial. Not any more than you did.' She paused, choked back the tears. 'So, for God's sake, William, pull your head out of your arse. Cause we're both just doing what we have to do, for your mother's sake, and you damn well know it.'

'As I said. You can always leave.' William spoke sternly, struck a match, lit the newspaper, circled the bonfire with rocks and kept his eyes fixed firmly on the task in hand.

With the fury rising up from her toes, she began to pace. Tried to think of a way to make the peace, to get William to talk to her. Like he used to. 'Me and Thomas, we used to come here, you know.' She waved her hands above her head, spun around in a circle. 'It was where we came when we wanted to escape the others.' Pausing, she took in a deep breath. 'Which makes you so much more like him than you know. He wasn't too fond of other people either. Not really.' She knew she was rambling, biding for time. Wished she could get him to talk. Ask him what he'd meant about her being embroiled in something she wasn't going to like.

'We used to wrap potatoes in foil, cook them in the embers and eat them for supper. I remember you joining us once.' With an attempted smile, she nervously pointed to the place where he currently knelt. 'There used to be a big log, right over there. Near the shed.' She furrowed her brow, took note of the tree that now lay beside the fire. 'It wasn't as big as that one and the shed, it was in a different place, over there.' She remembered the way they used to sit beneath the stars, lean against the fallen tree and use it as a backrest. It was also the place where she and Thomas had first made love, and undoubtedly, where on many an occasion, she'd sat in the shadow of the moon, totally naked.

She ran a hand nervously through her hair, flicked it backwards. Then, as she'd watched Thomas do a hundred times before, she now watched William light the fire, and blow on kindling until the drier pieces of wood took hold, and with a mild look of satisfaction crossing his face, he leaned back against the log. Nodded proudly. Then without warning, William stood up. Walked directly towards her and unexpectedly, he placed a hand on each of her shoulders.

'Let's get one thing straight, Lizzie.' He paused, searched her eyes. 'I don't give a flying fuck how many times you came here. Or what you did or didn't do with my brother. I don't want to hear it. Not ever. Do I make myself clear?' He let go abruptly, stamped back to the fire, began poking it with a stick. 'Now do as I ask. Get in your God damn car and go. Before you become a pawn in her God damn games.' He stared into the flames. 'She might look like a frail old woman, but she isn't. And what's more, she always gets what she wants. Whether we like it or not.'

21

ELIZABETH

Present Day - Friday Night

Feeling as though the air were about to explode in her lungs, Elizabeth did all she could to keep up the pace. She sprinted as fast as she could along the path. Her pumps were slipping and sliding as she went and with the torch in her hand, she held onto a tree, kept her eyes on her feet and on the sludge that moved beneath them. It was like running on a treadmill that changed direction, first one way, then the next and on other times, it went in both directions, all at once.

With her senses on high alert, she took in every sound; briars crunched underfoot, they scratched at her ankles and with a hand guarding her face, she wafted away the low-hanging branches, random spiders' webs that glistened brightly with rain, while all the time watching her feet, dodging knobbly roots underfoot and fearfully, after hearing one unusual noises too many, she was still sure she wasn't alone and that someone else was in the woods, with her. And like before, she had no idea who it was, or what they wanted.

Glancing back over her shoulder with terrified eyes, she stared longingly into the narrow stream of bright yellow torchlight. Waiting. Hoping. Wishing William would follow.

'Maybe you're right. Maybe I should leave.' She whispered into the darkness, 'The sooner I go, the better.' She closed her eyes, thought of all the wine she'd consumed at dinner, tried to work out how much she'd had to drink and how long it would be before she could safely drive.

Slowing her pace, Elizabeth felt her breathing accelerate. It had been years since she'd been out for a run and even longer since she'd done it at speed. And although stopping wasn't the brightest thing to do, she had no choice, took a moment to lean back against a tree and look up through the branches. Then, with her heart leaping in her chest, she felt a hand land on her shoulder and with her torch waving wildly in all directions she heard herself scream as Jordan's face was lit up by the light.

'Lizzie, where the hell have you been? We've been looking everywhere for you.' Nervously, he looked over his shoulder, along the path, towards the lake and without looking directly at her, he kept his eyes on the path and the woods beyond. 'And William, where is he? Cause... Lizzie, no one can find him and...' He furrowed his brow, the look of pain shooting dramatically through his eyes. 'He's needed. He needs to come to the house. It's... it's an emergency.'

With a million questions firing around in her mind, Elizabeth stood on her tip toes, tried to work out how far from the Manor she was, whether anyone was still by the lake and whether or not they'd heard her scream. 'Jordan, you...' She lifted a hand defensively, felt the nerves rise through her. They began in her toes, worked their way up her legs, until every inch of her trembled inside. 'You're... well, you're scaring me and I... well, I'd really like to get past.' Squinting as he took a step back, she caught sight of the blue flashing lights, ones that lit up the Manor. 'What the hell happened?'

Twitching, Jordan shook his head. 'Lizzie. That's what I've been trying to tell you. It's Ada... Ada, she's dead.' He raked his hands through his hair, threw a fist at a tree, connected, and yelled with the pain. 'Up there, on the patio, just like that.'

Feeling her legs weaken, Elizabeth took a step to one side, and felt her breath catch in her throat. She couldn't breathe. Couldn't think. It was as though the world had stopped spinning. Her body felt numb and with her eyes fixed on the ground, she thought of William. He and Ada had never really been close, but that had been before and things could have changed. Staring at the trees, she knew he was still deep within the woods, by the clearing, and that someone would have to go to him. Someone had to tell him his mother was dead.

After what felt like an age, she turned, fought with her emotions. 'Hey, hey... Jordan. Jordan, look at me?' Elizabeth could see the turmoil in his eyes. 'Jordan...' Grabbing hold of his hands, she took short, sharp breaths. Knew how unpredictable he could be, how easily he could lose control. 'Jordan, Ada... are you sure?'

'Of course I'm bloody well sure.' With a shaking finger, he pointed at the Manor. 'I've told you she was on the patio.' Pulling his hands out of hers, he paced back and forth. 'She'd gone a really bad colour. I knew it was bad.'

'You found her?' Elizabeth inched along the path, moved herself closer to the lake, further away from where Jordan stood. 'And you're absolutely sure she's dead?'

'Lizzie, I wanted to help her, and I tried. Honest, I tried. I yelled for help, tried to resuscitate her, but...' He shook his head. The dark grey eyes stared into the distance. 'I was too late. And now... now they'll blame me, won't they? They'll think I killed her.' He paused, let out a deep, meaningful sob. 'Lizzie... it's all happening again...'

22

LIZZIE

Ten years before

The early evening darkness has descended around a campus that's already given way to the end of another term. The normal village atmosphere has gone. The hustle of a constant party, that's warm and inclusive has ended. And most of the students have already gone home for the holidays. Leaving the place to feel cold, eerie, and without much of a purpose.

Walking hand in hand with Thomas, I look up and into his piercing blue eyes. 'It's so good to have you here, even if you did have to bring Jordan with you.' I feel pleased. He's rarely on the campus, being a trainee doctor he spends most of his time away on placement and I feel resentful that since Jordan started going out with Tilly, he's turned into Thomas's shadow and expects us to hang out with them at all times of day and night. I wish for time to go backwards to the days when Thomas would visit, spend time in my room, sleep in my bed, and I now wish we'd already left for home, like everyone else. Before once again, we're surrounded by the others.

Instead, we're still on the campus and now we're walking along the main road, into town, looking for pubs, for places where Jordan wants to go and celebrate his birthday. Thomas's voice is getting louder by the minute and it's only now that I realise just how much we've already drunk. I press my lips tightly together, begin to suspect that Thomas has been taking back shots, hitting the tequila, or sneaking the drugs. Something he'd promised he wouldn't do. Not tonight.

'Hey, are you okay?' I pull him towards me, press my lips to his.

'Only one more term to go.' Thomas slurs. 'Then, we get to follow our dreams.'

His hands hold onto me, much tighter than I'd like. It's a sign that he's already finding it difficult to walk, and deep inside, I ache for the gentle, loving way he normally is and as I loosen his grip, I feel the weight of his body slouch against mine and with force, I throw my arm out to one side, where I grab at the wall and lean heavily against it.

Realising just how close we are to completing our education, I'm both terrified and excited in equal measures. I try to imagine what our lives will be like once I finish uni, and once Thomas has graduated. I glance up and into his eyes and remember the promises we made. They're promises I'd love to think we'll keep, and dreams I desperately want to hang onto. Lovingly, I keep my eyes on his, sink deeper into the kiss and cheekily, I flick my tongue in and out of his mouth and try to ignore the sour taste within. It's the taste of tequila, and something that confirms my earlier fears. Reluctantly, I step away and choose to ignore it. I don't want to spoil the night and instead, I give him one of those looks we normally share, a look that promises him what's to come and I wish for a bedroom, or for the privacy of the clearing. For any space where we can be totally alone and for a time when Thomas isn't trying to be someone he isn't, just because his friends expect it.

As he grabs and releases my hand, I think of the reality. The size of my uni bedroom we often have to share. Of the bed that's smaller than a single, and the communal kitchen that's right next door. It's not really big enough, or private enough for two, especially two people who want to do so much more than sleep. Once again my hand goes out to where Thomas was stood, I realise that he doesn't respond and only when I look over my shoulder, I see that he's moved away. He's now stood by the bus shelter and with the smart lighting coming on and off as he moves past the sensors, I see the guilty look on his face and the way he hurriedly pushes his hand back into his pocket.

'What are you doing?' I ask, and watch. He has the look of a naughty child, one whose obviously up to mischief.

'For God's sake, Lizzie,' he throws at me, 'it's nothing... it's just...' Holding out his hand, I see the small white tablets, the way he sheepishly looks at the floor. 'It's Ket... come on, don't be angry, it's the last party of term...' he pleads, 'plus, it's Jordan's birthday and we... we're supposed to be having fun, aren't we?'

I watch as he puts the tablet in his mouth, gives me a surreptitious smile. Holding his hand out and towards me, he offers a tablet to me and furiously, I knock his proffered hand away, watch the tablets fly up and through the air. Swallowing, I feel an immediate guilt. The drugs are something we often do, but Thomas had promised that for just one night, we wouldn't and tomorrow, we'd wake up fresh and actually be in a position to remember what happened the night before.

'Jesus Lizzie, what do you think you're doing. That stuff's expensive.' Thomas's anger alerts both Jordan and Tilly and I hear both of their giggles as they scramble across the tarmac and through the darkness. Both are on their hands and knees, searching for the drugs. Everything they do is a game and for a moment I watch the way they comically roll around and once again, I'm the one on the outside, the one that's different, wishing I could be more like them.

'Oh, you can't waste these.' Sitting on the pavement, Tilly laughs out loud, throws one of the tablets into her mouth, then with her arm in the air she laughs and screams. 'We're having a party... whoop.'

Vehemently, I sit on the curb and in my frustration, I kick at the dirt by the side of the road to unveil a tablet. Swallowing hard, and even though it's covered in dirt, I consider taking it. It's less than we'd normally have but could easily take away the edge, allow me to join in and party with the others. It's something I wish I could do on a daily basis but being out of control isn't my thing. Slowly, I reach forward. Pick the tablet up, then I look over my shoulder to where the other two have moved away from the main road and are now lying on a grass verge. They're a mass of arms and legs and have become a little more amorous than normal. It's a sight I should be used to. After all, it's the way we live our lives. And to see them practically naked and twisted together is nothing short of a normal day. I just can't understand why Thomas is sitting so close. What his hands are doing in the darkness and in my temper, I throw the tablet back at the gutter, stand up, and crush it angrily beneath my foot.

Walking away. I give the occasional glance backwards. See the shape of bodies, lying prone on the ground. The erratic movement and noise. Tonight, it's something I don't want to see. And while reeling in my anger, I head towards town, close my eyes, lean against a wall.

Then, with no warning. I hear a high-pitched scream. One that cuts through the air. It's an obvious scream of distress, that stops abruptly. 'Tilly...' I lift the skirt of my dress and run back in her direction. I'm further away than I'd thought and as I bound the corner, I see Thomas and Jordan almost nose to nose, the tension between them palpable. 'What happened, where's Tilly?' My scream seems to break the tension as all eyes look into the shadows, to where Tilly is lying on the tarmac. Her beautiful skin, looking cold, lifeless, and grey.

With my heart racing in panic, I throw myself at the floor, immediately turn her head towards me and feel for a pulse. 'Thomas...' Terrified, I scream for help. See the way he and Jordan are still tussling in the darkness. The aggression is growing between them and I'm at a loss of what to do. How to react. Saving lives is what they're trained for. Not me. But as I look from one to the other, I see the glazed look in their eyes. The way their reactions are delayed and how unresponsive they seem to be. 'For God's sake,' I try again, 'one of you... phone a fucking ambulance. Now.'

As Thomas pulls his mobile from his pocket, I grab Jordan's hand and pull him down to kneel beside me. 'You need to do the compressions... I'll... I'll do the breaths.' Pinching Tilly's nose, I tip her head to one side, listen for breathing, then wait for Jordan to begin. But instead of pressing down on her chest, Jordan jumps to his feet, moves swiftly away.

'I can't... Lizzie, I can't do it...'

'Jordan, she needs you.'

His head is shaking from side to side, the fear in his eyes could cut through ice and even though he knows how quickly time runs out, he walks away and punches a wall. Turning back to Tilly, I know I'm her only hope. I have no choice but to help her and automatically, I press my hands up and down on her chest, begin the compressions to a stupid tune.

'Nelly the elephant, packed her trunk...' It's something I

remembered from the first aid course I'd taken some years before, a song that kept you in time to the rhythm. '...off she went with a trumpety trump. Trump... trump... trump...' Stopping, I blow into her mouth. Two long breaths. Nothing. No response. No sudden gasp for breath like you see in the films. And once again, I sing the tune, compress her chest. Continue to breathe for her.

'Tilly, come on. Tilly,' I scream, and with my eyes darting from side to side. I tune into Thomas. Overhear the conversation he's having on the phone. 'Tilly.' I begin the compressions again. Blow into her mouth. Pray for a response that doesn't come. 'Come on Tilly. The ambulance, it's coming. Isn't it, Thomas.'

I see him pause, nod, then close his eyes. 'Jesus mum, she isn't breathing. And I... I don't know what to do.' He runs a hand through his hair. 'Yeah. Okay. But we might need you... you know, in a legal capacity.... are... are you allowed to represent me?' Again, he pauses, and I feel my temper flair.

'You're phoning your mother?' I'm filled with disbelief, try to quickly establish whether an ambulance is coming or not. But the look on his face tells me that the call hasn't even been made. That his main focus had been saving his own skin, phoning his mother, asking for help.

'Of course I'm phoning my mum. She's a barrister. A good one. She'll know what to do.'

Standing up, I grab the phone from his hand, keep one eye on Tilly, on her prone, unconscious body. In my heart, I know she needs the compressions, the inhalations. But the sooner the emergency services get here, the better chance she'll have.

'Don't be stupid. Who you phoning?' Jordan grabs the phone. Throws it at the floor. Leans over and touches Tilly. Takes her pulse. 'As soon as they know she's dead, the police will come. They'll ask questions and we... Jesus Lizzie, we need to work out our story. We need to know what to say.'

Turning back to Tilly, Lizzie drops to her knees, continues the compressions. Refuses to give up. 'What to say? Seriously. We tell them the truth.' I scream as once again, I prepare to blow into her mouth, move her head to one side, feel a warmth on my hands, and instinctively I know it's blood. 'She's bleeding. Jordan. You need to help me. She's dying.'

Searching the area around me, I see where Jordan's gone. He's taken himself into a corner, where he's crouched and physically shaking. Looking up at me with the eyes of a wounded spaniel he holds his arms out wide. 'Lizzie. She's already dead.' He pauses, sobs. 'Can't you see that.'

'No, Jordan. I can't. But I'm not the wannabe doctor around here. Am I? You are.' Closing my eyes, I want to turn back time. Change the last ten minutes. Remove it from time, from history. Bring Tilly back. 'What happened?' I scream again, feel the shaking begin. Every part of me is tense, shaking with emotion, with fear.

'She just collapsed. Didn't she, Jordan.' Angrily, Thomas shouts the words. Tips his head questioningly to one side and breaths in long drawn breaths that remind me of a raging bull waiting to run. It's enough to make Jordan look up and in his direction.

Faltering, Jordan presses his lips tightly together. Shakes his head. Then with the fear of God in his eyes, he nods. 'Sure, that's exactly what happened. She'd walked away from us. She just collapsed and when we went to her, we knew she was already dead.'

Panicking, I look from one to the other. I know that one of them is lying. I just don't know who and with a mind full of uncertainty, I jump to my feet and feel Thomas's arms fold themselves around me and with my mouth so dry, I can't swallow, I wait for answers, hope that the truth will be told or for Thomas to give me reassurances that just don't come.

23

ELIZABETH

Present Day - Friday Night

Edging away from where Jordan stood, Elizabeth nervously furrowed her brow, shook her head. 'But... that night...'

'Look, I know what you're going to say.' Jordan closed the space between them. His hands, a scramble of fingers all steepling, then twisting tightly together as he desperately tried to hide his anxiety. 'But that was way back then, and now, now I've changed. I've learned how to cope, how to do the right thing. I went to lessons, took multiple first aid courses...' He gripped her by the shoulders, 'You have to believe me.'

'Jordan, you left medical school because you couldn't resuscitate. Not when it mattered.' Elizabeth inched further away, heard a twig snap beneath her foot. 'You froze. Panicked. And Tilly, she died and...' Her mind snapped back to that night, to the way he'd curled up in a ball, looked up at her with lost, terrified eyes. 'And... that kind of fear, Jordan. It doesn't just go...'

'I paid the price, didn't I?' He began to pull at the neck of his sweater, his breathing both heavy, and rapid. 'I quit med school, didn't I? I saved both of you from being implicated. Said I'd found her, right there in the road. And I... well... I got to work all the crappy mundane jobs ever since. While you lot got to live the high life, with your fancy degrees and your well-paid jobs.' He paused, shook his head. 'It was all his fault. I could barely afford to eat. I couldn't risk putting the heating on and everything was on a budget. My whole life, ruined. Like it was all my fault. But it wasn't my fault, was it?' Turning, he stared at the Manor. 'I protected him. I lied for him. And I did it because... I thought he liked me.' Turning back to Elizabeth, he took another step forwards and with his face just inches from hers he curled his lip. 'Do you know how many of you got in touch after I left? How many of my so-called friends offered me support?' He shook his head. 'None of you. Not even Thomas.'

It was a feeling Elizabeth knew well. And for the second time that night she'd been accused of not getting in touch. Of not giving enough support.

With her heart pounding in her chest, Elizabeth narrowed her eyes, and stared at the memorial. 'Well, as you can see.' She lifted a finger up to point, felt a weight bear down on her shoulders as the reality of Ada's death hit her. She was gone. Just a day before a memorial she'd wanted so badly. 'Thomas is dead. He could hardly pick up a God damned phone and check up on you, could he? And the others. None of them really knew Tilly. She was at the uni, but not really part of our group and you'd only been going out with her a few weeks.' Swallowing hard, she tried to step away. Remembered the way that on his mother's advice, she and Thomas had left before the emergency services had got there. How Jordan had taken the heat and told them how he'd been walking through the streets, came across her body and of how he'd tried to help her.

Lifting a hand to wipe away the tears, Elizabeth felt his hand grip her wrist. 'Jordan, what the hell do you think you're doing. Get off me.'

'Why, Lizzie? Why didn't you get in touch?'

It was a fair question. She couldn't say that she and Jordan had always been friends, but they had been very alike, the two with the most in common.

'I guess I blamed you... for bringing the drugs. For giving them to her.' Twisting her arm against his hold, Elizabeth felt the burn, the pressure beneath his fingers. 'Jordan. You're hurting me.'

'I will hurt you.' He growled. 'Tilly put the drugs in her own mouth, I didn't force her. So I swear, if you breathe a word of what really happened that night, we'll both end up in prison... do you hear me?'

'Why the hell would I go to prison?' With anger searing through her, Elizabeth pulled her arm out of his grasp, couldn't believe he'd threatened her, or tried to implicate her in Tilly's death. 'I tried to help her, whereas you... you panicked. I mean, what kind of a wannabe doctor does that?'

With an immediate reaction, Jordan jumped backwards and gave out a loud, animalistic scream. Falling to his knees, his face twisted painfully. His hands went to his head, and with newly formed fists, he punched himself repeatedly in his temper. Elizabeth jumped backwards, held her arms out protectively, and scoured the floor, looking for a potential weapon to protect herself if need be.

'Lizzie, we made a pact. And a pact is a promise. You can't tell them. Not now. Not ever.' He finally screamed, 'And you know the truth, you know she was dead the second she hit the floor.'

Seeing the rage in his eyes, Elizabeth felt her stomach jump in unison with her heartbeat and her body trembled with fear. Fixing her eyes on where Jordan stood, she could still hear Ada's words ringing in her ears: 'One of them knows who killed my son.' They'd been words Elizabeth had previously dismissed. Whereas now they spiralled around her mind at speed, and she looked at Jordan with suspicious, narrowed eyes.

Had Ada been right? Had the killer returned to the scene? Had Jordan wanted him dead? After all, not only had he blamed Thomas for his failed career, but he'd also resented the group and everyone in it. What she didn't know was whether or not he'd blamed Ada for the advice she'd given to her son just moments after Tilly had died. And whether or not his resentment could have possibly led to murder.

24

ELIZABETH

Present Day - Saturday Morning

After tossing and turning for most of the night, Elizabeth stared at the luminous red numbers that shone out much too brightly from the clock on the sideboard through painful, sleep-deprived eyes.

With her mind working overtime, she flipped the duvet to one side, jumped out of bed, flung open the curtains, and made herself comfortable on the window seat. Where dreamily, she kept her eyes fixed on the horizon. Waited for the sun to show itself. For the bright orange glow to shimmer in the distance.

For some reason, she felt desperate for the start of a new day. Even if it were a day she couldn't look forward to. Not when she knew that the police had arrived in force. That the circus had begun. And by the look of how many of them had turned up in forensic white suits the night before, it was a circus that would carry on for a number of days.

Last night's rain had left the fields with a misty look to the grounds and even though the lake had been the place where her worst nightmare had begun, in the early morning light, it now had a look of serenity. A soft amber glow dusted its surface, which emphasised the perfect symmetrical reflections that showed on the water's surface, making it hard to believe that anything bad could have ever happened in the waters below.

Jordan's face had flashed in and out of her mind all night. And with a deep, internal fear, she went over again what had happened. How he'd reacted. The way he'd spoken about Thomas. Every word had felt as though it were a twist on the truth. A truth quite easy to bend when the person you're accusing is no longer around to defend themselves. Which left her with a dark doubt settling in her mind. She had no idea what had really happened that night and at the time, she'd been unbelievably naïve. She'd wanted to believe every word Thomas had said and without question she'd allowed him to steer her away from the scene, take her back to the campus, where she'd curled up in his arms and sobbed like a child. Each memory of that night had haunted her for years, especially the way Jordan had frozen beside Tilly's body and the way she'd had no choice but to resuscitate Tilly alone. Just one of the reasons why the idea of him trying to resuscitate Ada now just hadn't rung true.

'They were liars,' she whispered through the window and to the trees. And with a finger resting against the glass, she drew a face in the condensation. A circle. Two dots for eyes, a long-twisted mouth. 'She died and I still don't know why... or how.' Her eyes went back to the bed, the same bed she'd once shared with Thomas. It was a place where she'd had so many dreams, so many hopes for the future. Yet now, she felt as though every night spent here, with Thomas, had been a time of deceit. She could no longer believe anything he'd ever said and angrily, she swiped at the window, wiped away the small face, she'd drawn there. 'He covered for you... Jordan covered for you.'

Thinking back, it was more than obvious a cover up had happened and while she kept her eyes on the pending sunrise, she could still hear Thomas's words, the way he'd pleaded his innocence, repeatedly. He'd said that Tilly had simply collapsed. And how at the time, Lizzie had desperately wanted to believe him, to think that it had been nothing more than a catastrophic accident. One that neither Jordan or Thomas had caused.

'Stupid. Stupid. Stupid. You believed them because you wanted to,' she whispered angrily, 'nothing more. Nothing less.' She still couldn't believe how much she'd loved someone who could be so cruel. But she had. She'd been totally blindsided. Smitten by both him and his lifestyle. His charm. And without a doubt, she now knew he'd manipulated everyone around him. Including her.

Tipping her head backwards, Elizabeth slumped back against the panelling, wished she were at home. Considered calling her dad, telling him what had happened, but couldn't bring herself to do it. He'd already said how he thought the house was cursed and to let him know that Ada had died would make him worry.

Thoughtfully, she cast an eye around Thomas's old bedroom. It was a room she'd once loved. A place where she'd always felt safe. Running a hand down the bed post, she tried to imagine how it would have been if Thomas had lived and whether or not she'd still be coming here, or whether Ada would have got her own way and the relationship would have ended. Everything had changed, yet somehow, it was still very much as it had been. And now, instead of sleeping in a Manor, she still slept in her childhood room, a place where her single bed stood in the corner and her dressing table, squashed into the corner, was always covered in perfumes and make-up.

Sitting on the edge of the bed, she remembered the days after

Thomas had died, when she'd gone home, hid in her room for what had felt like years. She'd been so young, and so naïve. Unlike now, a time in her life when she stopped wanting to hide and instead, she felt the need to get the answers to the questions that had plagued her mind for the past ten years and with a quivering smile, she nodded. Ada had been right: 'that lake, this house, it knows what happened that night and someone in this house knows who killed Thomas Kirkwood.' One memory after the other flashed through her mind until she took a deep breath in. 'I'm sure I know what happened too.' Elizabeth whispered out loud, 'I just have to find a way to remember.'

25

LIZZIE

Ten years before

'Oh my God, I love your an ensuite.' I shout the words through the closed door and for the second time that day, I climb out of the shower and wrap my hair in a large, white towel. My body in another. 'Thomas, you have no idea how luxurious this is, and how lucky you are.' I gasp with amazement, do a twirl in front of the mirror. 'I'd kill for a bathroom of my own.'

Frowning, I compare it with home, where our bathroom is old, stained, and chipped in places. It's a bathroom I share with my dad, with every visitor that comes to the house, along with half the neighbours who simply pop in for coffee.

'Lucky?' he shouts back. 'Everyone has an en suite, don't they?' Sticking his head around the door, he gives me a childlike smile, waves a finger up and down. 'And make sure you're dry before you come out this time, I bet you don't get away with doing that at home.'

Wiping the steam from the mirror, I feel my heart drop through my stomach. Realise that Thomas has no idea where I live. No concept of knowing the way I grew up or the life I'm used to. And quickly I do as he says, plug in the hairdryer, begin wafting it around and with my attention diverted, I begin counting the bottles of aftershave, the numerous creams, shampoos, and body creams that line the shelf. 'How many of these do you actually wear?' I pull open the door, peer into the bedroom. Where I see Thomas's feet precariously poking out from under the bed. It's a sight that makes me laugh as I imagine the bed eating him whole. 'Oh my god, what on earth are you doing?'

'I thought you were getting dry?' he says sharply while scrambling out from under the bed and once he emerges, I can see the annoyance that crosses his face, the way he rubs at his hair, pulls at his sweater, thoughtfully looks me up and down. 'You're not dry.' He states the obvious, points to the floor, to the damp footsteps I've trodden in with me.

Gasping, I feel as though I've done something wrong. I begin to retreat. Then, suddenly, I feel a tug on my towel, it falls from me, making me laugh as I watch Thomas jump up to his feet, bounces up and down in front of me.

'I think one of us needs to go back in the shower.'

Lifting my chin with his hand, I take pleasure in the way his mouth moves slowly over mine, the way he moves to drop soft, gentle kisses along my shoulder blade. His fingertips move slowly, sensually across me. And with an overwhelming feeling of arousal and need, I lean back against the architrave, use it for support and lift my legs until they circle his waist.

'Well, one of us?' I arch my back, press myself against him, give him a smile, 'One of us is wearing far too many clothes.'

26

ELIZABETH

Present Day - Saturday Morning

Jolted by the unexpected memory, Elizabeth held her breath, stared at the architrave, at the ensuite door, and then back to the bed. She still had no idea what he'd been doing beneath it, or why he'd used the sexual distraction tactics to make her forget. Albeit, at the time she hadn't seen them as a distraction at all, but now all her memories of Thomas were clouded. Every image showed him in a very different light. And as though a light switch had been clicked to brighten the memory, Elizabeth realised he'd been so much more calculating, than she remembered.

Inquisitively, she knelt by the bed. Lifted the vallance. Shone the torch that William had loaned her beneath. Sighing, she flicked the torch from side to side and with the bright beam of light saw nothing but a badly fitting carpet.

Sliding beneath the bed, she wafted a hand at a cobweb. Saw the way the carpet easily lifted, the piece of broken floorboard beneath. Reaching out, she nervously ran her fingers along the rough wooden surface, all the time knowing that Thomas could have possibly been the last person to have touched it and while holding her breath, she wondered what he could have hidden there. Moving closer, she felt the wooden base of the bed bang against her head. She winced with pain, then with a determined effort, she inched carefully forward. Lifted the board. Shone the torch inside the cobweb filled hole and grimaced as she saw a book, tatty and damaged, and a curled-up notebook.

Blowing the items free of cobwebs, Elizabeth grimaced as she noticed the multiple slashes that went across the cover and what looked to be two bodies twisted together that had been almost obliterated. Forcing the pages apart, Elizabeth could only just read the title: *Lady Chatterley's Lover*. D. H. Lawrence. Turning the book over in her hand, Elizabeth lay back on her belly, looked back under the bed, tried to work out why Thomas would have hidden a damaged book. Especially when it looked as though the damage had been inflicted on purpose. 'Maybe he didn't like the story.' She murmured, knowing that only Thomas could answer the question. Something else she'd never understand, notably because Thomas had always been so fastidious with his books. Even turning the corner of a page had been frowned upon.

Raising her eyebrows, she flicked open the notebook and immediately recognised the typical doctor's scrawl that had become Thomas's writing and with a sense of excitement, she read through the odd, random sentences he'd written. Found amusement in the way that there was no transition between them. That nothing really made much sense, and that most of the words looked as though they'd been written during a drug-induced state. And after flicking repeatedly through the first few pages, she pursed her lips and felt a sense of disappointment. She'd somehow hoped the book would be a permanent record of his inner most thoughts but instead, they were nothing more than the ramblings of a drunk.

Ran out of champagne – bummer

Another tough day, big exam and my patient died. Some days suck.

If he goes near Lizzie again, I swear I'll knock his head off.

Cricket, just 145 runs to the West Indies... Bangladesh are gonna whoop their ass.

Time to play the field. Look at my options.

With nothing to link the sentences together, Elizabeth could only guess when they were written, what had happened, or why he'd felt the need to climb under a bed and write them down. But then, she skimmed forward, turned to the very last page in the book. Saw the last thing Thomas had written.

School is done. Mother is right. I have to tell her it's over, and tonight, right after the party.

27

ELIZABETH

Present Day - Saturday Morning

Feeling as though she'd been punched in the gut, Elizabeth leaned against the bed. A turmoil of thoughts and questions began to spin violently around in her mind as she read the sentence, over and over.

Confused, she threw the book onto the floor, went over all the promises he'd made her. Had everything been a lie? A way of him having it all, until he decided not to. Until he planned to end it, just as Ada had demanded. He really was going to conform to her wishes. Again, she picked up the notebook, flicked the pages back and forth.

I'll toss a coin, heads mother wins, tails we leave.

Gasping, Elizabeth dropped the book. She didn't want to read any more, or to know what his thoughts had been. She didn't even want to know who he'd been speaking of, couldn't bear the thought that it might have been her. All she did know, was to have written it down, must have meant something. And now, more than anything else in the world, she wanted to hate him.

Furiously, Elizabeth stared at the door, cursed out loud. Ada had been the only person who'd known the truth, the only one who could have answered her questions. And now, it was much too late to ask. Looking back on the day before, she wished she'd thrown a barrage of questions in her direction, asked her if she'd known he was planning to leave, planning to escape the Manor and take her with him. But then, how would she have known? Unless he'd told her.

Pacing up and down the room, Elizabeth tried to make sense of what she'd read, how she felt. Her whole life, all her thoughts and dreams, had been based on a lie. On a relationship she thought she'd had. When the truth was, she could have moved on, met someone else, and had a family of her own. Something she'd always dreamed of doing.

She rubbed her eyes, blinked repeatedly. Every part of her ached. Her head throbbed and her stomach turned. The sour taste of bile hit the back of her throat with force and quickly, she ran into the bathroom, spat out in the sink. Cupping her hands, she gulped at the water straight from the tap. Scrutinized herself in the mirror, saw the dark shadows that lingered heavily beneath both eyes and the way she'd dragged her hair up and into a tight and unflattering topknot after being caught out in the rain.

'He really was going to finish it with me.' She repeated the words. Could still see Freya lying on the grass beside her, the smug look on her face. *Darling, Thomas has done the rounds with everyone here. More than once. And mark my words, he'll most probably take another round with them all before he settles down. Chooses himself a wife.*

She could see each memory, just as vividly now as it had been then. Every word, clear and calm. A whole summer throwing itself at her. Like bullets, fired in rapid succession. 'You're so stupid,' she said out loud. 'You should have known.' Her mind went back to that night in the lake, to the words he'd said when she'd questioned his love. *Whatever happens, you know I'll always love you. Don't you?* It had been a simple enough answer but in his own way, he'd already told her his intentions. She'd just closed her mind, chosen not to hear it.

Looking around the room, she wondered again why she was here. If Ada had hated her so very much, why had she invited her? Why had she been welcomed into the fold like the long-lost daughter-in-law, who'd finally come home?

Anxiously, she dropped her clothes to the floor, pulled her hair out of the topknot, and stepped into the shower. It was all she could do to wash the past away, and purposely, she allowed the water to hit her square in the face before it cascaded down her back in fast moving rivulets that reminded her of the night before and how scared she'd been out in the woods. She'd been lost and alone during a storm, certain someone was following her. But now the water was warm and welcoming and with her eyes closed tight, she turned away from the water, ran a hand through her wet tendrils of hair.

'You need to leave, and you need to leave soon.' The words echoed in the shower cubicle, bounced off each of the walls and threw themselves back at her with force, until she leaned against the wall, slid down it, and with her hands protecting her face from the water, she curled up in a ball and allowed herself to sob, to feel the emotion she'd held onto for so long. Finally, with a determination she'd never known, she picked herself up, and with a flourish, she flung a fluffy white towel around her body like a cape, and while glaring at herself in the mirror, she rubbed vigorously at the strands of wet hair. 'It's true. You have to leave. Once and for all. But before you do,' she growled the words, 'you need to find out what really happened, even if it kills you.'

28

THOMAS

Ten Years before

With the smell of hot coffee, croissants, and toast seeping out of the kitchen, Thomas stumbled in and threw himself at the kitchen table. He fell forward like a toddler, to almost lie on top of the table with his head lolloped against his arms. Then, with huge doe eyes, he gave the housekeeper a stare that was both pathetic and childish. 'Cookie, you need to feed me,' he drawled pathetically, used one hand to shield his eyes. 'I don't feel so well.' Sighing, he waved his other hand around under the table, felt for the spaniel he knew would be there. 'Hello boy.' Again, he stared up at the unimpressed housekeeper. 'At least you're pleased to see me, Alfie, aren't you?' He tickled Alfie's ears, smiled as the puppy nuzzled in.

'You shouldn't drink so much.' Sliding a slice of toast across the table, Mrs McCulloch patted him on the shoulder, gave him an affectionate squeeze. 'Every time you're home, you come into my kitchen, looking like this.' She paused, shook her head. 'Trouble is.

Life's a big party and you, well, you just don't know when to stop, do you?' She laughed as she spoke, pulled a face at the boy she'd watched grow into a man. 'I've told you a thousand times, drink some water before you go to bed.'

Grunting, Thomas lifted his head by an inch. Slowly, he pulled the toast towards him, took the smallest of bites, and closed his eyes as though by doing so, he'd chew more easily. 'Cookie, I'm a grown up all week. I have to work so many hours, and do you know what, Cookie, patients, they go and die on me, it isn't nice.' Again, he nibbled the toast. 'When I'm home, I like to have a bit of fun, party with friends. Not too much to ask, is it?' Then, with much more effort than it deserved, he sat up, rested his head against a hand and from a distance, he blew at a mug. 'Is it hot?' He rolled his eyes up to where the housekeeper constantly wiped at work-tops, her nervous demeanour along with the way Alfie ran back and forth to the back door, stirred his interest. Listening more care-fully, he could hear a whispered conversation. 'Who's out there?' he chelped, as another bite of the toast was taken. 'Is that William I can hear?' Moving his chair quickly backwards, Thomas went to stand up, thought better of it.

'You mind your own business and get that toast down you. It'll do you good.' She pushed the mug of hot tea closer to him. He lifted it to his lips and blew at the surface before taking a tentative sip. Then flopped back down to use the table as a bed. 'And what's more, I need to know how many I'm feeding tonight. Are your friends staying and what about young Lizzie, is she going to be here?' she questioned, while all the time keeping one eye on the back door as it slowly creaked open. 'Ah, Anna. You're... you're back from the shop, are you?' Giving the young girl an indignant look, she flicked her head to one side. 'Master Thomas here. He was just telling me how many we're feeding tonight. Weren't you, Thomas?'

With considerable effort, Thomas lifted his head from his arms, nodded suspiciously. 'Just Lizzie tonight, I think the others are going home later today. You know, people to see, families of their own, homes to visit.' He curled his lip. 'Maybe you should try it every now and then, Anna. Surely, you get time off and have family you'd like to see. Don't you?'

Shuffling on the spot. Anna's cheeks flooded with colour. 'Not really. I don't really have any family. Not any more. My mum went to live down in Cornwall and I don't really see her.' Twisting her hands together nervously, she looked around the kitchen for something to do. Turned to the sink and began running the tap.

'Right, Anna. Now we know that. You can go down the garden, pull me half a dozen beetroot, some green beans, and a basket of new potatoes. If you would. There's a dear.' Mrs McCulloch smiled at a flustered looking Anna, who turned off the tap and scurried back outside and in the direction of the gardens.

Rolling his eyes, Thomas leaned his head on his hands, tipped his head to one side, watched Anna leave and then, with a satisfied grunt, he nibbled at the toast. 'And that's why she leeches all over my family, is it?' He pushed the plate to one side, gave the remaining toast to a waiting, Alfie. 'Because she doesn't have a family of her own to pester.'

Pausing, Mrs McCulloch stirred a pot. Gave Anna time to move down the path, out of earshot. 'So, all your friends.' She emphasised the word *all*. Smiled. 'They're going back home today, are they?' She gave him a wry smile, 'First time in over a week. They do like to come here, Thomas, don't they?'

Sitting back in his chair, he picked up the mug and took a sip of the tea. He knew the housekeeper was, in her own way, defending the girl. Pointing out that his friends were constantly here, leeching off the family too. 'You might want to remember that my friends were invited.' He growled. 'I like them being here. Unlike her, who constantly steps out of line and if she does it once more, I'll have her dismissed. And, without notice whether she has somewhere to go, or not.'

'I know you're not fond of her, Thomas, but she really is a good girl. And if I'm honest, I don't know how I'd manage without her.' Mrs McCulloch threw back submissively. 'Anyhow, young Miss Lizzie. Does she have any plans to go home this week?'

Sighing, Thomas closed his eyes. He could still see the way Lizzie had been curled up in his bed. The way her hand had been held flat beneath her cheek, like a temporary pillow. The soft moaning and mumbling sounds she'd made, between deep sighs, and gentle smiles. It was more than obvious that she loved being here at the Manor, with him, in his bed. But his mother was right; she didn't fit in, not with the people they mixed with. Besides, now he was almost qualified, he'd be invited to functions full of young girls. One's who'd know how to act in polite company. But would any of them run barefoot through the woods, make love to him in a lake, or lie beside a bonfire with him, toasting marshmallows? It was that side of Lizzie he'd miss, along with the laughter that lit up her face and the glimmer of mischief that was always sat deep within her eyes.

Sighing, he knew not to dwell on the thought and arrogantly, he shook his head, then immediately wished he hadn't as the nausea rolled in his stomach. It was just a month to graduation. To a time when decisions would have to be made. A time when he'd half promised his mother that he'd do what she'd asked. Follow his career and mix in the right circles. It all felt like a Victorian existence. A way of life, where everyone had a role to play in society, something he thought the world had left behind over a hundred years before. Yet here he was, trying to comply, and doing what was right. Or he could ignore it all, leave it all behind, keep his promise to Lizzie, and take her with him.

Thoughtfully, he picked up the mug of tea, slurped it like a child and tried to remember if he'd actually made a promise to her. Or, whether during one of their mad, inebriated, planning sessions, he'd simply nodded in all the right places, looked interested in her suggestions, and smiled at a time that had ultimately made her happy. After all, hadn't he always been very careful? He'd worded things quite specifically. Answered in ways he knew wouldn't come back on him. It was a craft he'd mastered over years, had cleverly learned how to manipulate a situation, made sure he didn't inadvertently promise anything he didn't want to and could normally turn the situation around to a place where the outcome would end up in his favour. An art he'd found particularly useful when dealing with his mother. Who, being a barrister, had always been more than ruthless in her questioning.

'Cookie, have you got a coin?' He held his hand out, saw the housekeeper's questioning look. 'I need to toss a coin, it's important. I need to decide.'

'And what decision is that?' Striding into the kitchen, Dominic Kirkwood pulled out a chair and sat down at the long oak table. 'Morning, Cookie. My usual please.'

Ladling porridge into a bowl, Mrs McCulloch placed it on the table in front of Dominic. 'There you go, sir. I'll bring you some jam, I've got a jar of that strawberry in the pantry. The one I made earlier in the year.' She announced, 'I've saved it, just for you.'

'Ah, thank you, Cookie.' Dominic pushed a hand in his pocket, pulled out some loose change. 'Here you go.' He tossed the coin at his son. 'Make your decision, then smarten yourself up. Your mother will be down shortly, and we'll be expected to sit with her in the dining room while she eats her breakfast. Although. I have no idea why she can't eat in here with the rest of us.'

Studying the coin, Thomas rolled it over and over between his fingers, as though by studying it and polishing it, he'd get the result he wanted. Then, he tossed it in the air. Caught it in one hand and slammed it down on the counter. 'Heads, I do what mother wants. Tails, me and Lizzie, we'll go and backpack around the world,' he whispered the words beneath his breath, knew which outcome he wanted the most and stared at his hand, until eventually, he dared himself to move it.

29

ELIZABETH

Present Day - Saturday Morning

On reaching the bottom of the stairs, Elizabeth rolled her gaze back to the top. It had been the first time in her life she'd come down without watching where she stepped and instead of holding her breath, she'd purposely stepped on all the places where she knew the creaks would be, just to prove they were still there. Exactly as they had been. Sadly, it was just another reminder that there was no one left to be quiet for and that as well as both Thomas and Dominic, Ada was gone too. Now, only William remained, along with a few other guests. Most of which had already left the night before, leaving just the few who'd already drunk far too much to drive, either before or after Ada's death had been announced.

'Now then, there you are. I did wonder if you'd come through to the kitchen. Just like old times.' Mrs McCulloch gave her a welcoming smile, held up the coffee jug, waved it in the air. 'I seem to remember you loving my coffee.' Without waiting for an answer, she poured it into a mug, pushed it along the kitchen counter. 'Here you go, my girl. Get that down you.' With a penetrating gaze, she looked Elizabeth up and down. 'Oh, my girl, you haven't had much sleep either, have you?' She paused. 'And those beautiful eyes, so full of tears.' She shook her head, pulled a sheet of kitchen roll from the stand, passed it to her. 'It all been such a shock, hasn't it?'

Picking up the mug. Elizabeth sipped at the contents. She looked across the kitchen, to where bread had been sliced, ready to toast. A serving bowl full of grapefruit stood on a tray, next to pots of yoghurt. Small, puff pastry tarts, some sweet, others savoury. A speciality Mrs McCulloch had always made, one she remembered fondly.

'You said either, meaning more than one of us... who else didn't sleep?' Holding her hands out, palms up, she tried to feign a smile. 'Or were you just meaning that none of us slept very well?'

'Oh, I was meaning young William. He was up with the larks. Went out for an early walk. Right back to the clearing, said he'd forgotten to do something important. Something that just couldn't wait.' Looking through the window and towards the lake, Elizabeth wondered how he was, and whether she ought to follow him. Getting lost once had been more than enough and the thought of doing it again felt like too much of a trial.

'I see.' She didn't really see, but furrowed her brow, tried to look everywhere apart from at the elderly housekeeper, who had always seemed to know when they'd been lying or bending the truth. Cookie has always been the one who'd sneaked them treats, baked them cakes, and made them biscuits. The one person they'd turned to if and when things went wrong.

'Now then,' Mrs McCulloch said, 'Would you like some breakfast in here, with me. Or shall I have you a place laid in the dining room, with all your friends?' She paused, looked at the door. 'Although, you're all in the smaller Rose Room today. Seeing as the police still have the grand hall all taped off.'

With the tears threatening to fall, Elizabeth shook her head, felt the squeeze of Mrs McCulloch's hand on her shoulder. 'Oh, Cookie. I'm really not hungry and to be honest, I don't really know why I'm still here... but it is good to see you.' She immediately fell into the woman's embrace. Rolled back the years, remembered all the good things Cookie had done for them.

'We're all thinking the same, my lovely.' She interjected. 'I have no idea what I'm doing here either.' Pulling out a stool from under the counter, she perched, lifted a mug of coffee of her own to her lips. 'I got the invitation. Just like you. Quite a surprise, it was. And I didn't feel like I could say no. So here I am.' She picked up her coffee, took a sip. 'And now, William. He's the only one left and I reckoned that he'd be needing some help, so...' She held a hand up in the air. 'So, here I am, back in the kitchen. Making the break-fasts with Anna, just like before.'

'I've taken the croissants through, and Timothy, he's already in there. He's asked for some porridge. So now I'll have that to make too,' Anna grumbled as she entered the room, then stopped in her tracks as soon as she realised that Elizabeth was sat there.

Smiling, Elizabeth pretended not to hear, looked the woman up and down. She was dressed in a pair of black denim jeans with a black shirt. Typically respectful and very different to the strict looking maids uniform she'd worn just the day before.

'Well,' Mrs McCulloch said, 'you can either make it fresh, which will take forever. Or you can zap one of these and if he asks, tell him you made it earlier.' She opened a cupboard, pulled a packet from it, and as she passed it to Anna, she pointed to a microwave. 'Go on, put that in a dish, add the milk.'

Anna looked at the pouch as though it were filled with poison.

'I don't think William would like us doing that. He likes the food to be fresh,' she insisted.

'Well, if that were always the case, then he wouldn't keep ready mix in his cupboards, would he?' The older lady gave a smile, and once again pointed to the microwave. Looked pleased when Anna took the bag from her and did what she asked. 'There you go. That's how to do it.'

Watching the exchange, Elizabeth sipped at her coffee and looked around for something to do, for something she could help with. Felt uneasy in the way Anna watched her through one corner of her eye, without looking directly at her. It was more than obvious that the two women were having a power struggle and she decided that to join in would simply add to the fireworks that were already waiting to explode.

'Hi, it's Anna. Isn't it?' she eventually said, 'I remember you. You worked here before. Didn't you?'

Rushing across the room to stand in front of a pile of strawberries, Anna nodded, then began to chop the fruit in half, before placing each strawberry in turn in a huge silver bowl.

'That's right,' she replied, 'I'm part of the furniture, been here so long; I don't know what else I'd do.' Anna answered calmly, the colour reaching her cheeks as she awkwardly pulled off a blue latex glove and held out a hand to shake Elizabeth's. 'I'm surprised you remember me. I barely ever spoke to any of you.'

Returning the handshake, Elizabeth felt her cheeks colour with embarrassment, her body bristle at her touch. It was true; Anna had been like a part of the furniture. She'd been very good at blending into the background. Keeping herself to herself. Just one of the people who would have witnessed their constant parties and outlandish behaviour without being noticed. She'd also been sweet on William. A union that Thomas hadn't liked and the main reason he and William had battled so often.

Giving Elizabeth an awkward, unreadable smile, Anna went back to the chopping board, to the mountain of strawberries, and looked up at the clock. 'William should be back soon. I'm sure he'll want to see you.'

Elizabeth kept her eyes on the bottom of her coffee cup. Doubted that William would care she were there, especially after the night before when he'd demanded she should leave. And now that Ada was gone, there really was no reason to stay. The memorial was the last thing William had wanted, and she fully expected that he'd insist it were cancelled.

'Actually,' Elizabeth said, 'I think I'll get off. You know, before he gets back.' She paused, smiled. 'Do you know where my car keys are?'

'They're hung up. By the security cameras.' William stepped in through the back door, leaned against the architrave and with a pensive smile, he pointed across the room. 'You're not a prisoner.'

'I... well, yes, I didn't think I was.' She lied, felt her heart pound with the uncertainty of not knowing what he'd say next. And in anticipation that he'd ask her to leave, she took a step closer to the bank of keys and immediately spotted the diamante teddy bear keyring that hung on the rack.

Sighing, he poured himself a coffee. 'Although you might need to hang around.' He held the coffee mug up in the air. 'The police, they said they want to speak to as many people as they can. Try and get to the bottom of what really happened, start gathering alibi's etc, just in case the post-mortem comes back as suspicious.' He spoke with a matter-of-fact tone, had a distant look in his eyes, and following a slurp of his coffee, he placed the mug down on the counter. Walked across to the security cameras and began to fiddle with the leads.

'Suspicious?' Elizabeth felt the colour drain from her face. 'It couldn't be suspicious, could it?' With her mind doing a somersault, she went through the list of people at the gathering, the same people who'd been there the night Thomas died and the words Ada had said to her. *That Lake. This house. His friends. They all know what happened to my boy. I know they do. And you... you have to help me find the truth.*

Gasping, Elizabeth held onto the worktop, used it for support and felt an arm go around her shoulder. Relaxing into the hold, she looked to see Mrs McCulloch guiding her back to her seat. 'I... well, I was in the woods. With you, William.' She stuttered the words, watched for his reaction.

Standing back, Mrs McCulloch raised both eyebrows, 'Enough gawping, Anna. Let's go and finish laying the table.' She picked up a pile of cutlery from a tray. 'I suspect the others will be down shortly, and we don't want to let the side down, do we?'

Grabbing hold of Mrs McCulloch's arm, Elizabeth held her gaze. 'But they won't want to speak to me, the police, will they? I mean, I didn't see her. Not after dinner. But...' She did remember leaving the table and asking Ada if she'd like to walk with her. Tried to work out if they'd still be talking about her death if she had. 'I walked to the lake and fell to sleep. Then everyone turned up, started jumping in the water and I couldn't bear to watch, so I made an escape and headed for the clearing.'

Pinching a strawberry from Anna's pile, William pressed his lips tightly together. 'I should probably thank you, you know, for coming back. For letting me know about mother.' He paused, continued to pick at the strawberries. 'It was good of you. Especially after... you know.' With a sidewards glance at Anna, it felt apparent that William was omitting the details of what had really happened. Didn't mention the way he'd shouted at her, demanded she left, or that she shouldn't have come here in the first place.

Going back to the clearing had been the right thing to do. Even though the idea of walking through the woods, in total darkness, with just a torch light for comfort, had been just a little more than daunting. She'd been nervous about getting lost again, especially with Jordan lurking around. And even though she'd stood in the edge of the tree line, waited for him to go back to the Manor, she couldn't be sure he had. After all, she still didn't know who else had been there, in the trees, following her every footstep.

With a sigh, she could still see every puddle, every branch, every part of the path she'd walked. Although getting back to the clearing hadn't been difficult. But telling a grown man that his mother was dead had been the worst thing she'd ever had to do. She could still see the mixture of emotions that had crossed his face. The look of both disbelief, followed by grief, then a confusion that was quickly followed by what had looked to be a flash of relief. Every emotion had contorted his face and the blood simply drained from his features. For a moment, she'd thought he might collapse, right there, in the clearing. Then suddenly, like someone had wound him up, he'd come back to life. Worked out what did and didn't need to be done. And systematically, he walked around the clearing, put out the fire, made sure the tools were stashed, the shed locked.

Looking lost and alone, William stood beside Mrs McCulloch, looked through the window, stared out. Then, automatically, he reached out, clenched the woman's hand. Without warning, his bottom lip began to tremble. He closed his eyes and took a deep breath in. 'I should go see to Alfie; he's still at the cottage?' he said by way of explanation. 'He'll be needing a walk and...'

'Never mind all that big, brave talk. Come here.' In a swoop of her arms, Mrs McCulloch pulled him into her hold, rocked him back and forth like a child. 'There, there. You know you don't need to act all brave in front of me, don't you?' She whispered. 'I've known you since you were the littlest of boys, you spent hours and hours sat at my table, baked your first biscuits right here and there's no point in my telling you that your mum and I were the best of friends. You know the truth. We didn't always see eye to eye over a lot of different things, but I am sorry she's gone and...' She choked back a sob. 'I am sorry for you too. For your loss.' She paused, sniffed. 'And I'm here for you, for as long as you need me. You do know that, don't you?'

Welling up with emotion, Elizabeth turned away. She couldn't bear to watch a grown man sob, especially William, and she knew that in Mrs McCulloch's arms, he'd reverted back to being a little boy. It was more than obvious that right now, he felt safe, protected, and loved and it seemed fitting that Mrs McCulloch was here, looking out for him, just as she always had been.

'Your kitchen,' Mrs McCulloch continued, 'it's in safe hands. I'll stay and do all I can, just until you get the funeral organised.'

Looking Mrs McCulloch directly in the eye, William blinked back the emotion, smiled. 'I'm really glad you're here,' he whispered. 'As I said yesterday, the place really isn't the same without you.'

'Get away with you.' Stepping back, she flicked him with a tea towel. 'Now, go on, go and see Alfie, he'll be waiting for you, wondering why you haven't been home.'

'You... you still have Alfie?' Holding a hand to her chest, Elizabeth walked across the kitchen, peered over his shoulder as though she expected to see the puppy stood right behind him.

'Of course, I do, although, he isn't the puppy you'll remember.' Wiping his eyes dry of tears, William gave her an apologetic look, a half-smile.

'I'd still love to see him.'

'Well then, today's your lucky day cause Alfie loves visitors.'

With a smile, Anna dropped her knife. Went to take off her apron. 'Can I come and see Alfie?'

'Not right now missy, you can see him anytime you want.' Mrs

McCulloch gave William a wave of her hand. 'William and Lizzie, they have a lot of catching up to do. And us, we've still got at least twelve guests to feed, haven't we?' She paused, rolled her jaw, and watched as Anna replaced the apron. 'They'll all be up soon. All wanting their breakfast and it's down to us to make sure they get it.'

Watching on, Elizabeth saw the way Cookie had taken control of the kitchen, and the way that even though Anna had quickly become subservient, it was more than obvious she didn't like it. And with a firm, fast movement of her knife, she began to chop the strawberries with a lot more force than she previously had.

Whereas Cookie kept her gaze fixed lovingly on where William stood, gave him a wink, then while wiping her hands on a tea towel, walked up behind him and opened the door. 'Go on, get yourselves gone, before I change my mind and find something that only you can cook in the kitchen.'

30

WILLIAM

Present Day - Saturday Morning

Feeling as though he needed something to do, William picked at the garlic chives that grew next to the cottage door, while keeping one eye on the way Alfie's whole body moved with the obvious excitement at seeing Elizabeth; he began to whine, in a high-pitched yowl.

'Alright, alright, that's enough, settle down.' Slapping his hand against his own leg, William couldn't help but smile as Alfie paid him no attention at all and instead, he affectionately wrapped himself around Elizabeth's ankles, sat down on her feet, and looked up at her with the biggest, most adoring eyes. 'He remembers you.' William whispered, 'It's as though you've never been away.' Giving her an affectionate smile, he watched Alfie sit as close as he could, pressed himself tightly against her. As though by touching, watching, and sitting so close, she wouldn't be able to move. Not without him knowing.

'Oh, I'm so pleased you're still here,' she giggled, pulled her feet out from beneath him, knelt on the floor, and allowed him to lollop against her. 'You're such a good boy, aren't you?' She looked up, caught William's eye. 'You have no idea how much this means to me. I've often thought about him. Wondered what happened to him and now, now I know... don't I?' After ten long minutes of kissing and fussing, she stood up, brushed the dog hair from her jeans, began to walk along the gravel path with Alfie close behind. 'And you live in the cottage now. I didn't realise.'

Pulling the front door to a close. William nodded. 'I sure do. I moved out during the hotel's renovation.' Holding out a hand, he joined in the fussing of Alfie. 'Decided that a hotel was no place for a dog, not with the food hygiene people breathing down my neck all the time and... well, we kind of like having a place of our own, don't we boy?' Picking up a stick, he threw it along the path. Then shook his head in disgust as Alfie flopped to the floor, gave him the dirtiest look. 'I have no idea why I have a dog. You don't play chase. You won't fetch sticks. Might as well throw the damn stick and fetch it myself.' He'd tried to laugh through the pain. A pain that came and went, in waves of emotion. He couldn't believe that his mother was gone and now, he felt lost, empty, and strangely without purpose. He'd rarely ever needed her, or gone to her for advice, not since being a child. But even so. She'd been his mother. She'd always been there. Whether he'd needed her or not. And now, well, now she wasn't.

He took long, deep breaths. Subconsciously, he knew that Lizzie was watching his every move, waiting for the unhappiness to hit, for his world to stop turning and ultimately, for him to break down with grief once again. She played with Alfie, threw sticks that for her he happily seemed to run after, and with the odd smile here and there, she kept the conversation going and right now, he was grateful for the small moment of normality they shared. For being so forgiving, especially after he'd treated her so badly. And now, seeing her compassion, he wished he hadn't taken the annoyance he'd had with his mother out on her. She hadn't deserved it and he knew he should apologise.

'William...' she whispered, disturbing his thoughts. 'I need to tell you something...'

Standing by the lake, she gazed aimlessly at the water, at the overhanging willow that stood beside it. The very same tree he'd felled in temper shortly after his brother's death. It had been a reminder, no one had wanted to see. But ironically, over the years it had sprouted new growth and was now, once again a fine-looking tree which had showed how much it had wanted to live. Annoyed, he'd left it be. Especially when felling it again would be nothing more than a waste of his efforts.

Waiting, he hoped she'd continue. Hoped she'd once again talk about something random, something that would distract his mind and for just another few minutes, keep the reality at bay. 'Go on...' he finally prompted.

'There's a book, actually there's two books.' She finally replied. 'I found them.' As a sob left her throat, colour immediately flushed her cheeks, and her hand went to her face in embarrassment. 'They were hidden under the floorboards, under the bed, in Thomas's room.' Sheepishly, she averted her gaze. 'I know I shouldn't have been digging around, but...' She paused, furrowed her brow. 'One of them is just an old, battered book. But the other, it's a bit like a diary, with things Thomas wrote and, well I guess it belongs to you now.' She nodded as though the affirmation helped.

Standing back, he took a breath, saw the discernible amount of pain that crossed her face, the obvious discomfort she felt. It was more than obvious she'd read something personal. Something she hadn't wanted to see. And he felt an overwhelming need to protect her. To stop the pain his brother had caused.

'Do you want to sit down? I'm willing to risk it if you are.' He placed a hand on the grass, sat down, and leaned against the tree trunk, hoped that Lizzie would join him. 'Not too wet and if I'm honest, I thought it'd be worse, after the rain.'

Smiling, apprehensively, she sat beside him, deep in thought.

'You okay?' He bumped her with his shoulder. Caught her gaze with his. 'I hate him for hurting you.' Tapping his thigh, he smiled as Alfie flopped down by his knee. Rested his head against his leg and gave him a sorrowful look.

'How do you know he's hurt me?'

'Because I know you...' He closed his eyes, wanted to tell her how often he'd seen her pain, how many times he'd wanted to comfort her, but hadn't.

'He was going to finish it. That night he died. It says so, in the book.' She lifted a hand, palm out. 'I know he was under pressure to end it. I overheard them talking.' Running a hand down Alfie's back, she pursed her lips, 'Don't ask, but...' Dabbing at the corner of her eye, she bit down on her lower lip. Paused. 'I'd really hoped he wouldn't.'

'Under pressure?' William sighed. He didn't even know why he'd asked the question. It was more than apparent where the pressure had come from; his mother had made it more than obvious to all concerned that Lizzie wasn't good enough. Not for her son.

Leaning back, Elizabeth closed her eyes. 'I don't want to say, not now, not after...' she stopped, her eyes once again filled with tears. 'I still can't believe she's gone, William. It doesn't seem fair. Not now. Not this weekend. Not before she got her wish.' Reaching out, she once again laid a hand on Alfie's back, twirled the fur between her fingers. Smiled as he leaned around, licked her hand.

'And what about you Lizzie. What did you wish for?' he whispered. 'Was it fair, or right for you?' Pausing, he turned his body to hers, but avoided her gaze. 'I knew, back then what she'd done. What she asked him to do. I didn't agree with it, but there was nothing I could do, not when Thomas always did everything she asked. I should however have been a good friend and told you what I knew.' Pausing, he dropped a hand on top of hers. 'Do you want to tell me what you heard, back then?'

Hesitating, Elizabeth accepted his hand, held it back. 'I'd overheard them. The night I tried to release you from the cellar, via the coal chute.' She closed her eyes, the emotion crossing her face as she struggled with the words. 'God only knows why I thought it a good idea for you to climb out that way.' She gave him an apologetic smile. 'I was on my way up to bed, when I heard footsteps and because I didn't want to run into Thomas, I hid behind the chesterfield. Then Ada, your mum, came and bumped straight into Thomas, asked him to end it. She said I wasn't a suitable match, that he could do much better.'

Not wanting to hear any more, William intertwined his fingers with hers and squeezed her hand, looking down at them thoughtfully. 'You were more than fucking suitable.' Growling the words, he felt his stomach leap with affection. 'And if Thomas had listened to her, then he was being ridiculous...' he puffed up his cheeks, blew out with frustration. Didn't really know what he wanted to say. All he knew was that Lizzie was hurt, that all these years later and because of his family, she was still suffering.

31

ELIZABETH

Present Day - Saturday Morning

Sitting in the Rose Room and to one end of a dining table, Elizabeth sipped at her coffee. Cookie had been right; the room was considerably smaller than the one they'd sat at the night before and feeling puzzled, she tried to work out whether or not she'd ever been in this room before. With a quick look over her shoulder, she tried to remember the layout, the way the house had been and felt sure that this room had previously been a library where Thomas's mother used to sit with a book on her knee, a wistful look on her face and a full view of the garden, which she seemed to enjoy. She was sure that it was also the place she last remembered seeing Thomas alive, before they'd gone to the lake.

Using her fork, Elizabeth cut the salmon into small, mouth sized pieces. Then systematically, she moved both that and the scrambled egg from one side of the plate to the other. Made a facade of pushing the food onto her fork, only to flick it back off like an actress pretending to eat.

With the large oak door in her line of sight, she watched as the others were shown into the room. Took note of their expressions and the surprised way they all took a double look. All of them, without exception, had turned and inquisitively tried to look across the hallway and into the Grand Hall, where the room had been taped off, and portable shutters had been placed in front of the door, blocking it from view.

'Seriously,' Henry spooned fresh strawberries into his mouth, waved the silver spoon around in the air. 'I feel pretty bad that we're still here. But we couldn't have driven last night, could we Patty? Not after all that wine.' Puckering, he turned to his wife, pressed his lips against her proffered cheek. 'Do you think we should leave? I mean, I'd rather stay cause that bed is bloody amazing.' With a seductive smile, he paused, placed a strawberry between his lips, leaned in towards his wife and sensually passed the fruit to her. 'It's so big, you could get lost in it. Couldn't you, darling?' he laughed, then quickly added. 'Not that we did.'

Holding onto his arm, Patty happily joined in with the sensual exchange. 'We were having the most amazing night.' She blushed, answered coyly, in almost a whisper. 'Until Henry opened the curtains. He wanted to look at the lake but saw the blue flashing lights, they literally lit up our room.' She held tightly to his hand. 'Such a shock.'

'First I heard was when Jordan bounced into the Grand Hall, screaming like a banshee.' Patrick said as he pulled out a chair beside Henry, took a seat at the table. 'Never seen anyone shake so dramatically in all my life.' Picking up a napkin, he spread it out across his lap. 'Any chance of some tea? I could seriously murder one.'

Gasping, Patty held a hand to her chest. 'Henry came down,

didn't you darling?' She sat forward in her seat, pushed the tea pot towards Patrick. 'We knew that flashing lights would mean something bad. But... we never thought for a minute it could be Ada. I couldn't believe it when Henry came back up the stairs and told me what had happened.'

Sweeping into the room, dressed in a simple black trouser suit, Lucy placed a hand on Elizabeth's shoulder, kissed her on the cheek. 'Morning, my darling. I bet you're in pieces, aren't you?' She made a pretence of waving a tissue in front of her eyes, dabbing at the corners. 'Good job we all brought suitable clothes, isn't it?' Using a finger, she pointed up and down her outfit. 'I was going to wear this for the memorial.' She grabbed at a slice of toast, dropped it onto a side plate. 'Now, what were we all talking about?'

'Henry was asking if we ought to stay, or go,' Elizabeth filled in.

'Well, I must say, I do feel a bit awkward about staying.' Lucy bit into her toast and waved it around in the air while she chewed. 'The family, they'll need some privacy.'

'The officer I spoke to last night,' Freya interjected, 'he said they'd want to speak to us all.' She paced around the edge of the room, held a sobbing Louisa to her shoulder, rocked her from side to side and with a look of apology, she closed her eyes, leaned against a wall. 'I have no idea why, maybe it's me being so upset about what happened, but she simply won't settle. She hasn't slept, not a wink, and I'm so bloody tired.'

'Here, give her to me.' Holding out her arms, Lucy took Louisa from her and surprisingly, she sat on the floor, leaned against Timothy's leg, and rocked the baby from side to side in what looked to be a well-practised manoeuvre. 'There look, she likes you.' She looked up at Timothy as she spoke, winked.

'What if I don't want to stay?' Patrick interrupted. 'I mean, they can't hold us hostage, can they? And what about all the guests who've already left?' Reaching across the table, he picked up the salt, sprinkled it liberally over his eggs.

'Patrick,' Freya continued, 'you're hardly a hostage now, are you?' She pointed to the plate of food he'd begun digging into. 'If we're all here it makes it easier for them to talk to us. Saves them tripping all over the country tracking us down.' Flopping into a chair, she picked up the tea pot, poured herself a cup, leaned back, exhausted. 'Although. I could do with going home. Louisa isn't sleeping and I have the other two to think about.' Tipping her head to one side, she kept one eye on where Louisa now slept peacefully in Lucy's arms, gave her a loving smile. 'Billy and Elsie, the twins, they're just three years old. I've never left them before, and Chris, he's probably pulling his hair out by now.'

'Darling girl,' Lucy cut in. 'Chris is a grown man. He's more than capable of looking after them and if he isn't, it's about time he learned.' She stood up, walked around the room, continued to rock Louisa from side to side. 'They'll be having the time of their lives.'

Picking up his cup, Timothy ran a hand through his long, ginger beard, flicked the random flakes of pastry from it, before slurping at his coffee. 'I couldn't resist the croissants, they were amazing.' He peered inquisitively around the room, through the door and towards the grand hall. 'And that porridge, that was superb too.'

Smiling, Elizabeth could still see both Mrs McCulloch and Anna debating the porridge in the kitchen. 'I must send my thanks to the chef.' He paused, thoughtfully. 'Has anyone seen William this morning?' He picked up another croissant. Began to eat. 'I hope he's okay.'

Trying to ignore the question, Elizabeth sucked in a deep breath. She'd left William at his cottage door less than an hour before, when he'd made it more than clear that he had no intention of coming to the Manor. Not unless he had to. The last people he wanted to see were Thomas's friends. 'I didn't want a memorial,' he'd said, 'I didn't want any of them here. And now this has happened, I want them here even less.' He'd stood close, gently lifted a hand, moved a strand of hair from in front of her face. 'Apart from you. I know it didn't sound like it yesterday, but I am pleased you're here.' He paused, nervously stepped from foot to foot. Ran a hand thoughtfully across his short, neatly trimmed beard. 'And I'm so sorry for what I said. I was just angry at mother, and you really didn't deserve it,' he'd whispered, leaned forward, gently kissed her on the cheek. 'Can you forgive me?'

With the memory fresh in her mind, Elizabeth felt the heat flood her cheeks. She kept her eyes averted, switched on her phone, and while still listening to the others, she scrolled, read through the three different kinds of messages that jumped up, onto the screen, and sighed. There were one or two enquiring ones. Then, a sharp and demanding one that came from her father.

Elizabeth. Worried about you, are you okay. xx ps: I can't find the bread. Do we have any? x

Pushing the plate of scrambled egg and smoked salmon to one side, Elizabeth sat back in her chair. Turning the phone over and over in her hand, she considered responding to her father, knew whatever she said would worry him. But she couldn't lie and with a pointed finger, she tapped at the screen.

Sorry Dad. Things got complicated. Ada died and of course, the police came, and we have to give statements. Nothing to worry about. I'll be home as planned, Tuesday. x ps: Look in the cupboard next to the cooker. Bread is in there. xx

She thought of all the extra goodies she'd put in that same

cupboard. The ones that her father had obviously missed and with a smile, she switched off the phone, placed it back in her bag.

'Was there something wrong with your breakfast?' Anna leaned in, picked up the plate and gave her a worried but affectionate smile.

'I'm fine. I'm just not very hungry.' Returning the smile, Elizabeth thought about the text, wondered if she would stay while Tuesday. Or whether William would want everyone to leave, just as soon as they could.

Looking out of the window, she felt a sense of nostalgia as she saw Bobby the gardener walking past. Once again, he was dressed in his shorts, wellington boots, and a body warmer. A look he'd often sported over the years, but today he had an overwhelming look of sadness about him, a trudge to his step as he pushed the wheelbarrow across the grounds and to a spot where he stopped, and lifted a hand in acknowledgment, as William walked towards him.

With bittersweet thoughts about the funeral arrangements, a part of her hoped he'd ask her to stay. That once again she'd get the opportunity to see Alfie and walk with him just one more time. After all, he was no longer the same bundling puppy she fondly remembered and now, rather than bouncing around as though he had springs for feet, he plodded at a pace not much faster than a snail. It had been a pleasure mixed with pain seeing him again, much frailer than he had once been. A time that had ended with William apologising, leaning forward, and kissing her gently on the cheek. A soft, friendly kiss that had brought a heat to her face she hadn't expected.

Staring at the tablecloth, at her cup and saucer, she thought about William and about how much he'd changed. He was now a grown man with broad shoulders, a short, trimmed beard and the most attractive smile she'd ever seen, rather than the awkward teenager, she fondly remembered.

'Hello. Earth to Lizzie.' Timothy's voice cut through her thoughts. 'Have you seen Jordan today?'

'What, no...' She looked from one to the other. 'I haven't seen him since last night. He came to the woods, told me about Ada...' she briefly remembered him heading towards the hall as she'd stood in the treeline. Couldn't be sure he'd actually got there. 'But I went to find William. To tell him about his mum and as far as I know, Jordan came back here. Didn't he?' Staring intently at the doorframe, and to the hallways beyond, she remembered the footsteps in the woods, the sound of someone moving through the undergrowth, the inbuilt fear that told her someone else had been there.

32

WILLIAM

Present Day - Saturday Night

'So, you're saying she was murdered?' William punched out at the living room door, closed his eyes for a beat, and felt his stomach turn in somersaults. 'Are you serious?' He looked carefully between the two officers. The palpable look on their faces was firm, unyielding, and told him all he needed to know. 'You really think someone hurt her. Don't you?'

After Thomas, it was the news William had dreaded the most. He had spent the last twenty-four hours since his mother had died walking Alfie, avoiding the others, and torturing himself with the thought. He'd lost count of the times he'd been back and forth to the clearing. Of the menial tasks he'd done that hadn't really needed doing. It had all been a way of killing time and keeping his mind busy. It was as though life had gone full circle. History was repeating itself and the whole feeling of déjà vu that came with it.

'It's certainly looking like a possibility, Mr Kirkwood.' The female officer looked down at her notebook, squinted in the subdued lighting, turned to her colleague, and gave him a long and enquiring look. 'PC Palmer will give you some more details.' She hesitated, furrowed her brow. 'That's if you want to hear them.' Pressing her lips tightly together, she waited momentarily for a response that didn't come. 'We always ask, because some relatives want to know, and others, well, they don't and... we fully understand either way.'

Nodding slowly, William flopped into an armchair. Felt Alfie sidle up beside him, and automatically, he placed a hand on his head, began to stroke. 'It's okay, boy. It's okay. That's right, sit down.' Sighing, he waited for the young officer to speak, saw the way he nervously read and re-read his notes. Wondered how many times he'd been out to deliver bad news, or to give relations the low down on how their family member had died. Finally concluding that he looked a little green around the gills and that today was most probably the first time he'd been issued with the task.

'Mr Kirkwood,' he began. 'Early toxicology reports show that your mother had ingested large amounts of both alcohol and ketamine.' He looked up, caught William's eye. A nervous emotion crossed his face and while slowly exhaling, he glanced around the room, looked for reassurance. 'Her current health conditions, along with the fact that a scarf, or an item similar to a scarf, appears to have been tightened against your mother's neck to severely restrict her breathing, are thought to have been contributary to her death.'

'She always wore a scarf. A silk one that matched her outfit.' He tried to picture her on the patio, tried to remember what outfit she'd been wearing, but couldn't. All he could remember was the red mist that had descended, the moment she'd made her demands, quickly followed by the barked-out threats she thrown at him, before he'd walked off.

PC Palmer paused and took a breath, 'An eyewitness says that they removed the scarf from your mother's neck and tossed it to one side, before attempting resuscitation. I can confirm that a scarf was found at the scene and has been taken for forensic examination.' He cleared his throat, once again looked up and into William's eye. 'Your mother, she'd been drinking?'

William chose to ignore the question as spontaneously he lifted a hand to his neck, gently massaged his carotid artery, tried to swallow. 'So, what are you saying? She took her own life, or...?' he paused. 'Or that someone took it for her.'

'We're right at the beginning of the investigation, Mr Kirkwood. We still have a lot of questions before we determine what really happened.' Sergeant Baguley sat forward in her chair and spoke gently while tipping her head to one side, half listening to the radio attached to her shoulder. It had noisily burst into life and with a pensive smile, the Sergeant turned it down until finally, only a crackling noise rumbled in the background. 'Do you know of anyone who might have wanted to hurt your mother, Mr Kirkwood?'

Shaking his head, William pressed his lips together. It wasn't that he couldn't think of anyone who might have wanted to hurt her. The fact was he could probably name too many. A lot of people who'd been to the house over the years, most who'd left with their tail firmly between their legs. 'There's so many.' He whispered. 'She seemed to piss everyone off at some point. Including me.' Realising what he'd just said, he stood up, pushed open the window, took in a deep breath of fresh air. 'I... I'm really sorry, I need a minute.'

Leaning on the windowsill, he raked a hand through his hair, stared across the grounds, at the Manor. The night was drawing in, lights flicked on and off in the guest rooms and he counted the windows until he reached the room that had once been Thomas's, wondered whether Elizabeth had stayed, or as he'd initially demanded, whether she'd packed a bag, got in her car, and gone. Alarmingly, he could still see the deep-seated look in her eyes, the flash of emotion she'd given him when he'd tried to apologise and how, just for a moment, he'd wished he'd known Elizabeth before she'd met Thomas. It had been a thought he'd very quickly shook from his mind. *Don't be crazy*, he'd told himself over and over. *She loved your brother, not you.*

Bending down, he made a fuss of Alfie. Stroked his ears, his side, and then gave him a half smile as he flopped to the floor, lifted a leg, offered up his stomach for William to tickle. It was as though the old boy had already guessed that something was wrong, that Ada was gone and that from now on, he had no choice but to make the most of it being just him and William.

'What are we gonna do now, boy?' He closed his eyes, thought about all the effort it had taken to refurbish the hotel. The debt he'd gained, along with all the sleepless nights. 'Do you think we'll stay?' He was talking out loud, forgot that the police were stood right behind him. 'Or is it time to go?' Again, he reached down to ruffle the old dog's ears. 'What do you say, boy?'

Holding back the tears, William could still see his mother's face, the way she'd lifted her chin in a formidable manner and angrily, he slammed his hand down on the window ledge.

You're the only one who can do it... he could still feel his temper lurch as he remembered her words, could still hear the disbelief in his voice as he'd shouted his retort and physically, he'd felt his anger grow to an intolerable level. Determined to defy her ridiculous request, he'd refused to continue the conversation and had stormed off towards the woods. Even if that refusal had meant him losing the Manor, and all he'd worked for.

'Your mother?' Sergeant Baguley disturbed his thoughts, 'She'd been drinking.'

'Yes.' William chuntered. 'A couple of doubles, that's all. Normal for her.' It had always been true that after dinner, his mother had often had a drink, her own way of relaxing of an evening. 'It helps me think,' she'd often said. Especially during the nights when she'd have no choice but to sit up, pawing her way through court papers, looking for the answers her clients needed. But last night something had been different and of course, the last drink had been more than a double. A way of emptying the bottle. And he remembered she'd picked it up and knocked it back in one. 'Oh my God, you think the ketamine was in the whisky?'

'We'll know more once forensics have completed their enquiries.' She added, flashed him a supportive smile, 'There's a long way to go, I'm afraid.' She looked over her shoulder at the young PC. 'The hotel. It has CCTV, doesn't it?'

Feeling nauseous. William nodded. 'I took her some whisky, right before she died. I poured it. I could have fed her the drink that killed her.' He stared at Alfie, tears filling his eyes. 'What if...'

'And you know which bottle the whisky came from?'

'Of course...' He bit down on his lip, determined not to cry. Not in front of the officers and anxiously, he threw open the door, stepped outside, inhaled as deeply as he could. 'You'll need to come to the hotel,' he said. 'There was a bottle, in the kitchen.'

'Was?'

'It was empty, I'll take you with me, see if it's still there.' He turned, gave them an apologetic look, 'We keep it separate as it's an expensive blend, hence why she had a bottle all of her own.' Feeling himself retch, he tried to control his breathing, took short sharp breaths as he remembered the way he'd had to fiddle with the security cameras, with the leads that had been loosened.

'Shall we go?' Sergeant Baguley began to march along the gravel path and onto the hotel's driveway. Then she stopped, glanced over her shoulder to where PC Palmer remained in the doorway. 'You don't mind if PC Palmer stays behind, do you... takes a look around?' Again, she waited for him to nod, knowing full well he had no choice but to give his approval. 'We like to get a full picture of all the people involved. Helps us in the long run. You do understand, don't you?'

'Do I need a lawyer?'

Falling into step beside him, Sergeant Baguley thought carefully before she finally spoke. 'Do you feel as though you need one, Mr Kirkwood?'

33

ELIZABETH

Present Day - Saturday Night

With the sound of doors opening and closing along the upstairs corridor, Elizabeth lay on the bed, looked up at the clock, tried to work out which voices she could hear and which she couldn't.

Feeling sure that most had gone down to dinner, she left the bedroom, inched her way along the landing until she reached the place where the staircase split. All those years ago, she'd seen a tiny window, hidden in the ivy. It had been a clue to the house's secrets and the reason she'd begun to study the multi-faceted roofline. The shape and structure of the building that had indicated another level and following a boisterous day by the lake, she'd escaped the others, found her way through the maze of corridors, and into the attic, where she'd found the privacy she'd needed.

Climbing the final set of steps, Elizabeth placed her hand on the doorknob, felt the excitement build within her. It was just a room full of disused and discarded items, but when she'd been up there before, amongst the family's heirlooms, she'd felt as though she belonged. And now, ten years later, she took in a deep breath, hoped that the items remained, that both the rocking chair and the chaise longue were still in place and that once again, she'd get to sit on them both, relax, and put the last two days behind her.

Pushing open the door, she flicked on the light. But then she took a step back, felt the shock wave hit her and stood with her mouth wide open. The room contained nothing but a small wooden trunk. One that stood to one side of the room, right under the window. An obvious stepping stool someone had placed there and used it to look out through the window. All the other items were gone, the room now void of its treasures.

Slowly, she made her way to the trunk. Felt inquisitive as to what the view would be like and who would have used the trunk as a step and quickly realised that if she stood on her tip toes, she could just about see through the tiny window, with its overgrown ivy, the tip of the monument standing proudly beyond.

'Lizzie?'

Jumping at the sound of William's voice, Elizabeth felt herself topple precariously to one side. 'William. I'm so sorry. I shouldn't be up here, not without permission but... I was... I was up here, kind of reliving my youth.' She smiled, awkwardly. 'The attic. It was my favourite place in the whole house, somewhere I came. You know, before.' She paused. Wanted to say the right thing and had no idea how she'd explain. It had been a time when she'd dreamt that the Manor would one day be her home. Whereas now she was nothing more than a guest. *One who's outstayed her welcome.* 'During the last couple of months before Thomas died, I noticed the roofline, found the attic, and used it as a place to hide from Thomas's friends.' She eventually said. Laughed, nervously. 'I was so doubtful over Thomas's feelings for me, it was the only place I could go to think, to get some solitude.' She fretfully paced across the floorboards, heard her own footsteps echo beneath her. 'I used to love being alone up here.' Aware of the way his eyes searched hers, and with the colour flooding her cheeks, Elizabeth turned and paced across dusty wooden floorboards.

'And now?'

'Now what?'

'Do you want to be alone?' He shifted. 'I guess I'm asking if you'd like me to leave. Give you some space?' He turned, placed a hand on the doorknob. 'If I'd known it was you, I wouldn't have raced up here quite so quickly.'

Laughing timidly, Elizabeth ran a hand through her hair, tossed it backwards, almost seductively over her shoulders. 'William. This...' She held a hand out, swept it outwards. 'This is your house. It's me that shouldn't be here.' With an apologetic look, she headed back towards the door, gave the room a final look. 'I just wanted to see it again. To see all the things that used to be here.' She stopped, turned, pointed to one of the corners. 'Right over there. There used to be a rocking chair. I'd sit in it for hours. Rocking, pretending. Sometimes, I'd borrow a book from the library downstairs. There was a chaise longue, right over there and I'd lie on it and read, or take a nap.' She strode from one part of the room to the other. 'There was a Christmas tree, a box of decorations. Things I remember your father bringing up from the cellar when the rain got in.' She stopped, held a hand to her mouth as though in shock. 'And a baby's crib. Right here. It stood, right here.' Exhaling, she longed for the room to be full, for all the items to be returned. For William to go back to being the young, carefree teenager she'd known and loved.

'Yeah. My mother. She had a clear out. Got Bobby to get rid of all the items we didn't want right after Dad died.' He tapped the trunk with a finger, 'And for some reason, the only thing she wanted to keep was this.' He knelt down, slapped the lid with the flat of his hand. 'It's full of things that belonged to Thomas. One or two things that might have been hers. I doubt it contains anything of mine.' He shook his head. 'There was nothing I ever did to make her feel proud. The prodigal son who didn't go to law school as she'd expected.' A look of sadness crossed his face. A memory too many that made him furrow his brow, with a pain that was obvious to see.

'William, you might not have gone to law school, but look at this, look what you did. I'm sure she was proud of you.' The thought back to the barbed comments Ada had made about the house and how Thomas would have never done what William had. They were words that had been filled with so much venom; she knew that for his sake, he didn't need to know them. 'And for what it's worth.' She lay a hand on his shoulder, gave him what she hoped would be a convincing smile. 'I'm proud of you; this house, it looks amazing. And you...' She tried to think of something appropriate to say but couldn't and instead, she reached out. Lay a hand on his. 'Seriously, you've done so well since I last saw you.'

With eyes sparkling with unspent tears, William smiled back at her. Nodded a silent thank you. 'How about,' he took a step forward, gave her a hopeful smile, 'we take the trunk down and look through it together?'

Closing her eyes for a beat, Elizabeth felt the trembling inside her begin. Her friendship with William was back and this time, she had no intention of letting it go.

34

ELIZABETH

Present Day - Saturday Night

'Well, I'm kind of pleased you went snooping. I'm glad of the distraction.' William said as he rested the trunk against his knee and waited in the corridor for Elizabeth to slot the key into a new and shiny brass lock that had obviously been fitted quite recently to Thomas's bedroom door.

Sighing, she realised how unusual it felt to unlock a door that had previously been a part of a family home, one where locks hadn't been needed and where she'd let herself in and out without invitation. Now, the key created a formal separation. Between now and then. One she wasn't sure she liked.

'I've wanted to look through this for a while,' he continued, as thoughtfully, he lowered the trunk to the floor. He knelt down beside it, leaned against the bed, wiggled to get into a comfortable position, made himself at home and even pulled at the quilt, to use it as a cushion squished up behind him.

'So why didn't you?' Elizabeth paced nervously back and forth to the window, looked through it and at the lake, where a single light shone up at the memorial, lighting up Thomas's name. It was a sight she didn't need to see, and quickly she pulled the curtains to a close, clicked on the lamp to give the room a soft, amber glow. Fidgeting with her things, she moved a makeup bag from one side of the room to the other, picked up a bottle of perfume and without spraying it, put it down again. Couldn't escape the overwhelming feeling that sitting down with William in the room she'd shared with Thomas felt strange.

'I don't really know. I guess it felt wrong.' With pursed lips, he gave her a pensive smile. It was a smile that told her how strange he felt too and quickly, she tried to brush the feeling to one side, to consider how many times they'd been alone together. How many hours they'd simply been together in the days following Thomas's death. Sometimes they'd sat in total silence or walked by the side of the river. And on other days, they'd gone out for a drive, and avoided being anywhere near the Manor.

'It was something that meant a lot to her.' William continued, 'and if I'm honest, I was always a bit scared she'd catch me snooping.' Looking up, he caught Elizabeth's gaze. Tapped the carpet beside him. 'These were the things she'd deemed important,' he said. 'And I guess there could be things in here I don't want to see. Things that make everything seem real.'

'Like what?' She moved across the room, sat on the carpet beside him. Reaching up, she grabbed at one of the many crisp, white, cotton pillows, pushed it behind her. 'That's better,' she laughed, 'Do you want one?'

'No. I want to see what's in here. But if I'm honest, I'm a little scared to open the lid.'

Using a finger, Elizabeth traced the carvings that stood out on top of the box, took note how each swirl was a perfectly carved twist. One that could easily be imagined into any shape you wanted, and like she did with clouds, she stared as hard as she could, saw the shapes turn into faces and suddenly, she could see Thomas scowling back at her. It was an image she didn't want to see, one that had no place in her present day and to escape the image, she closed her eyes, rested her head back against the pillow.

'Sometimes, the past is better off being exactly that. Don't you think?'

Furrowing his brow, William moved forward until his leg was curled up beneath him. 'Do you think that's where the trunk is better off?' he said. 'Maybe being lost was the best place for it... out of sight and all that...'

'William.' Slowly, she moved her fingers along his lower arm, pushed her hand into his, and squeezed tenderly. 'I don't think it was ever lost.' She hesitated, 'I think your mum, she knew exactly where it was, and I still owe you an apology. I really shouldn't have been up there, snooping around.'

William tipped his head to one side, saw her confusion. 'If I'd known it was you, I'd have left you to it.'

'I still don't understand how you knew anyone was up there?'

He laughed. 'I was messing with the security cameras. Some of the wires had been coming loose. It's happened a few times recently and a tiny alarm went off, gave me a warning that someone was up there.' Sliding his fingers across the trunk, he moved to the lock, massaged it between his thumb and fingers before unhooking it from the clasp. Tossing it to one side, he flashed her a look as it landed on the carpet. 'The police, they wanted to see the security from Friday night,' he added.

'And...'

'There was nothing to see.'

'What?'

'The wires, they'd worked their way loose. So right now, I have the police dusting it for fingerprints.'

'Well, that's good, isn't it?'

'Not really, all that dust all over my kitchen and for what? We're all in and out all day and at some point, we all touch the monitor or keyboard for one reason or another. It'd be easier to say whose fingerprints wasn't on it.' Staring at his hands, William twisted them tightly together. 'Which is crap, cause... they already think mother's death was suspicious.' He stood up, ran both of his hands nervously through his hair, stared up at the ceiling. 'They're saying she'd ingested ketamine, a possible overdose and now, now the footage is missing, it makes us all look guilty.'

'Ada would have never taken drugs,' Elizabeth suddenly blurted out. 'She despised them. Told us more than once how much she hated anything to do with them. In fact, she was always having a go at Thomas, telling him how stupid he was, how irresponsible.' Pausing, she looked William directly in the eye, hesitated before speaking. 'Which means that someone else gave them to her without her knowing?'

He stared at an imaginary spot on the trunk, swallowed hard. 'Well, the police, they're speaking to everyone. They're probably going to pull the kitchen apart, test everything, but their focus will be on her whisky. She had a bottle that was kept on the side, just for her.'

Flopping onto the bed, Elizabeth grabbed at a pillow. Held it tightly in front of her, like a form of personal protection. She wasn't sure what she was afraid of, or what protection she needed. All she did know was that for just a while, she felt better holding onto it. 'They think someone killed her?' Feeling as though a tonne of weight had just landed on her shoulders. She couldn't speak. Could barely focus. The thought that Ada had been right made the nausea take over and with the pillow pulled tightly against her, she closed her eyes, hoped she wouldn't vomit. Someone in this house could have been responsible for Thomas's death, and now... Ada was dead too. The question was, was that same person responsible for killing them both? It was a feeling that made her tremble nervously inside.

'Sure... they've turned the back study into an incident room, gave me quite a grilling. And now, they've started speaking to the guests, to the staff, one by one and... they'll want to speak to you too.' He raised his eyebrows in an apology. 'Sorry... but...' William's voice broke into her thoughts, 'anyhow, do you still want to do this? While we're in the mood?' He pointed to the trunk.

Shuffling to the side of the bed, Elizabeth leaned against it, looked between the trunk, the wardrobe, and her car keys that still lay on the dressing table beside her handbag. 'William. Please don't take this personally, but I'm going to leave. So many bad things happen in this house, and my dad, he already thinks it's cursed. And... I can't lie... I'm starting to think he's right.' She stared helplessly at the door. At the shiny brass lock. 'I mean, do you feel safe, right now, in this house?'

Standing up, William heaved a sigh. 'Lizzie. I don't know, all we can do is lock this and hope for the best.' Turning the key, he gave the door a satisfied nod. 'If we stick together, we'll be just fine.' He pursed his lips, caught her eye. 'There is only one problem I can think of.'

'What?'

'I wish we'd have locked ourselves in one of the rooms that has a mini bar full of wine and chocolate.'

'The other rooms have chocolate?'

'Well, no. But... right now, I wish they did.' He smiled. It was more than obvious he was trying to lighten the mood. 'Seriously. If we stick together, nothing can go wrong. Can it?' He pushed his hands into his pockets. 'But I must admit, I am hungry...'

As though on cue, her stomach growled. But quickly, she shook her head. 'I... I don't want to go down. Not tonight. And if someone could have drugged Ada, what's to say we won't be next?' She picked up her handbag, rummaged through it. 'I have one of these,' she held up a squashed Mars bar. One that had seen better days. 'It isn't very big, but I'm willing to share.'

Laughing, he picked up the phone. 'I have a better idea. Hi, it's me, William,' he said. 'Did I see Cookie making one of her famous quiches earlier?' he paused, 'Great. If there's any left, could I get two portions, salad on the side, new potatoes. Oh, and a bottle of the good Malbec, unopened. Actually. Make that two. Yeah, I'm in Thomas's old room.' Placing the phone back on the hanger. He held his hands up in the air. 'Voila, dinner is ordered. Oh, and before you get worried. I saw Cookie make the quiche herself. I also saw her eating some and if she's willing to eat it, so am I. What's more, there's been a multitude of occasions when I probably deserved it, and...' he smiled, 'she didn't kill me then and I have no reason to think she'd hurt either of us now.'

Elizabeth smiled. It was a bold statement, but true. Cookie had never hurt anyone. She'd always been the most loving, kindest person Elizabeth had ever met, and only that morning she'd witnessed her hugging William like one of her own, with emotions that just had to be genuine.

Turning her attention back to the trunk and to the way William had knelt beside it. Elizabeth smiled reassuringly, saw the nerves that appeared to surround him, the way his hand went back and forth to the lid, the way he almost opened it, then stopped, waited, shook with anticipation. Then, determinedly, and in a single swift movement, he threw the lid backwards and peered inside.

Elizabeth dreaded to think what Ada had decided to keep, especially after emptying the attic and disposing of so many of the treasures that had been there. She knelt beside William and nervously leaned against him. Watched the way he lifted one item out of the trunk at a time. Until an old leather wallet was revealed and immediately, her hand shot out to pick it up. It was a wallet she recognised. One she clearly remembered Thomas using. And while biting down on her lower lip, she allowed her fingers to trace the initials that were engraved on its surface. TMK. Thomas Matthew Kirkwood.

'I don't remember this. Do you?' William held up an old Nokia phone. It had soft grey buttons, where some of the alphabet could no longer be seen. All worn out through constant overuse.

Putting the wallet down, she took the phone from him, turned it over in her hand, ran her fingers across the buttons and took note of which had been used the most. 'I don't think it belonged to Thomas. He had one of those Galaxy ones. It was a white one with the stylus, wasn't it?' She cast her memory backwards, could clearly see Thomas with the phone in his hand, tapping away on the screen with the small stylus that slotted in and out of a hole at the bottom.

'Then whose was it?' He tossed the phone to one side, continued to dig through the box, lifted one item out after the other, studied it, before placing it with the other items beside the trunk.

'Did you see this, it's beautiful.' Elizabeth opened a small, hard-covered book. Turned each page to see a different flower. Each one carefully pressed between the pages. Along with small notes and poems. 'Do you think these are love notes?' She handed one to William, saw the smile disappear and, in its place, a wistful look replaced it.

Leaving William to read through the notes. Elizabeth picked out various items of baby clothing. A pair of socks, a white christening gown, two tiny shoes. 'It's hard to believe these ever fit you.' She held them up, wiggled them around in the air. Then playfully, she held them next to William's feet. 'No way, they can't have ever fit you, can they?'

Gently taking the shoes from her, he placed them on top of the gown. Pushed them away and stared aimlessly into the air. 'They weren't mine,' he eventually replied. 'They belonged to my brother. A brother born before Thomas.'

'But I thought that Thomas was the eldest?' Elizabeth frowned, kept her eyes on the shoes.'

Taking her hand in his, he threaded his fingers through hers. 'No, Thomas wasn't the eldest. We, Thomas, and I, we had another brother. He was the eldest. The one who ironically should have inherited the Manor.' He closed his eyes for a blink. 'It should be him that's sat here, not me.'

'So, where is he? Why have I never met him?'

'Because he died. Just a few days after being born, at least three years before Mother had Thomas.' He paused, looked her in the eye. 'We didn't really talk about him.'

'Oh my goodness, I didn't know.' Elizabeth felt her eyes swim with tears. 'And Ada... oh my God, poor, poor Ada.' It was a thought that rocked Elizabeth's mind. She couldn't imagine what it would have been like for her to lose one child. But to find out that she'd lost two was awful and she stared at the gown, at the other tiny items of clothing that were now scattered around them on the floor. 'Maybe, that explains why she was so very protective. Why she acted the way she did.'

'Elizabeth.' Speaking gently and almost in whispers, William held his arms out as though he were about to hug the room. 'There is so much you don't know. And this house, it has so many secrets.' He reached forward, lifted a pale-blue box file from the trunk, flipped back the lid. 'Don't get me wrong, I wanted to do this, and it feels right that we do it together. But it does feel a bit like we're opening a shrine. Digging up a past that should probably stay buried.' William whispered, as one piece of paper after the other was lifted out of the box, carefully read, and then placed in a pile. 'And as for your dad's theory about it being cursed, I just hope for all our sakes it isn't.'

Flicking her gaze from William to the trunk and then across the room to where Thomas's notebook still stood on the dressing table, she had the sudden urge to read the rest. She felt confused, began to question everything. She'd been uneasy about coming back. But now, she wished she'd never been here at all.

'William...' She lifted a hand to her chest, placed it over her heart. 'So many bad things happen here and... do you know what, I really am gonna go.' She spoke at speed, stood up, began to collect items from around the room, tossed them into a small, canvas bag. As though an afterthought, she grabbed at the notebook, tore out a blank page, hurriedly wrote her name and address on it. 'I'll leave you my contact details. You know, for the police.'

'Lizzie.' Jumping up, William caught her by the hand, turned her towards him, wrapped his arms around her. 'Please don't go.' He rocked her gently from side to side. 'Other than Cookie, you're the only ally I have left and...' He paused, gently pushed her away. 'I'm being unfair. Aren't I?' Defeated, she saw his arms drop to his side. 'Look, sorry. Just do what you have to do.'

Closing her eyes, Elizabeth took in a deep breath, waited for the anxiety to subside, for the common sense to take over. Right now, William needed her. Needed someone he could rely on other than Cookie, who'd already taken on the running of the house. Sighing, she dropped to her knees, began to search through the box. Tapped the floor beside her. 'Come on then.' she said. 'If you want me to stay, you could at least sit down here and help me.'

Laughing, he sidled in beside her, took the piece of paper out of her hand. 'Oh my God, I'd forgotten about this; this was when Thomas won the egg and spoon race. The same year that our mum entered one of the adult races and ran it in a pair of Louis Vuitton heels.' He shook his head from side to side. 'She complained to the organiser when she came last. Said she should have been told to expect adult participation.' He pointed to his feet and pulled a face. 'Oh, and the shoes, were covered in mud, totally ruined.'

Amused, Elizabeth laughed and leaned back against the bed. 'I can imagine that happening. Ada did dress impeccably.' Rummaging, she pulled one sheet of paper out after the other. Kept up the routine of passing them to him. 'Here, look at this one.'

'What is it?'

'Looks like an old email or maybe one of those faxes. It's so faint, I can barely read the words.' She stared at the faded parts of the paper, tried to make out what it said. Could just about see the start of what looked to be Ada's name. 'I think I can make out Thomas's name, and... yes, that says...' She suddenly stopped speaking as she spotted the name Matilda, knew it stood for Tilly. Quickly she scanned to the bottom, looked for other clues as to what it all meant and felt her breath catch in her throat as she saw a figure, followed by zero's and quickly, Ada's words came flooding back. *The last time you got yourself into trouble. It cost me a lot of money to get you out of it. Just imagine how much it would cost me if you did get this girl pregnant*. Feeling anxious. Elizabeth tried to push the sheet to one side. Looked at her watch. 'I hope the food comes soon. I'm starving.'

'It shouldn't be too long now.' He reached across her, picked up the sheet, held it up to the light. 'I think I can see a signature at the bottom. Is that Jordan's name?'

'I'm not really sure.' Elizabeth lied, quickly took the fax from him and placed it back down on the floor as she continued to work her way through the box file full of papers. The words were clearly there to see and yet again, she did all she could to work out what it all meant. Only now there was proof that Thomas had done something wrong. That Tilly's death hadn't been the accident he'd made out and that Ada had stepped in and paid Jordan off. It was a thought that wouldn't leave her mind and cautiously, Elizabeth stared at everything in the room apart from that piece of paper. She wished for an ethereal force, for Ada to appear, for her to answer all the questions she wanted to ask. But Ada was gone. As were both Tilly and Thomas. None of them were there to answer her questions. And now, only Jordan knew the truth.

'Food's here.' William jumped to his feet, answered the door to see a waiter stood in the doorway, pushing a small hostess trolley. It had a white cotton cloth, shiny silver cutlery, two stainless-steel plate covers that had been positioned carefully over the food, with two wine glasses placed beside it. On the bottom tray stood the two bottles of Malbec William had ordered, alongside two covered dessert bowls. 'Thanks, Geoffrey,' he said to the waiter, before pushing the trolley into the room. Studying the bottle and with a nod of approval, he opened the wine, poured a glass, and passed one to her. Then he held his out, clinked it with hers and for a moment, she kept her eyes averted, went over and over the night Tilly had died. Tried to decide whether or not she should tell William all she suspected. But to tell him was to involve him. And now that both Thomas and Ada were dead too, she didn't know if she dare, not when it was becoming more than apparent that knowledge had consequences.

35

ELIZABETH

Present Day - Sunday Morning

Drifting in and out of a restless sleep, Elizabeth pulled the quilt up and over her shoulders, snuggled down beneath it, and sleepily began to remember where she was as she listened to the sounds that moved up and down the corridor outside. Hearing a door slam to a close in the distance and footsteps walking past, she jumped, turned against the pillows. Then she honed in on the noise that came from behind her, the gentle sound of breathing. A breathing that wasn't her own.

Closing her eyes as tightly as she could, she took short, sharp breaths. Impulsively, she wanted to turn, to run and hide, but couldn't bring herself to move and in her half unconscious state, she imagined Thomas lying behind her.

With her eyes squeezed tightly together, she felt her fingers tighten around the duvet, moved her legs slowly towards the edge of the bed, and felt her heart miss a beat as she felt a hand land gently against her shoulder.

'Hey... are you okay?'

With her mind leaping back to the present, Elizabeth found herself smiling at the sound of William's voice, began to remember the evening before and felt herself blush with the memories.

'Morning...' She exhaled, and while not knowing where else to look, she kept her focus on the small wooden trunk. It still stood by the side of the bed. The random pieces of paper still scattered around it. Lying on top of it all was the old mobile phone, its battery flat. 'I didn't realise you were going to stay...' She didn't know what else to say, her body tingled with nerves and timidly she climbed out of bed, walked across the room, ran her fingers across the edge of the silver dinner tray. It was still stood on top of the hostess trolley. The plates all stacked, the glasses empty, along with the two bottles of wine they'd happily drunk. One bottle quickly following the other. 'We... I...' She turned, spoke slowly. 'In fact. Remind me. Why are you still here?'

Propping himself up against the pillows, William could see her confusion, gave her a broad, sensuous smile. 'I didn't think you'd mind. You were scared and maybe just a little bit more than drunk.' He held a hand in the air, his finger and thumb held closely together. An indication of a measurement much smaller than the two whole bottles they'd managed to devour. 'Oh, and someone should tell you. You talk in your sleep.' He stood up, walked across the room but kept a respectful distance. 'You seemed to be having a bad dream. I didn't want you to wake up alone.'

'Oh, I see.' She feigned a smile, tried to remember the dream. Somewhere in the back of her mind, she could see herself running, falling, taking a leap from a great height and then... then what? What had happened? She stared at the floor. Was there water? A river? The danger felt real, her heart rate quickened, and fearfully, she grabbed at the bed, held onto the post.

Taking a quick step towards her, William reached forward, gently moved a strand of hair from in front of her face. 'Lizzie, look at me. Are you okay?' Gripping her elbow, he manoeuvred her across the room towards the bed. 'Here sit down, you've gone really pale.' He kept a hand on hers. 'Not the normal reaction I get after sharing a bed with a woman.'

Blushing, she looked down at the floor, then at him and then quickly away. 'And of course, you must share your bed with random women all the time?' She said, then quickly, she tried to backtrack on her words. 'Actually, I shouldn't have said that. It's none of my business...' She held a hand out to the bed. 'Anyhow, the bed belongs to you and you can sleep in it whenever you like.'

He winked, playfully. 'First, I wouldn't class you as random and secondly, it was okay for me to stay, wasn't it? And before you ask, I was a perfect gentleman. Slept on my own side all night.' He pointed to a row of pillows that had been purposely positioned down the centre. 'Which helps when the bed has enough room for a football team.'

Looking at his watch, he picked up the bedside phone, dialled for reception. 'Hi. It's William,' he said. 'Can you send me some coffee up?' He paused, listened. 'Yeah, that's right. Actually, I'm starving. Could you send me a couple of rounds of toast to go with it?' He looked across at where Elizabeth stood. 'And some of those little pastries, the ones that Lizzie likes.'

Trying not to look in his direction, Elizabeth listened to him finish the call, ran a hand through her hair, caught her reflection in the mirror. She was still wearing the same clothes she'd worn the day before, and desperately, she wished for a shower, for a change of clothes and for some of those tiny little pastries William had just ordered for breakfast. Already she could taste the apricot jam within, the soft flaky pastry, and the icing sugar that Cookie always sprinkled on top.

Kneeling down, she picked up the old mobile phone, looked at it more closely, and took note of the soft, rubbery buttons, where some of the more prominent letters could no longer be seen; the overuse and constant texting was more than obvious. It had been a phone that had failed to give up its secrets. One they hadn't been able to charge, even though they'd searched for a lead but hadn't found one.

'We must have a charger for it somewhere,' she remembered saying as she'd searched through the box. 'I mean, surely if they'd kept the phone, they'd have kept the charger too?' It didn't look like a phone she recognised, and she'd wondered whose it might have been. She knew Thomas had kept a lot of secrets of his own and like the notebook, those secrets could still be buried within this house. Lying on her belly, she'd pulled herself under the bed, checked the hole in the floor, just in case there had been anything else left in it.

'It was worth a try.' William had said as he'd topped up the wine, passed a glass to her. Then, casually he'd draped an arm lovingly around her shoulders. 'Don't worry. I've got a box full of old chargers up in the loft, at the cottage. There's bound to be something that fits.' He'd smiled, pulled her in a little closer. 'It could be the battery. Or why don't we just transfer the SIM card into a different phone? See if that works.'

She'd settled into the hug, relaxed against him. 'This wine is lovely.' Holding the glass up in the air, she studied the colour. 'Do you see how it coats the side of the glass?'

Nodding, William had swirled his drink around the glass, 'Last time I remember you being on the wine, you were down in the kitchen.' He'd bitten down on his lip. 'Do you remember?'

A distant memory had flooded back and nervously, she'd felt

the blush rise through her body until it landed heavily on her cheeks. She'd swallowed hard as she spoke. 'I think I know where you're going with this.'

'You almost kissed me.' He'd chuckled, poked her playfully in the ribs. 'And yes, you'd definitely been on the wine, or was it champagne?' Raising his eyebrows, he'd tipped his glass to clink against hers. 'I often wondered what would have happened if you had kissed me. My mother would have hated the scandal.' He'd laughed playfully. 'Although I guess by the next morning, you wouldn't have remembered. You were so drunk, you could barely walk.'

Allowing her mind to run on overtime, Elizabeth had thought about the night she'd almost fallen down the stairs and ended up in the kitchen. It had been one of those happenings that had come back to her in waves, just a little at a time, like a scrambled jigsaw. Until eventually she put all the pieces together. It was true; she had initially thought he was Thomas. But so many things had told her he wasn't: the fresh breath, the aftershave, the way he'd been calm and gentle with her. So many clues she'd chosen to ignore. And now, she wondered what might have happened, and how things would have turned out, if she hadn't been in a relationship with his brother. With her whole-body tingling with nerves, she'd pressed her lips tightly together. Allowed the question to hang in the air. 'William. If I'm honest, I think I knew it was you,' she admitted guiltily. 'I'd been so angry with Thomas. I'd already worked out that our days were numbered.' She'd allowed her gaze to land on William's lips. 'I guess I held on much longer than I should have.' Taking his hand, she'd twisted her fingers with his, squeezed. 'I always felt close to you, and in the days after Thomas had died, we spent a lot of time together.' She'd raised her glass, took a large gulp of the wine. 'I have to admit, I depended on you. Felt as though we were getting close. But the more time I spent with you, the more confused I got. So, I left.' She'd paused, 'It was the right thing to do.'

Holding her gaze, William had taken in a breath. 'He didn't deserve you... I often thought that.' He'd closed his eyes, considered his words. 'I have to admit, I used to wish you were with me, not him and when you left... it killed me.' He shook his head slowly. 'And I decided that I should leave too. I couldn't stay and that's when I went to London, thought it would be the easiest way to forget all that had happened, but couldn't. Every day I kicked myself, wished over and over that I'd taken my own feelings into consideration. There were so many times I'd wanted to kiss you.'

Feeling confused, she'd tightened her grip, couldn't bear to let go. The breath had left her body, her mouth had turned dry, and her mind had questioned everything past and present. She'd gone from one thought to the next, knowing that whatever she said next could define the rest of her life.

'And now...' She'd held her breath as she whispered the words. 'What do you want to do about it now?'

With his arm still draped carefully across her shoulders and with a slow, but firm movement, he'd pulled her towards him, 'What I want is to kiss you.' He'd leaned in close until he was so close she could feel the warmth of his breath against her cheek. 'Lizzie, I feel guilty for wanting you. I felt guilty back then and I feel guilty now. But I really can't help it... I want you, like I've never wanted before.'

Leaning in, Elizabeth had pressed a hand against his cheek, guided his mouth towards hers.

'I know we'd both had a lot to drink, but by the look on your face,' William's voice brought her back to the present, 'you either don't remember the kiss, or you're regretting it, and if that's the case, I owe you an apology.' He mumbled the words, pursed his lips. 'It had been a hell of a day and... do you know what, it shouldn't have happened.' He closed his eyes, raked his hands angrily through his hair.

Feeling insulted by the apology, Elizabeth kept her eyes on the curtain. She couldn't respond, couldn't speak, and with her gaze moving up to the rail, she spotted where a small spider's web had gone between the rail and the coving. She had the urge to climb up, to knock it off but the anger inside made her go over his words until they were spinning violently around her. Annoyed, she wanted to throw the apology back, to pretend she regretted it too.

'William.' She began. 'I do remember the kiss. And I'm so sorry you feel the need to apologise.' She snapped, held up a hand, palm forward. Closing her eyes, she felt her lip tremble, the stress building up within her. 'I'll make sure it doesn't happen again.'

'Lizzie... don't...' He paused, reached out, gently lay a hand on her shoulder. 'Don't be like that.'

Shrugging him off, Elizabeth stepped away, watched him slam angrily into the bathroom. Feeling hurt and humiliated, she glared at the bathroom door. Once again, she felt rejected, humiliated. Couldn't believe they could have shared a night like the one before, only for him to retreat to a place of safety and apologise for the fact it had happened. Turning away, she moved back to the window; she still wanted to move the cobweb and, in an attempt, to do so, she threw open the curtains. Placed her hands on the windowsill and stared across the grounds at the lake beyond. 'What the hell?' she growled under her breath. Her eyes fixed on the memorial. 'Is there something I don't know about,' she shouted in the direction of the bathroom. 'Like a memorial that's still going to happen?'

'What? What are you talking about?' Opening the bathroom door, he poked his head around its edge. 'There is no memorial.'

'Then,' Elizabeth chipped in, 'you might want to tell the others that.' She waited for him to stand beside her, pointed to the place where Thomas's friends were all sat on chairs, beside the lake. All dressed in black, looking as though they were all about to start a service.

'What the hell are they doing?'

'What time is it?' She searched the room, looked for a clock.

'Breakfast time, that's what time it is, and much too early for a bloody memorial. Yet there they are. Waiting.' He reached past her, banged on the window, pulled on the catch, then took a step back. 'Do you know what? They can wait. They can sit there all they like. I really don't care.' A tentative look flashed across his face. His hand went to her cheek, came to rest behind her neck. 'What I do care about is you. And... Jesus Lizzie, of course I'm not sorry I kissed you. It was something I'd wanted to do for years. But this morning, I was stupid, I panicked. I thought you regretted it and, well... I was kind of trying to give you an out if you wanted one.'

Holding her breath with anticipation, Elizabeth felt him pull her close, and sensitively he flicked her hair back and over her shoulders, tipped her head backwards, and once again, he pressed his lips to hers. It was just a graze at first, a tease and with a playful smile, he began to surround her mouth with soft, gentle, tender kisses.

'I like you kissing me,' she whispered as he took a final step forward, pressed her back against coldness of the wall.

'I like kissing you too.' One kiss followed the other, until without warning his lips left hers, followed a path down her neck and unexpectedly, she felt herself moan in a moment of surrender. Melting into his touch, she felt his lips capture hers in a tense and more demanding way. With each kiss, the intensity heightened, and while holding her breath, she felt his fingers move over her shoulder. It was a moment of pure pleasure. A time when desire took over and Elizabeth felt the heat sear through her, as time after time, she felt his lips re-capture hers.

'You're so beautiful.' He whispered the words against her cheek, took a step back, stared deep into her eyes, saw the sparkle within. 'I've always wanted you, Lizzie. I... I meant what I said. I always wished I'd been that little bit older. That you'd have met me first.'

Hearing the enormity of his confession, Elizabeth turned to the window, felt the anticipation within her. The need to be touched. To be held. 'I think,' she whispered, 'I think we should leave the others to whatever memorial they're having and well, I think we should close these and you know... have a reunion of our own.' Reaching forward, she pulled at the curtains, needed the privacy they gave. Pulling him across the room, and towards the bed, she stared into his eyes, unbuttoned his shirt, and allowed it to drop from his body, as her fingertips ran across his defined, chiselled chest. And even though the room had been cast into a semi-darkness, with just a shard of light spilling through the gap in the curtains, she looked into the deep grey of his eyes, took note of the way they shone back at her, the way his hands moved slowly and seductively across her body.

Taking his time, he deepened the kiss. Allowed his hands to gently arouse her. 'Lizzie.' He paused, searched her eyes with his. 'I want to make love to you, so much,' he whispered, 'I've always wanted to make love to you.' He smiled, searched her eyes with his. Pressed his body tightly against her, and with a gasp, she could feel his arousal and moved sensually against him.

'William.' A yell came from the corridor, followed by a rapid, knocking against the door. It was a sound that made Elizabeth's heart leap out of her chest. It was more than obvious that something was wrong, that William was needed and quickly.

'I'll get it.' William rushed to the door, and before opening it, he rubbed vigorously at his face with his hands. Readjusting his jeans, he pulled a face. It was a comical twist of his mouth that was quickly followed by a furrowing of his brow, a way of him showing his obvious discomfort. 'It'll be the breakfast.'

Opening the door. He looked out and onto the corridor, saw an anxious-looking Anna pacing up and down. She moved quickly between the door and the top of the stairs, then back again.

'William, I'm so sorry.' She took in his state of undress, looked past him to where Elizabeth stood. 'You might want to get dressed; you need to go to the cottage... quickly.'

'What's happened?' William reached for Elizabeth's hand, squeezed it affectionately.

'It's Alfie.' Turning, Anna headed back towards the staircase, looked over her shoulder, gave both William and Elizabeth accusing looks. 'He's sick,' she shouted. 'On top of everything else, Alfie is sick.'

'Sick? He was fine yesterday. He's old and a bit wobbly, but he was fine.'

'Johnny, he stayed with him last night, just like you asked and this morning, they went for a walk.' She paused, pointed through the window. 'Alfie, he grabbed at a wasp or a bee or something... and his face, well it's all swollen. Like a big balloon.' She held the palm of her hand in front of her face. 'Johnny thinks he needs to go to the vet and says that you need to go with them.'

36

ELIZABETH

Present Day Sunday - Morning

Throwing herself into the shower, Elizabeth stood under the water, leaned forward, and placed her hands on the opposing wall. Moving slowly from side to side, she allowed the heat of the water to massage her lower back. Took pleasure in the way the water hit her body and still she couldn't believe that one of the most tender moments of her life had been followed by such heart-wrenching news. Images of Alfie flashed up in her mind, and with a deep, and profound sadness she thought of the puppy she used to know, wished he could go back to being the bumbling, bouncy character she remembered so well. With tears stinging the back of her eyes, she gasped. It had only been the day before when he'd lain beside her, his head resting on her knee, and now she wished she'd gone with William to the vet but she hadn't wanted to intrude.

'One kiss doesn't make you a couple' she whispered under her breath, as she climbed out of the shower. 'It doesn't mean you're a part of his life.'

Checking her mobile for the tenth time that hour, Elizabeth clicked through her messages. Replied to one from her father and another from Aunt Peggy. Tapping at the screen, she scrolled, found the number William had given her before he'd left and hesitantly, she tapped out a message.

Here if you need me.

Staring at the words, she realised how crass it sounded. How pathetic and needy. And immediately she deleted it, threw her phone at the bed, considered her options and with the curtains once again thrown open, she took in the early morning mist and the way it drifted eerily across the lake, towards the group of friends who'd remained sitting by the memorial. All the strange happenings that seemed to have begun the moment they'd arrived had pulled them all together as a group. A group that didn't include her in it and now, she watched the way they interacted. Wondered which one of them was lying, which one had killed Thomas, or Ada. Whether the same person had killed them both.

Pulling her black trouser suit out of the wardrobe, she slipped it on and pulled her hair backwards into a simple but neat chignon and placed a silver hair clip in her hair before smiling at her appearance in the mirror. 'Even when you're not feeling your best, look professional.' She whispered the words her father had often said. Then gave herself a last look up and down before closing her eyes, wondering if the killing had stopped, whether Ada had been the last, or whether she or William were next on the list and with a mind full of indecision, she cautiously made her way down the stairs and into the hallway where forensic tape still blocked the entrance to the grand hall. A distressing reminder of what had happened and what was to come. And with the need of some fresh air, she ran past the dining room, pulled open the front door, and walked out of the Manor.

37

ELIZABETH

Present Day - Sunday Morning

Walking out through the same door she'd entered just two days before, she took a deep breath, thought about how frightened, alone, and anxious she'd felt. And how things had changed. Even though she still felt anxious following Ada's death, her feelings were now mixed. For the first time in years, she had hope for the future and with a skip in her step, she made her way down the ramp, kept one eye on William's cottage. Thoughtfully, she leaned on the balustrade, looked for tell-tale signs that William was home. But the cottage stood quiet. There were no lights in the windows. No car in the driveway.

'Please let Alfie be safe,' she whispered, closed her eyes and disturbingly, she began to expect the worst.

'Hey Lizzie, you coming to the memorial?' Patrick ran to stand beside her. 'And where the hell were you at dinner last night? Hey?' He lifted his eyebrows. Gave her a questioning look. 'We thought you'd have come down and joined us. But word has it you were just a bit busy. Bit tied up, someone said.' He sang the words and held his hands together, as though they'd been bound.

'I was tired,' she lied. 'It was an emotional day. I stayed in my room.' Even from a distance, Elizabeth saw the way the others had turned. Looked over in her direction.

'Yeah sure, I've used the tired excuse before too.' He took her hand, and even though she tried to pull it free, he held it tightly in place, led her across the grass, and down to the lake. 'Slept in Thomas's old room, did you?'

'What's it got to do with you where I slept?' She snapped back, and painfully she wrenched her hand out of his. 'Let go of me.'

'Darling, ignore him. He's only jealous because he isn't getting any. Either that or he's still pissed off that last night, the police were interviewing him for the best part of the evening. By the time he got out, there was only Timothy and I still up. And if I'm honest, we only lasted another half hour, then called it a night.' Pushing her arm through Elizabeth's, Lucy steered her away from the lake and towards the edge of the woods. 'He's never changed, darling. Still besotted with you. Last night he kept asking where you were and what you were doing.' She paused, pursed her lips. 'Should have seen his face when someone mentioned William being up there, in your room.'

Puzzled, Elizabeth threw a look over her shoulder. 'What the hell's it got to do with him, who I have in my room?' She watched the way Patrick distanced himself from the others. Sat apart from them, staring at the water.

'He's always been a bit odd.' Lucy chipped in. 'Don't you remember the way he used to act at uni? Always lurking around, dropping into places where he shouldn't have been.' She pulled a face. 'And, if I'm honest, I was pleased when he, Thomas, and Jordan went off to their placements, was kind of nice that we didn't have to see them every day. Talking of Jordan, have you seen him?' She pointed to the trees. 'He headed this way the other day and I don't think anyone's seen him since.'

'Did anyone try his room, get the staff to let you in, make sure he's okay? Or maybe he left?'

'Yeah, his room was checked. It's all as it was, all his things still in there.'

Panicking, Elizabeth felt her mind spin in in somersaults. 'Do you think we need to call the police, or maybe, maybe we should search for him?' She pointed to the woods. 'Quite easy to get lost in there these days.' She spoke from experience.

'Don't be silly, darling. He could be dangerous.'

'No, I don't think so...' She could still see the look in his eyes, the same look he'd had the night Tilly had died. A look that should have told her he'd known the truth all along, and deep down she knew he'd seen what had happened to Ada. But just like before, he'd chosen to keep quiet. To keep the truth to himself and now, he was missing too.

Looking at the treeline, she thought about the night she'd been lost in the woods. She'd been sure that someone had followed her and cautiously, she stared at the trees, felt her stomach flip with nerves. One too many things had happened. All were unexplained. None of them solved and for a moment, she felt as though the trees were surrounding her, wrapping their branches around her throat, squeezing until she couldn't breathe.

'Lucy, he was scared. I saw it in his eyes.' She eventually said. 'He was terrified of something, or someone and...' she pointed to the trees, 'I just don't know who.'

38

ELIZABETH

Present Day - Sunday Lunchtime

'Urgh, what's this?' Patrick poked suspiciously at the undergrowth with a stick, his feet prancing back and forth as he leaned forward to take a better look. 'Ah. Don't worry. False alarm, it's just a smelly old t-shirt.' He pulled the faded, muddy garment out of the hole. Tossed it to one side. 'God, that stinks.' Screwing up his face, he took a step back. 'Jordan...' he shouted, kicked out at a tree stump. 'God knows why we're still looking; it's more than obvious he's long gone. Isn't it?' Once again, he struck out at the thicket. 'And not a minute too fucking soon if you ask me.'

Elizabeth gave Patrick a look of annoyance. She didn't like the way he continually cursed and still wished she'd searched with one of the others. 'Best we stick to one girl and one boy. Safer that way.' Patrick had shouted earlier, while quickly taking the extra step, to stand by her side. 'Maybe you and I stick together, Lizzie. Henry will be with Patty, obviously. Which leaves Lucy and

Timothy to bring up the rear.' He'd pointed with authority, took the lead. 'If we fan out, and stay in earshot, we should be okay.' With everyone nodding, Elizabeth had found herself going along with the plan. A plan that had left her both thoughtful and suspicious.

As they walked side by side, she threw her mind back to the days before Thomas had died, clearly remembered the barbed comments Patrick used to make. The piercing glares and the way she'd often overheard him telling Thomas about his huge mistake, and that sending her home would have been the best solution for all. 'Mate, you know you can do better,' he'd once openly said, pointed between them both. 'You don't even look right together.' He'd nudged Thomas, made out he was joking. But the sideward glance had cut into her soul and told her all she needed to know.

Elizabeth stood on her tip toes, peered between trees that were all twisted together. The branches were warped, coiled, and made their own rules, as each one reached for what little bit of light they could find. Beneath them, thickets grew randomly. Some areas grew more thickly than others, with each bush, sapling, and weeds growth completely dependent on how much sunlight had managed to break through the dense canopy above.

'We've gone a long way past the clearing.' Elizabeth held onto a sapling, looked nervously over her shoulder, tried to judge just how far they'd walked. Wished for the familiarity she'd once known. They'd all stopped at the clearing and checked for any sign that Jordan could have been there, before fanning out in different directions to walk through a darker, denser area of the woodland. And now, she and Patrick were close to the other side where the river could be heard and the sound of birdsong slowly returned. For some reason, the topography in this area was different. The ground was much softer, almost boggy. And the idea of finding Jordan this far into the woods felt far less likely.

Looking down, she felt pleased she'd had the opportunity to change. She'd donned her favourite comfy pumps, along with a pair of jeans, previously torn in accordance with fashion, but which were now shredded beyond repair. More rips had been added, some in all the wrong places, along with the multiple scratches that now covered her legs, arms, and face.

'I can still hear the others.' Patrick pointed through the trees. 'Henry and Patty. They're somewhere over there, and...' he stopped, listened, 'yes, I can hear Lucy's voice. She's shouting Jordan's name. So, she and Timothy must be a couple hundred yards in that direction, probably closer to the river than we are.'

Closing her eyes for a beat, she thought of the river, of the stepping stone crossing, of a night she and William had used them to escape the others. Shaking the memory from her mind, she looked over her shoulder. 'I'm worried about Freya. She's the only one of us that's all alone. She must be feeling quite abandoned.' Pulling her phone out of her pocket, she held it high above her head, waved it around, hoped for a signal.

'She was hardly alone. Was she?' Patrick continued to poke at the bushes. 'She has Louisa attached to her, all day long. And for the life of me, I have no idea why she brought a baby to a bloody memorial.' He paused, sneered. 'Anyhow, from what I can gather, Anna was heading her way. Said something about organising some refreshments. Setting them up, next to the memorial.' He looked at his watch. 'They'll be waiting for us to find Jordan and take him back with us.'

'Do you think we will?'

'Will what?'

'Take him back?' Thoughtfully, Elizabeth continued to poke at the undergrowth. Tried to look for anything that appeared out of place in the hope they'd find a clue to Jordan's whereabouts. It had been a couple of hours since they'd left Freya behind. 'I can't go in

the woods, not with Louisa, she's far too young to go on a search,'
she'd said. 'I'll wait here and when the police come, I'll tell them
what you're doing. Send them in to find you.' She'd smiled, hopefully. 'And when you find him,' she'd gulped, 'phone my mobile. I'll
get you some help.'

Elizabeth had gone over and over the words: 'When you find
him... I'll get you some help.' Initially, Elizabeth had thought it a
peculiar thing to say and now, she simply felt both ridiculous and
paranoid. Jordan was missing and none of knew where he was or
what condition he'd be in once they found him and the thought
that he might be dead made Elizabeth's shoulders physically drop.
She took in a deep breath, glanced back over her shoulder. They
were so far from the lake, from the clearing and with every step,
she felt more and more uneasy and with a sigh, she began to
wonder if the trip was futile. They'd left the original path behind,
followed another track where the undergrowth had been flattened.
'Look, someone's been down here.' Patrick had said as he'd
grabbed her hand, pulled her behind him. She felt her skin crawl
with tension and kept looking behind, wondering how far they'd
go, and considered leading them all out of the woods, back to the
riverbank. Where, if it were still there, they could use the stepping
stone bridge as a way of them all getting back to the house without
going back the same way they'd come.

Stopping, Elizabeth leaned against a tree. Took a deep breath
in, tried to listen for the sound of the others: of shouting, of footsteps, of leaves crunching beneath their feet. But instead, she was
met with an eeriness she couldn't explain and for the first time that
day, she actually felt grateful for the noise Patrick made. He was
stood in one spot, constantly swishing his stick back and forth in
an attack of the bushes. It was a sword-like fashion that grew with
intensity, until finally he was decimating whole plants at a time,
with a single wrathful swipe.

'Feels spooky, doesn't it?' Patrick stopped swiping, moved towards her. 'In fact, I can't hear the others at all now, can you?' He stared at her feet, looked thoughtful, then he allowed his gaze to travel upwards, until it stopped and came to rest directly on her breasts. 'I expect they've all gone back to the house,' he sneered, 'left us both in the woods, where anything could happen.' Taking another step forward, his body was inches from hers and as she tried to take a step backwards, she felt the hard bark of a tree behind her. It was a moment of panic; a moment when she could feel his breath on her face, the way his aftershave hit the back of her throat with force.

'Patrick, what...' She coughed nervously, shuffled her body to one side. Looked over her shoulder. Felt the need to move, to shout, to find both Lucy and Henry, to surround herself by others. 'What are you doing?' Again, she tried to move. 'Whatever it is, I don't like it, and you're scaring me... so...'

'Lizzie. Lizzie. Lizzie.' His hand shot out, grabbed her wrist. 'You don't need to be scared.' He gave her a sickening, repulsive smile. Placed the flat of his hand against her cheek. 'You know how much I like you,' he said. 'I've always liked you. You know that.'

With her heart rate accelerating, Elizabeth felt her stomach lurch. Once again, she felt totally alone, with no one to help her. The difference this time was that she was deep in the woods. Miles from anywhere. With Patrick.

'Lucy...' she shouted out, 'where are you?' She searched the woodland behind where Patrick stood, hoped for once that someone would come. Then, without warning she felt the pain in her face as his hand clasped itself tightly across her mouth.

'Jesus, Lizzie. Shush. Don't do that. Christ. Has no man ever made a bloody pass at you before?' He paused, growled the words. 'You didn't seem to mind William staying in your room the whole night so obviously you must be up for a good time while you're here.'

With her eyes darting from side to side, Elizabeth tried to scream, to avoid the way his piercing, dilated eyes stared into her soul. She struggled to move his warm, clammy hand away from her mouth and without warning, she began to retch repeatedly.

'You're revolting,' he sneered as he moved his hand away, wiped it down his jeans in disgust, then returned it to grip her wrist, tightly.

'Patrick. I need to go back now.' Her voice quivered and she spoke quickly. 'I don't feel well. I need to get back to the house. To the police. I still didn't speak to them. In fact, they could be here any minute.' She hoped that mentioning the police and the fact that they could be following them might jolt him back to reality. That he'd take a step back and leave her alone. Instead, she felt her arm pushed high above her head, and his mouth land heavily against hers, with his tongue darting in and out of her mouth. She gagged as the sour taste of drugs hit the back of her throat.

'Stop.' She managed to scream. 'Get the hell off of me.' Lifting her leg, and with as much force as she could, she kicked out, connected.

Watching him bend in two, she heard a long, guttural scream leave his lips. It gave her enough time to turn and run. She aimed for daylight, for the river, a place where she knew an escape and frantically, she scoured the landscape. Looked for the path. For somewhere she'd be able to move easier, to run faster. 'Lucy...' she screamed, 'Lucy... where are you?'

'What the hell... I'm here. What happened?' Appearing from the edge of the trees, Lucy rushed towards her. 'Are you okay?' She paused, hurriedly looked over her shoulder. 'Tim, Lizzie's all upset, come quickly.' Lucy opened her arms, pulled Elizabeth in. 'Darling. You look like you've seen a bloody ghost.'

'What did I miss?' Tim rubbed a hand through his beard, gave her an inquisitive look. 'Did you find him? Did...' He looked beyond her, into the trees. 'Where's Patrick?'

Taking a step back, Lucy held Elizabeth at arm's length, kept tight hold of her shoulders. 'Did you find him; did you find Jordan?'

Between them, they threw the questions like bullets, and Lucy waved a hand frantically in the direction of where Patrick emerged, his face scarlet; he could barely breathe and the minute he saw Lucy, he slid down a tree and onto the ground. 'Darling. Go and look... they came from over there.'

Shaking her head, Elizabeth felt her chest tighten, her heart pound audibly, her eyes fill with tears. She kept her eyes on Patrick's. Saw the terrified look of apology he threw in her direction. 'I'm sorry,' he mouthed. And for a moment, she simply focused on the silence. On the way the whole woodland around her had stilled. Then, from somewhere in the distance, Henry's scream echoed through the woods, bounced from every tree. A sound so shrill, so piercing, that they all knew that Jordan had been found.

39

ELIZABETH

Present Day - Sunday Night

Sitting by the fire with her legs pushed tightly beneath her, Elizabeth glanced around the room. It was full of soft lighting, candles, and the biggest, cushion-filled settees she'd ever seen. For a cottage, it was spacious. Its décor, a perfect blend of greys and reds. And she wondered if the house had had a woman's touch and if so, who that woman had been.

Giving off an involuntary shudder, she leaned forward, stabbed at the coals with a poker, and did all she could to enrage the flames. Having grown up in a mining village, stoking a fire was something she'd done at least a few thousand times before and with a knowing glare, she carefully fed the flames with kindling, which she circled with lumps of coal and finally, a large piece of kiln-dried wood was precariously balanced on top.

Satisfied with her efforts, she sat back, crossed her arms around herself. Then, as she rested her head back against the settee, she closed her eyes, listened to the way the logs crackled and for just a few minutes, there was a silence that surrounded the room. Until the door opened and a rain-soaked William walked in with Alfie trotting in close behind him.

'Hey, boy... come here.' She patted her leg, pressed her bare toes into the thick, cushioned rug, and as he approached, she ran her fingers through Alfie's long, wet fur. He'd settled down by her side, rested his chin lovingly against her knee, and looked up with his usual, wounded spaniel eyes. It was a look that had gained him so much in the past. A way of getting exactly what he wanted. 'Urgh, you're all wet, you need a towel...' She laughed as he curled in, closed his eyes.

'That should be him settled for the night and I suspect he won't need to go back out there again.' Taking off his waxed jacket, he hung it over the newel post at the bottom of the staircase, ran a hand through his rain-soaked hair and pointed to the door. 'Police are still out there.'

Nodding, she tried to make sense of the day. Couldn't get the image of Jordan's lifeless body out of her mind and the immense relief she'd felt less than an hour later when William had arrived at the scene. Seeing him had been exactly what she'd needed and without hesitation, she'd quickly fallen into his long and comforting hug. It had been one of those hugs that had lasted forever, where neither party had wanted to let go. A fitting end to what had been a long, cruel, and distressing day that had resulted in another death, another body, and much to the annoyance of police forensics, another relentless storm.

'I'm so pleased Alfie's gonna be okay.' She tried to change the subject, but felt the words catch in her throat and with a tissue in hand, she dabbed at sore, gritty eyes. 'I was so worried about him when you left this morning.' She paused, sobbed. 'I really wanted to go with you.'

'And I'd much rather you'd have come with us than become a witness to that lot.' He glared at the window, did all he could to control his temper. 'Can't remember if I told you or not, but the vet, he said he might have learned his lesson, might not go round snapping at bees any more.' He leaned forward, switched on a lamp, 'And the antihistamine, it'll probably make him a bit sluggish for a day or two.' He allowed his foot to press gently against hers and in a unified silence, they both stared into the flames, watched the way they danced warmly in the grate.

Glancing out of the window, Elizabeth could still see the rain. It beat heavily against the window, and in the distance, it lashed down in front of the police floodlights where they'd set up a base by the lake. As dusk had fallen, the lights had grown more and more brightly, until the mist had begun to descend and a distinct eeriness had reminded them all of the work being carried out, deep inside the woodland. It was a place where men in white, hooded coveralls now combed every inch of the area where Jordan's body had been found. Most were on hands and knees, their fingertip precision leaving no stone unturned. All in the hope that answers could be found.

Sighing, Elizabeth hoped that the lights would go out soon and that the work would be finished. It was a deep and profound thought that made a numbness press down on her shoulders. It weighed heavily and she felt as though she'd been strapped into a rucksack. One full of rocks that she couldn't take off, no matter how much she wanted to.

Standing up, William left the room, and returned just a few moments later with two mugs of steaming hot chocolate. It was a smell that filled the room, one that made Elizabeth's stomach turn. 'I'm so sorry,' she whispered as she placed it down on the hearth. Pushed it as far away as possible. 'I can't drink anything, not right now.' She ran a hand across Alfie's fur. Used slow, gentle, and rhythmic movements. 'You're such a good boy, Alfie. Aren't you?' she whispered. 'I have missed you.' Turning, Alfie gazed at her with devotion, licked at her hand.

'I think he missed you too.' William sat down beside her, uneasily reached forward, placed his hand over hers. 'It's okay you know, to be upset.' He nodded, swallowed. 'You've had one hell of a day.' He draped an arm around her shoulders, pulled her into a hug. 'No one should have to go through what you've been through today, especially after last time.'

Elizabeth knew he was referring to Thomas, to the way she'd found his body and the parallels that had joined that day to this, and so soon after she'd returned to the Manor.

'They think he took his own life.' He finally said. 'The police. They're not suspecting foul play.' Slowly, he twisted his fingers with hers, made a big deal out of linking them together.

'When we started the search,' she paused, looked up and into his eyes, 'we hoped we'd find him, and alive. But somewhere deep down, I think we all knew we were looking for a body.' She squeezed his hand. 'It was Henry that found him, not me.' She thought about Henry, the way he and Patty had clung together by the side of the river. 'And at least Patrick didn't try anything more. He did apologise.' She could still see him, disappearing down the riverbank, offering to raise the alarm, to bring the police. While she and the others had walked to the water, and while keeping a distance, they'd clung together and waited in silence.

'Well, you'll be pleased to know Patrick has gone.' William said, protectively. 'And before someone else tells you, yes, I may have stood in the doorway of his room and told him he had no choice.' He gripped her hand, lifted it to his lips, dropped a kiss on her fingers. 'I won't have anyone attacking you, not like that.'

'I really don't know why it bothered me so much.' She blew out through puffed up cheeks. 'For God's sake, it isn't like no one's made a pass at me before.' She ran her other hand over Alfie's ears, felt another appreciative lick in return. 'But he seemed different; his eyes were dilated, piercing. I'm sure he was on something.' She rested her head against William's shoulder. 'He scared me.'

Cupping her chin, William lifted her face, looked deep into her eyes, pressed his lips tightly together. Sighed. 'You have no idea how beautiful you are. Do you? I'm not surprised men want to kiss you.' He kissed her gently on the forehead. 'Does this hurt?' He touched the side of her face, where a pale, grey bruise had appeared. 'Saying that, I could kill him for what he did.' He ran a hand down her side, to rest on her hips. 'I don't ever want anyone to hurt you again,' his eyes implored hers, 'and ... right now, I really want to stop talking and kiss you myself.' She felt his lips touch hers. His mouth moved slowly, sensually and in a quick, fluid movement, he straddled her knee and just as she had that morning, she responded urgently to his kiss. Unbuttoning his shirt, she felt the desire increase, her tongue teased his and with the anticipation building, she lifted her jumper, pulled it up and over her head, dropped it to the floor.

Pointing to the stairs, she smiled seductively, 'Shall we?' Catching the deep, sensitive look in his eyes, she thought carefully about what was about to happen. About the guilt that had previously torn them apart. 'William, I do want this,' she buried her face in his neck. Then, without effort, he picked her up and carried her towards the stairs.

Pushing open the bedroom door, he lowered her to the floor. The shirt that was still hanging from his shoulders was immediately pulled off, thrown to one side. Then slowly, he began to kiss her. Every touch was one of meaning. Every kiss, pure passion. 'I've always wanted you.' He smiled provocatively as he spoke, his lip curling sensuously. 'I always hoped you'd come back.' With eyes that sparkled, he seemed to search her soul. 'Lizzie. I want this. Us.

So much. But... Suddenly he stopped talking as though he'd been hit by a thunderbolt. Took a step backwards.

'What is it?'

'There's something I have to tell you.' He finally said, then paused, turned, leaned with his back against the post of the bed. 'Lizzie. I'm not a Kirkwood.' As soon as the words left his mouth, panic filled his eyes. 'Thomas and I, we had different fathers.' He gazed around the room. 'Mine wasn't Dominic. He was someone Ada had fallen for. One of the staff.'

Moving towards him, Elizabeth closed her eyes for a blink. She wondered why he was telling her now but smiled. 'William. When I first saw you, I was shocked. All I could see was Thomas and how much you were like him. But now, now I really look, I can see that you're not like him at all.' It was true; he and Thomas might share the same square jawline, but the eyes, the smile, the personality, they were all very different. 'Is that why he was so horrid to you?'

Nodding, William stood up, walked across the room, clicked on a soft, glowing lamp. He looked down, sorrowful. 'The Kirkwood line, it should be passed to a Kirkwood. The next in line. Mother, she knew we were treading a fine line and that if anyone found out, the will would be contested.' Once again, he held out his arms as though he were surrendering to his fate. 'And that night. The night she died... she demanded I do something for her...'

Elizabeth reached for him. Held a finger to his lips. Moved in close and pulled him towards her. She didn't care about his parentage, whether or not he'd keep the Manor or what Ada had asked. If anything, she felt a deep sense of relief that William had only been partly related to Thomas. Half of her wished he hadn't been related at all. And now, everything made sense. The way Thomas had been, the constant one-upmanship, the bullying. 'William. Seriously. None of it matters. Not to me.'

'But there can't be any secrets. Not between us. Not if...' He sighed and then purposely, he took a step away from her walked to the window and nervously, his hands went up to his head as though struggling with his thoughts.

'William. I was never trying to catch myself a Kirkwood and it never really mattered to me that the others used to think I was. It doesn't matter to me who you are. Who your dad is, or was.' She paused, walked up behind him, considered her words. 'And right now... all I really want is for you to make love to me.'

Within seconds, William had turned. Her lips were crushed against his. His strong, muscular contours pressed her passionately against the wall. Then gently, he eased back, dropped a kiss against the bruise on her face.

'Jesus Lizzie.' He locked eyes, with hers. 'You have no idea how much I wanted you to say that.'

The words were soft, gentle, yet heart-breaking. Deep inside, her heart pounded. Nervously, her hands moved to the button of his jeans and in a single silent answer to his question she pulled at the button, then at the zipper and lifted her face back to his.

'I want you so much,' William whispered, between kisses. He skimmed her hips and thighs with one hand, as the other moved up her spine, she felt the currents of desire spiralling through her body.

Instinctively, Elizabeth arched towards him, her jeans now beside his on the carpet and as he manoeuvred her onto the bed, she heard the last piece of her underwear drop to the floor. Gasping, she felt William press against her, took short sharp breaths, saw his deep cavernous eyes once again lock with hers and gently she nodded. Every part of her ached, tingled with desire and with her arms held high above her head, she surrendered to his touch, and felt her breathing increase as every part of her melted into a pleasure that was both pure and explosive.

40

WILLIAM

Ten Years Before

'For God's sake, Mother. I don't want to go to the bloody party.' He snatched the suit from her hands, attempted to throw it at the bed, and felt his stomach plummet as dramatically, the freshly laundered suit bounced against the bed post and dropped onto the floor. 'You're creating nothing more than a damn circus out there. Everyone in dinner suits, champagne flowing, and God only knows how many drugs they're taking.' He closed his eyes, listened to the sound of a mini orchestra that seeped through the Manor. Up to now, he'd heard a mixture of tunes, all different styles. Most that grated on his senses and made his ears burn with pain. He couldn't imagine anything worse than going downstairs, dressed in a monkey suit and being any closer to it. 'And what's the music all about?' He held a finger up to the ceiling. Furrowed his brow. Listened. 'Classical, really?'

'Darling. Don't be obnoxious. Your aunts and uncles are here too. The music has been chosen to cater for everyone.' Picking up a bottle of aftershave from the dressing table, she sprayed it in the lid, and sniffed. With an obvious distaste, she screwed up her face, dropped the bottle, pushed it as far away as she could. 'William. Do it for me. You know that it'd make me very happy if you went down there. Showed your face. Maybe even make the effort to shake your brother's hand.' She gave him a hopeful smile, lifted a hand to smooth down her carefully coiffed hair. Then strutted across the room in her black evening dress, its perfectly positioned white piping giving her an air of elegance she'd always commanded. Typically, she moved in a fluid and theatrical way, like an actress taking centre stage for a final performance. 'Your brother. He did all that was asked of him. He finished med school, became a doctor,' she said in a voice that might have suggested that William didn't already know. 'He wanted to have a party and cele-brate with his friends. It wasn't too much to ask, was it?' She held a hand to her heart. Patted it in rhythm. 'Seriously William, you're being so difficult and you're giving me palpitations.'

Staring at the floor, William knew not to argue. It was a battle he was never going to win. Not with his mother playing with his emotions. It was an act she'd perfected over the years, like a highly skilled musician playing a finely tuned violin as part of an orchestra.

'You have to understand. I do as much as I can. For the both of you.' His mother continued, looked down as she spoke. 'But Thomas is the eldest.' It was a comment he should have expected. Thomas coming first, last, and foremost was something he'd had to come to terms with. Especially after their older brother had died, just a few short days after being born. 'Your brother, he has status. I thought you understood.' Her voice had now softened, her bottom lip quivered, and with her head bowed, she dabbed at her eyes, took a step towards him. It was a sight he couldn't bear to see and with a lump in his throat, he held out his arms and pulled her lovingly towards him.

'Okay, okay. You win. I'll get dressed.' He relented. 'I'll go down and kiss all the aunts and you know, pretend I'm happy.' He dreaded nothing more than being paraded in front of the relations. The people he barely ever saw. And with them all drooling over how well Thomas had done, he had every intention of making a fast appearance, before retreating back to his room. And as for shaking Thomas's hand; well, in his opinion, that was never going to happen.

'There's a good boy.' She patted his cheek and for a moment, William felt as though he were still a six-year-old boy, vying for attention from both a mother and a father who only had time for Thomas. And now, he resented the action. He didn't want to feel second best, not any more. 'Good. That's good.' She nodded, kissed his cheek. 'I'm pleased you've come round to my way of thinking cause our Thomas has quite a difficult night ahead of him. Poor boy's going to need all the support we can give him.'

'Why does Thomas have a difficult night ahead?' He asked abruptly, as he looked out of the window, saw Thomas stood on a chair, a bottle of champagne held up to his mouth. 'Looks like he's having a ball to me.'

'Dutch courage. That's all it is.' Ada said as she walked to the window. 'He's building himself up to do what's been asked of him and tonight, he'll put an end to that horrid relationship.' She took a step back, a smug smile crossing her face. 'After all, he can't possibly carry it on; he needs a wife who'll be his equal. Doesn't he?'

Feeling himself flare up internally, William moved to one side. 'What the hell have you done?' His eyes shot from his mother to the window, to a place where Thomas still stood in the middle of his friends and family who all danced on a patio, sipped at the champagne, and were surrounded by strings of coloured lights that blinked in rotation. It was a scene that reminded him of Christmas. A time he despised the most. 'My God, mother. You've insisted that he end it. Haven't you?' He kicked out at the suit, that still lay on the floor. 'What did Lizzie ever do to you?' He spat the questions out like bullets, glared out of the window, didn't trust himself to look at her. 'Is this what you did with my father? Once he wasn't useful any more, did you dismiss him too? Like one of the bloody staff?'

'William. I'm ashamed to say it, but as you well know, he *was* one of the staff.' She looked over his shoulder, through the window and narrowed her eyes at where Lizzie stood. 'And the Manor, well... it'll be here long after both you and I have gone. This house, it's a part of history. And the last thing it needs is a scandal.'

Heaving a sigh, William rested both hands on the windowsill and stared at Thomas, who constantly mingled with his friends in the crowd, and then at Lizzie, who stood to one side of the patio, looking up. She gave him what looked to be a half wave. A wave that was quickly dropped the moment she saw his mother walk up beside him. 'Of course, Mother. You're right,' he finally said. 'It'd be just tragic if Thomas fell in love with a girl from a mining village, wouldn't it?'

Giving him a radiant smile, Ada patted him on the shoulder. 'See, darling, I knew you'd understand.' She bent down, picked up the suit, passed it back to him. 'Now then, be a good boy, put this on.'

'Mother, I was being impertinent,' he said in retort. Took the suit from her and once again, he threw it at the bed where it landed successfully. 'So, it's okay to do what you want. So long as no one else finds out. Is it? So long as it doesn't cause a scandal. Is that right?' He was giving a nod to his mother's affair. An affair she'd promised had been a brief encounter. But something didn't sit quite right; there were things that weren't being said and answers he'd needed for far too long. 'There is one thing I've always wondered. My older brother, the one who died, was he a Kirkwood too or...?'

'William. Don't judge. We've all done things we're not proud of and well, I've learned from my mistakes. Have you?'

Sighing, he shook his head, knew that by avoiding the answer she'd told him all he needed to know. He also knew that continuing the argument was fruitless. He wanted to open the window, to scream and shout. To warn Lizzie what was about to happen. But knew how little it would help. Just like the times he'd been locked in the cellar. And while thinking back to those days, he could still see Lizzie's beautiful face leaning in through the coal chute, her eyes sparkling in the moonlight and even though she'd been terrified of Thomas, she'd done all she could to help him. Which brought him back to the present, to what was happening now, and he tried to decide what Lizzie would do. What she'd say. Would she say what she truly believed, or would she become compliant and take the route of least resistance? Narrowing his eyes, he searched for her in the crowd. Eventually finding where she'd moved to. She now stood to one side of the patio, half hidden by topiary. Her eyes had been lowered, and the heartbreak that crossed her face was clear to see as Thomas took Lucy's hand, and central to the group he began to dance provocatively with her in time to the music.

Stamping angrily across the room, William reached for the door, pulled on the doorknob. 'Mother, you can't keep dismissing people once you're done with them. Not everyone can have a status and Lizzie, my God, how can you be so cruel? She's amazing. She's kind, considerate. She has more good bones in one finger than most have in their entire body and personally, I don't understand why anyone wouldn't want her as a part of the family.'

'William, close the door while we're speaking.' Ada spoke firmly, fixed her eyes on the doorknob, on the corridor beyond. 'We have staff. Guests. You never know who might be listening, do you?'

Out of belligerence, William pulled the door further open, fixed his jaw, and pressed his lips tightly together. 'Where is he?' He asked. 'My father, what the hell happened to him?'

Stepping past, Ada pushed at the door, tried to close it. 'He did what was right.'

'Did you tell him to leave?' He snapped. 'I mean. You'd had two sons to him and what's to say there wouldn't have been another? Although Thomas landing right in the middle, well that was convenient for you, wasn't it? Quite a relief that you actually gave birth to a Kirkwood.'

'William, I'm not talking to you about this. Not with the door wide open.'

Relenting, William slammed the door, leaned against it, pushed his hands angrily through his hair. 'Mother, I have a right to know what happened. And whether you like it or not, I need answers that...' He pleaded through tear-filled eyes, walked to the bed, clung to the post, then sat on its edge. 'Well, they're answers that only you can give me.' He leaned forward, placed his hands in front of his face, squeezed his eyes tightly closed, and with a sob, he felt the emotion take over.

Feeling his mother walk to his side. William felt the sag of the bed as she sat down beside him, the pressure of her hand as she patted his leg. 'William... your father's never really been so far away,' she replied, unexpectedly. 'What do you really take me for?'

41

WILLIAM

Present Day - Monday Morning

Running along the opposite side of the riverbank, and along a path that was barely ever used, William felt the ground squelch beneath his feet and once or twice, he felt one of his feet slide from beneath him. Jumping over rocks, he avoided the places where the embankment had disappeared, worn away with age, and where tree trunks had fallen to lie on their side, and one that had almost formed a bridge over the water.

Looking across at the woods, he could still see the police activity, resented the intrusive way they were still digging their way through his woodland, causing damage that would take years to repair and with an angry shake of his head, he wondered what they were still doing, especially in an area so close to the river.

Feeling as though he'd been running for miles, he slowed his pace, caught his breath, and with a quick look over his shoulder to make sure he was out of sight of the police, he made his way along the bank until the place where six large boulders protruded out of the water. They were boulders he'd painstakingly rolled along the bank and on a day when the water had been so low, when he could easily paddle through it, he'd carefully created his very own stepping stone bridge. One that as a teenager had given him a short-cut between the woods and the house. But today, and following the rainfall they'd had the previous night, the water was high, and instead of the boulders protruding, they were now just beneath the surface, slightly hidden from view. With indecision, he tried to work out how easily he could use them without crashing into the water and being taken by the current.

42

WILLIAM

Ten years before

Sneaking through the trees in the early evening darkness, William homed in on the bonfire which, along with the smell of freshly baked potatoes, made his stomach rumble even before he got to the clearing.

It was the first time he'd been invited to join in with the others and he couldn't help but feel just a little excited. Walking towards the clearing, he puffed out his chest and with a final look at his watch, he made sure he'd arrive at the exact right time. A time that Thomas had said, and for once he didn't want to do anything that would rile his brother up or give him cause to change his mind.

Leaning against a tree, William spied the spot where Thomas was sat. He was leaning against the fallen tree, his face glowing in the light of the bonfire. From the outside, he looked to be in a good mood and sipped at a can of beer he held in his hand. While with the other hand, he stabbed at a small tin foil package that he'd rested on the floor. His boots had been removed, leaving his bare toes to wriggle around in front of the fire in an obvious attempt to warm his feet. It was an image copied by most of Thomas's friends, who either leaned against the fallen tree beside him, or lay on their bellies and without exception, each of them ate potatoes from a piece of screwed up tin foil.

It was like a scene in a movie, where everyone got along. Jokes and banter were passed around the group and more often than not, their laughter rippled through the trees. He'd always wanted to be included, to be a part of the clan. A group that Thomas had always pushed him away from and kept him firmly on the outside of, looking in. Until today when unexpectedly, he'd been invited to join them.

Scanning the group, he looked for Lizzie and moved his position until he'd circled the clearing and spotted where she sat at the other side of the fire, alone.

'Who wants the next one?' She shouted as she pulled a stick away from the flames, waved a sticky, hot marshmallow around in the air. Waited for one of the group to jump up and take it from her. 'Oh, watch your fingers.' She laughed as Henry tossed the marshmallow from hand to hand.

'Ouch, that's hot,' he yelped. 'You could have warned me.'

'Henry,' Lizzie laughed, 'you're a grown man that just saw me pull the marshmallow out of the flames. So seriously, which part of you didn't realise it'd be hot?' Standing up, she made her way across the clearing to where Thomas sat. She ran a hand lovingly through his hair, leaned forward, and dropped a gentle kiss on his lips. 'Is there one of those for me?' she asked as she reached forward, took a potato from the pile. 'In fact. I'll take a couple. One for William, you did say he'd be coming, didn't you?' She smiled, kissed him again. 'It's really good of you to include him. It'll be nice to have him around more often.' Prising open the tin foil that surrounded her potato, Lizzie searched the tree line. 'What time did you say he'd be here?'

'Nine o'clock.'

Thomas's words caused an uncomfortable ripple of laughter to circulate the camp. It was a laughter that made William nervous and immediately, he felt his body retract and as quickly as he'd arrived, he turned, made for an escape, and came face to face with a startled-looking Patrick who'd twisted his body to one side while he urinated into a bush.

'Going somewhere?' Patrick asked, as he hurriedly arranged his underwear, pulled up the zip of his jeans, and with a slow, menacing gaze, looked William up and down.

'I was going to go and get more drinks,' William lied, 'I'd only brought these and well... once I saw how many of you were here, I thought I'd best go get some more.'

'No need now, is there?' With a hand on his shoulder, Patrick led William through the treeline until they both stood so close to the bonfire, he could feel the heat scorching his face. 'Look who I found, skulking around in the trees.'

'I was early.' William dropped the carrier bag by Thomas's feet, tried to judge how welcoming his brother would be. Saw the immediate look of mischief that was followed by a sneer.

'Lizzie here saved you a potato.' Thomas tapped Lizzie on the back, tipped his head to one side. 'Good of her, wasn't it?'

Catching Lizzie's smile. William felt himself relax, took the potato from her outstretched hand, sat beside where she'd perched on a tree stump, close to one side of the fire. Looking into the flames, he wanted to feel a sense of pride that he'd been accepted into the group, that no one seemed to mind him being there and for once, his brother wasn't being unkind, jeering, or making him the butt of his jokes. But the earlier ripple of laughter still played on his mind, a nervous tingle travelled up and down his spine, and while slowly pulling the tin foil back on the potato, he kept an eye on where Thomas sat, and the whispered words that were slowly being passed around the group.

'Here.' Thomas tossed him a beer, 'Get that down you and finish your food.' He gave him a half smile, one that showed the malice viciously printed all over his face. 'After that, we've got a little game to play.' Thomas dropped onto his knees beside the fire, held his arms out and addressed the group. 'You all remember hunted, don't you?' He nodded, smiled, took in the laughter and encouragement of some, the gasp of horror from others.

Choking on his potato, William immediately felt the terror. Knew that Thomas was back to being his old self and that tonight, like always, he'd be at the centre of Thomas's amusement.

'What...?' Lizzie looked from Thomas to William. Then she twisted around, looked at the others. 'What's going on, what's hunted?' she questioned, saw the glint that lit up Thomas's eyes.

'What if we don't want to play?' William felt his eyes dart back and forth and his heart pound rapidly in his chest as he tried to work out which was the best escape route, the fastest one he knew. His knowledge of the surrounding paths was good; he'd run along them all of his life. The problem he had was Thomas knew the paths too. Knew exactly which one's he'd take, which meant he had to play smart and outwit his brother.

'What do you mean "we"?' Thomas asked, 'I can only see you objecting.'

Looking from one brother to the other, Lizzie gave them both a puzzled look. 'Seriously. Are you going to tell me what hunted is?' She tapped Lucy on the arm. 'Do you know what they're talking about?'

'Sure I do darling. It's a game where one person sets off running and we all chase them.' She pushed the last of her baked potato in her mouth, held a hand up until she finished chewing. 'It can be tremendous fun for most. We've played it before. However, saying that, the last person we chased ended up in the river and almost drowned. But that's rare. And probably a good lesson in staying away from the riverbank. Anyhow, Thomas has decided that tonight, it's William's turn to be hunted.'

Jumping to her feet, Lizzie took a step towards Thomas. Held a hand out to grip his arm, stared into his eyes. 'Thomas, I don't think we should play,' she shook her head, 'it doesn't sound like much fun for your brother. In fact, it sounds barbaric. Cruel. And...'

Pushing her roughly to one side, Thomas strode across the clearing, positioned himself in a way that William had no choice but to take a step backwards, with his back dangerously close to the bonfire. 'You'll play the game, won't you William?'

Feeling the heat, William knew that with one more step, with one push, he could easily overbalance, and end up in the fire. There was no escape and without a choice, he caught the terrified look on Lizzie's face and with slow, inward, breaths, he nodded his head. Gave her what he hoped would be a brave and determined smile. 'Lizzie, don't worry. I'll be fine.' He tossed what was left of the potato into the fire. Then, as quickly as he could, he stepped to one side, grabbed Thomas by the scruff of his neck and in a simple manoeuvre he'd mentally practised over a dozen times before, he turned the tables. Now, Thomas was stood with his back to the fire. The heat scorching the back of his hairline as William stared deep into his eyes, pressed his lips tightly together, and saw the immediate fear that flashed through his brother's face. The bravado had gone, and now he scrambled to take hold, to grip onto any part of William he could.

'Don't be silly, William. You don't want to do this.' He flicked his head from side to side, saw how the others had stood up, moved in close. 'Don't just stand there, help me.' He screamed, as his whole body began to shake relentlessly.

William knew how easily he could be overpowered, but when no one moved, he breathed out a sigh of relief. Then looked up to see Lizzie who'd knelt by the fire, her hands clasped tightly together as though in prayer and her eyes full of tears that threatened to fall. It was a sight that brought him back to earth. She was the last person he wanted to hurt and with a sudden movement, he threw Thomas to one side, heard him crash heavily into the floor.

Jumping up, Lizzie ran to William's side. Threw her arms around his neck. Squeezed him tight. 'Thank you,' she whispered the words in his ear, kissed him gently on the cheek. 'Now please, be gone before he gets up and realises you're still here.'

Taking a breath, William knew Lizzie was right. He had no choice but to run, to become the hunted. Knew that if the others played, they'd only be doing it because Thomas said so, that not all of them really wanted to play the game and with that in mind, he had to slow his brother down. Make it difficult for him to follow. With a swift movement, he jumped forward, grabbed Thomas's boots, and threw them as hard as he could towards the fire and with a satisfied look, he saw the sparks fly upwards as the boots began to smoke and melt in the embers.

It was enough to make William turn on his heel and with the speed of a gazelle, he headed for the protection and darkness of the trees. He knew how closely Thomas would follow and with his eyes darting from side to side, he quickly chose his path. Squinted continually and while changing direction, he leapt over bushes, from one bush to the other. Making sure no one could follow a trail. Eventually, he took the path that led away from the lake. The one that went through the densest part of the woodland, where eventually he knew he'd reach the river.

Breathing through lungs that burned, William could hear

Thomas and the others getting closer. 'Catch the little bastard and when you do, throw him in the fire.' Thomas yelled on the top of his voice, then with his hand bouncing on and off his lips, he made a noise that resembled an old cowboy and Indian film. A noise that made William's blood boil and with a resounding growl, he left the path, took the long way around, hoped that by doing so, he'd lose the group. Bounding a corner, he jumped over a fallen tree and headed towards the river, to a spot where he knew he could cross and get to safety.

'Quick, over here.' The sound of Lizzie's voice echoed through the trees and for a moment, he felt disorientated. Didn't know where the sound had come from. But then, like a vision she appeared from behind the tree, closest to the river. 'I knew where you'd be heading, I've followed you here before.' She smiled, held a hand out to him. 'Come on, we'll go back to the house. See if Cookie made an apple pie, I'm sure she did.' Encouragingly, she took his hand, wove her fingers between his, pulled him towards the river.

'Lizzie, crossing the river. It's dangerous.' He kept one eye on the woodland behind him, could hear the others getting closer, and with panic filling his mind he tried to decide what to do. To stay on this side of the bank was dangerous; they'd easily be caught. Now, he had Lizzie to think of too and with Thomas being so cruel, there was no way of knowing how he'd react if he found out she'd helped him. 'It's dark. Slippy. I'm not sure you should do it.' He looked around, dropped her hand and with his mouth growing dryer by the minute, he began grabbing at the lower branches of trees, swinging on them until they broke away from the trunk. 'People have drowned in there.'

'I'm not leaving you.' She took an unwavering step forward, held her hand out to his. 'And Thomas, well Thomas can stay in the woods. If he wants to act like an animal and all that... then let him.' She looked over her shoulder, then turned in the moonlight to give him a radiant smile. 'Come on, we have to go.'

Passing her one of the branches, William took the other. 'Use the branch as a walking stick. Poke it into the water below, until it goes into the silt. It'll give you an anchor, help with your balance, and let me go first, I'll test the stones, make sure they don't wobble and then I want you to step exactly where I do.' He gazed into her eyes for a moment too long and felt the desire tear through him.

She's your brother's girlfriend.

It was a thought that played on his mind. And no matter how cruel and nasty Thomas could be, it was still a line he knew he shouldn't cross. Couldn't cross. And quickly, he shook his head, turned back to the water. 'Lizzie,' he finally said, 'I've got you. If you fall, I'll be right behind you. Okay?'

Realising how much he meant those words, he took her hand and held it close.

43

WILLIAM

Present Day - Monday Morning

With his mind flicking back and forth to the past. William felt each of the memories hit him like a thunderbolt. Since Lizzie had arrived, the memories had come thick and fast. Even the ones he'd spent years trying to bury.

The crossing in the river had been one of those memories. It was a place he hadn't really been to since before Thomas died. Yet the night before, when Patrick had turned up at the hotel with news of Jordan's death, followed by a description of where in the woods the others were, the stepping stones had been the first place he'd headed for. His only thought had been getting to Lizzie, making sure she was okay and protecting her from whatever evil still remained in his woods.

During his rush to get to Lizzie the night before. Something had caught his attention, something unusual he hadn't liked, but with no time to stop he'd made a mental note to return to the scene, to investigate further and determinedly, he moved slowly from one path to the other. Made sure he was heading in the same direction, using the same paths, and stood with his hands on his hips, turned in circles, looked for the gnarly hornbeam, a tree that looked like no other with its oval leaf that had a furrowed, finely toothed edge. It used to be the biggest tree in the area, one that had stood alone for years. But now, it was surrounded by both English oak and yew, a tree that ironically symbolised doom or death. A tree he now wished he'd never allowed to grow. Moving slowly, he found the tree's masterful position, where he admired its gnarly branches that reached out in all directions. Beneath it, a small patch of freshly dug over soil, the cap of a whisky bottle clearly sticking out from beneath the surface.

Staring indignantly, he knew immediately that it was the bottle his mother had taken a drink from the night she'd died and that there were only a few people still alive who'd know this part of the woods. Who'd find their way both in and out of the woodland without getting lost. And Lizzie was one of them.

44

ELIZABETH

Present Day Monday - Morning

'Come on Alfie, let's go see Cookie.' Opening the cottage door, Elizabeth slapped a hand repeatedly against her leg, headed towards the Manor, and kept a cautious eye on Alfie who unenthusiastically hopped over the threshold to follow her. 'Where's William got to, hey?' She scanned the lake, the grounds, and then the woods, hoping to catch sight of him, running, walking, or sitting by the water. Disappointed that he wasn't there, she glanced back at the house and sighed. She'd hoped that they'd get up to have a long leisurely breakfast and still felt saddened by the way he'd jumped out of bed and gone for a run, right after making coffee. In his absence, she'd spent a lazy hour over breakfast, kept one eye on the door and when he didn't return, she set off for the Manor.

Reaching down, she touched the dog's side, felt the heave of his chest, noticed the way he continually panted as he walked and with some effort, he did a peculiar hop and a jump, rather than the bounce she'd witnessed just a couple of days before.

'That antihistamine sure packed a punch, boy, didn't it?' Putting Alfie's sluggishness down to the previous day's antics, his visit to the vet, and the fact that he'd slept so heavily, she slowly walked on but kept looking down. Sighing, she noticed how much the weather had dramatically changed. It had now turned clement and she felt concerned to see how much Alfie was panting and how often he stopped.

Without warning, Alfie gave her a look, and sat down in a way she'd have expected him to do on a hot summer's day, rather than a day like today, that was both dull and overcast. The small, angry-looking, grey clouds that had been floating around at sunrise had now merged together to form larger, more threatening ones, there was a new promise of rain, and feeling worried, she looked at where the river hugged the woods. She could hear how it rumbled in the distance and hoped that William would come back soon before the inevitable downpour began.

Holding Alfie's lead loosely in her hand, she rattled it as she walked in the hope that it would encourage him to follow and then waited as he pulled himself to his feet, and with a look of concern, she paid close attention to the way he took each step, noted the effort he made.

Looking back, she judged that they were almost halfway between the cottage and the Manor. A point in the middle meadow, where trees grew randomly. The exact place where ten years before, she used to lay for hours. All in the hope that Thomas would pay her some attention.

'What a fool you were,' she whispered to herself. 'Stupid bloody fool.'

Stopping in his tracks, Alfie gave her a sorrowful look and with a half-smile, she knelt down beside him, immediately felt the moisture of the wet grass as it seeped into her jeans. Giving Alfie a few tender strokes, she laughed at the way he snuggled in lovingly beside her and licked at her face.

'You're such a gorgeous, old boy, aren't you?' She dropped a kiss on the top of his head and with reluctance, she settled herself to lean against one of the trees. 'Oh well. Who needs dry jeans?' She laughed, 'And you wait till we get to the kitchen, I bet Cookie will have some leftover chicken.' Again, he turned, gave her all his attention, pressed his nose against her cheek. 'Oh, wow, you know the word chicken, don't you?'

With a jump, he bounced to his feet. Took a few steps forward. Then, he sat back down with a flop. It was a sight that left Elizabeth feeling deflated. Only yesterday, she'd felt relieved that he'd shown signs of recovery and now, rather than heading for the Manor, she wished they'd stayed at the cottage, curled up by the fire and thoughtfully, she tried to work out what she should do. How heavy he'd be. And whether she could carry him back to the cottage.

Moving onto her knees, Elizabeth leaned forward to run a hand across his fur, wished for all the years she'd missed and then smiled as Alfie inched towards her, until once again, his head was resting against her leg. Taking a deep breath in, he closed his eyes and sadly, he pretended to sleep. 'Don't worry, boy. You sleep for now; we can go as slow as you like.' She looked back and forth from the cottage to the Manor. Then, with half open eyes, she heard the sound of Bobby's wheelbarrow, the squeak that happened with each turn of the wheel. Looking up, she smiled through unshed tears. No matter how often she saw Bobby, or what the weather, he always wore the same peak cap, a quilted black bodywarmer, and a pair of jet-black wellingtons that were always covered in mud.

'You okay there, young Lizzie?' He kicked gently at the grass, knocked the mud from his boots and after feeling how wet the grass was with a hand, he pulled a face, sat down beside her, then affectionately, he held a handout to where Alfie lay. 'What's up with you then boy, hey? You're doing a bit of panting today, aren't you?' He paused. 'You keeping our Lizzie company down here?' He gave her a look of concern and in question, he furrowed his brow.

Sighing, Elizabeth had now resigned herself to the fact that everyone at the Manor called her Lizzie and that no matter how much she wished for it, no one was ever going to call her Elizabeth. Once or twice, she'd tried to remind them. But Bobby had called her Lizzie for as long as he'd known her and now, it would almost seem wrong to correct him.

'We're just taking a rest, aren't we boy?' She gave Bobby a fond smile, looked deep into his dependable eyes. Thought of all the times he'd looked out for them all; he'd been the one person who'd always had their backs and no matter how much it hurt, he'd always told them the truth. Between him and Cookie, they'd looked after them all, like the surrogate parents each one of them needed.

'When I was younger, I could set my watch by you,' Elizabeth finally said as she looked at the screen on her mobile phone. 'Seven o'clock you were always feeding the animals, the ducks, chickens, and rabbits. Then, by nine o'clock, like it is now, you'd always be stood by the back door, leaning on the architrave, with a mug of tea in one hand, and whatever Cookie chose to feed you in the other.' She pulled a face, held her arms out to her sides, made the illusion of being a big round ball. 'It's a wonder we're not all the size of a house.' Reaching forward, she touched his hand. 'So, what happened today? It's nine o'clock and you're not by the back door. Or is there something I don't know... and Cookie refused to feed you?'

Pulling off his cap, Bobby ruffled his grey, peppered hair that had now dramatically thinned beneath his cap. 'No, I'm just a bit out of sorts. A lot's happened over the past few days, hasn't it?' He sighed. 'And instead of chatting with the others, I thought I'd go down to the lake. I noticed that the sedges needed thinning out and well... I saw you sat here, and I thought I'd come over. I hope you don't mind.'

'Of course we don't mind, do we, Alfie?' She said. 'We were just sat here, having a bit of a rest, weren't we, boy?' Running a hand down Alfie's back, Elizabeth bit down on her lip. Did all she could to stop herself from bursting into tears. 'Bobby, I don't think he's too well.' She caught Bobby's eyes, saw the disquiet within them. 'He had a big day yesterday.'

'Yeah, Cookie told me what happened.' Again, his hand went to lovingly stroke the spaniel. 'Not a good idea to go round chewing on bees or wasps, boy, is it?' He pushed a hand in his pocket, pulled out a dog biscuit. 'I was going to pop over later and see him, so like I always do, I shoved him a biscuit in my pocket.' They both watched as surprisingly, Alfie leaned forward, eagerly took the biscuit from him.

'Well, there's nothing wrong with his appetite, so that's a good thing.' Elizabeth smiled with relief. 'Do you think he'll be okay?'

'He is getting old. But... well, we'll see.' Standing up, Bobby searched the grounds. 'Did I see William heading out earlier?' He turned his gaze on the cottage and stared at the front door as though he were fully expecting William to open the door and walk towards them.

'Oh, he isn't at home; he got up early and went for a run. Said he was going to go by the river.' She pointed across the meadow, to where just one or two of the forensic team remained. 'I think he was going to stick to the other side of the river. You know, keep out of their way. But...' she looked at her watch, 'he's been gone a really long time.'

'He got up early, did he?' He nudged her, shoulder to shoulder and began to laugh. 'Well, it's about time the two of you found some happiness. You both deserve it and I'd say there's been quite a lack of happiness around this place for the past few years.'

Looking down, she felt herself blush, didn't know how to respond, and decided to stay quiet in the hope that Bobby would see her discomfort, and change the subject.

'Come on then.' Standing up, Bobby held a hand out towards her. 'Seeing as this one isn't too sick to eat, we'll put him in the barrow, give him a ride, take him back to the kitchen. I'm sure both Cookie and Anna will want to make a fuss, and then...' He put his cap back on his head. 'I'll need to be getting on.' He held up an arm, swept it outwards and towards the grounds. 'There are things I need to do, before it's too late...' He paused, stared wistfully towards the lake, 'Everything's changed... and Lizzie... it'll never be the same. No matter how much we wish it were.'

45

LIZZIE

Ten years earlier

Feeling exasperated, I stand to one side of the patio, doing all I can to take in the ambience while all the time allowing the smell of incense to stimulate my senses. Each pot is a mixture of sage, lavender, and mint. A scent that's filled the air with a heavy, exotic smokiness, an idea Thomas had used to disguise the distinctive smell of cannabis that was already doing the rounds and being circulated by most of the others.

'This is good shit, isn't it?' Timothy took a drag of the joint, held it up in the air, then covered his mouth with a hand as he realised how loud his Scottish drawl had just sounded. 'Hey. Here. You want some of this.' I see the way he nudges Lucy, holds the joint out to her, then pulls a face as she quickly dismisses it.

'Darling, do I look like I want your second-hand joints?' She takes a step back, lifts a glass of champagne from a tray and throws him one of her dirtiest looks. 'This dress, it's a Norma Kamali, cost me a damn fortune and the last thing I want is for it to stink of bloody weed.' Amused, I watch as she runs a hand across the bright red, one shoulder dress and gives him a shimmy, just for effect. 'Gorgeous, isn't it?' Lifting the sunglasses from the top of her head, and even though the darkness was pulling in all around them, she places them over her eyes, gives him a broad, flickering smile. 'Jessica might want a drag though, she's always up for getting high.' Reaching up to where Jessica is dancing on a chair beside her, I see the way she playfully pushes a hand up the skirt of her dress. 'Jessica darling, Timothy has something for you.'

Standing back, I'm all alone. It's where I always prefer to be, something I'm used to and after many years of feeling like an imposter in the crowd, I realise how much pleasure I get from watching the others. How much I can learn from each and every one of them. Tonight, for the first time since Tilly died, Jordan has joined us. He's the one person I'd rather stay away from, and nervously, I've kept an eye on the way he keeps pacing moodily around the patio, While I've done all I can to keep him at a distance, I realise that I've already heard one too many of his excuses and can't bear to hear any more of his persistent moaning. They're stories that seemed to change every time I speak to him and now I'm no longer sure which story to believe. With annoyance, I watch the way he lifts the champagne to his lips. He's drinking directly from the bottle and unlike most of the other men who've dressed for the occasion and are wearing dinner suits with crisp white shirts and bow ties in various colours, Jordan has thrown on a pair of black jeans, a lightly patterned shirt, a pair of black sneakers. Interested I've watched the way he moves from person to person, has a brief interaction, then quickly moves on to the next. Whereas Jessica seems more than happy to drape herself across Lucy for all to see. The two of them have been dancing with no inhibitions, no boundaries, and feeling envious, I watch the way they kiss, wish I could be more like them, more in tune, more in love.

I'm not silly and I do realise just how many drugs they've been taking. I've watched as they've passed tiny pieces of blotter between themselves, carefully placing it on their tongues and smiling infectiously as the effects slowly take over their minds.

Deep inside, I'd love to do nothing more than join them, stand on a chair and with the live band playing in the background, I'd like to dance with the freedom they obviously feel. But to do that would mean taking the drugs and after the last time, I'm not sure I can. I didn't like the way they'd made me feel, the panic that had taken over my mind, or the hallucinations that followed.

Everywhere I look there's a smartly dressed waiter, a tray of champagne, appetisers that Cookie has been making for days and at least a hundred of Thomas's friends, relations, and staff who are all mingling together to form the biggest crowd I've ever seen at the Manor. Nervously, I smooth down my black, borrowed, evening dress, pull back my shoulders, and with a deep, inward breath. I wonder if this is how an actress feels as she walks onto a stage, all the eyes upon her. And even though I still haven't forgiven Thomas for the way he's treated William, for how tribal he was, the evil I saw in his eyes or for how the so-called game was played out just a few nights before, I still do all I can to give him what I hope comes across as one of my warmest, most radiant smiles.

Searching the crowd, I wonder if William is here. Or whether he'll stay in his room, just as he has since the night of the bonfire. Running my eyes quickly across the upstairs windows, I stop when I reach the one belonging to William. He's stood, with his hands on the ledge, looking out. Lifting a hand, I give him a timid half wave.

Only to drop it just as quickly as I see Ada walk up beside him, where she now stands, glaring out. Her face is full of animosity, a look that makes me take a step backward. I move as far out of her view as I can, only to turn and see the slow, provocative dance, that Thomas had just begun with Lucy and embarrassingly, the way our friends have formed a ring to surround them.

Shrinking into the background, I can't help but look back up at William's window, to see the way Ada turns theatrically, gives me a flick of her hair. It's an act I'm quite accustomed to and know that once Ada has decided what should or shouldn't happen, there was nothing I could do to change her mind. No matter how much I tried. After all, she thought I was feral, said that I didn't fit in and my dreams of belonging to this family, or of making a life with Thomas had now been firmly placed in my past. And all I wanted now was to get through this night and then leave with my dignity fully intact.

With one eye on Thomas, I hold my breath as he lets go of Lucy, climbs up and onto a chair, and confidently taps the side of a champagne glass with a knife. Jumping on the spot, I see the way he's begun to laugh hysterically, that the glass has shattered in his hand, and now he's stood there, with just the broken stem to hold onto. 'Oops, one down...' He turns to Jessica, carefully passes her the broken pieces, 'Be a darling, go get me another.' He pauses and everyone in the crowd sees the look of disgust that Jessica gives him. It's more than obvious that she too hasn't appreciated his dance with Lucy. And when she doesn't do what he asks, I see him flush with colour.

Leaning against the patio doors, I close my eyes. I want the floor to open up, for it to swallow me whole and with every ounce of concentration, I listen to the live band playing in the grand hall, behind me. Amusingly, they're successfully managing to drown out Thomas's speech. Each of the trio playing a mixture of instruments. Some of the songs are accompanied by guitars or keyboards. Others are sung a cappella, their harmonies perfect. And cleverly they go from modern to classical in what feels like the blink of an eye.

'...Lastly, I'd like to thank you all for being here. Now, please go and drink the champagne that my parents have generously provided.' A round of applause marks the end of the speech and I hold my breath. Now was the moment that Thomas and I have spoken of. The time he's going to walk across the patio and take my hand in front of everyone. It's a dance we've practised so many times and I hope that Ada is watching. That she comes to realise that I do know how to behave in public and that I'm not quite as feral as she thought.

'Lucy,' Thomas unexpectedly said, 'come on my darling, if you'd do me the pleasure. Let's show them a few more of our moves, shall we?'

With the words cutting through me like a knife, I feel the tears spring to my eyes. I feel confused, rejected. And with my heart feeling as though it's about to be torn from my chest, I make for the lake, run as fast as I can. In the distance I can see Bobby; he's pacing up and down, mobile phone in his hand. With a moment's indecision, I try to decide whether to run towards him or to divert towards the woods.

'Sorry. Got to go.' Looking uncomfortable, I see him push the phone deep into his pocket, and he strides towards me, puts his hands on my shoulders. 'Hey, come here, what's going on, why are you crying?' Protectively, he folds his arms around me. It's a hold I'm more than happy to fall into and with a sob, I begin to tell him what happened, about how cruel Thomas was and how right at this moment in time he was dancing with Lucy at a time when he should be dancing with me.

'I don't know why I try,' I sob. 'I'll never be good enough, not for Ada and now it looks like I'm not good enough for Thomas either.'

'Oh, my girl.' He pauses. 'I know just how you feel.'

'Bobby. Leave it. I've got this.' Thomas's voice makes us both jump as he bellows loudly above the music. His bow tie is uncharacteristically undone and it now hangs loosely around his collar, almost discarded. 'Lizzie, come on. I'm so sorry. Don't do this, don't get upset. Not here, not tonight.' They're the words I wanted to hear, but they feel just a little too late.

'Get off me.' Humiliated, I can feel Thomas's hand on mine. He's begun dragging me across the grounds like a child. It's one thing too many and my heart has taken on the percussion of a hammer drill, especially as I can see how many people have already turned. They're watching and I hate it. Kicking out, I catch him on the back of the leg. Smirk as I see the muddy footprint spoil his suit. 'You are not doing this Thomas, now do as I say and let me go.'

'Lizzie, seriously, stop it. We need to talk.' He turned, held his nose close to mine. I can feel his breath on my cheek, the sour smell of ethanol on his breath. It hits me in the face, makes me want to retch but instead, I hold my breath and glare at him with a look of detest. Until he looks away and once again, he tightens his grip.

'Oh, you want me to stop, do you?' Painfully, I yank my wrist out of his hand, take a swipe in his direction, and hear his yelp, as the flat of my hand catches his cheek. 'Oh, I'll stop alright. In fact, I have no idea why I'm still here.' Pulling my phone from my bag, I begin to flick through my contacts, I'm hoping that one of them jumps out at me, that I can find just one person I could rely on. One person who'll come for me and take me home.

'What are you doing?' Thomas shouts angrily. 'Put it down and Lizzie, put it down now.'

I hold the phone out of his reach, continue my search. 'I don't care what you say. I'm going home.' Desperately, I keep flicking through the numbers and feel tears flood my eyes as I realise there's no one I can call, no one who'd come and get me and because of that, I have only two choices. I either have to drive my car after drinking champagne, or stay for just one more night and wait until morning.

'Don't be crazy.' Thomas's voice moves up an octave as we move through the house, past the musicians who seemingly continue to play, no matter what happens in the room beside them. Pushing open the library door, and with a hand on my shoulder, he spins me around and even though I don't want to enter the room, he pushes me from behind. 'God damn it, let me explain.'

I blink repeatedly as the light is flicked on and as I practically fall into the room with tear-filled eyes, I realise now how stupid I've been, how much I've held onto the dream of being in love, of becoming Thomas's wife and how desperate I must have been just to be loved. 'Thomas, there's nothing you can say. Not any more.' I pause, flare my nostrils angrily, and point at the door. 'You were supposed to dance with me.' I go to slam out of the room but remember that the dress I'm wearing belongs to his mother and whether I like it or not, it's designer, expensive, and even if I wanted to storm out of the Manor in an explosive manner, I couldn't possibly take the dress with me. Or could I?

'Lizzie, come on.' He lets out a long sigh, pulls open a cupboard, points to the two large bags that are piled up inside.

Feeling confused, I'm unsure what they are, and I step forward to take a better look. 'What's going on? What am I looking at?'

With a smile, Thomas pulls me towards him and while staring suspiciously at the bags, I allow it. My resistance has gone. I no longer have the will to run, or the desire to escape. What I really want is for Thomas to love me, to revert back to being the man I'd fallen for and embarrassingly, I hear a sob leave my throat. Hate myself for feeling so needy but give him a smile as he lifts a hand, pushes my hair back into place. Leaning in, I feel his lips touch mine and for a moment, I close my eyes, remember why I'm here.

'They're for us, silly.' Once again, his lips grazed mine. 'We talked about it, didn't we? We've always said we'd leave, right after graduation. Get ourselves a little bit married, travel around the world.' He pauses, pulls one of the bags out of the cupboard, unzips it and shows me a pile of paperwork, two burgundy passports. 'I thought it was what you wanted.'

'But...' I furrow my brow and point at the door. 'Out there, you... you danced with Lucy. You... I mean. You did it in front of everyone.' I thought back to the dance, to the way Thomas made sure that everyone, including Ada, had seen.

'Of course I did.' Looking directly at me, I can see the sparkle within his eyes. The smile that crosses his face. 'I have to make them think they've won. But they didn't. They can't know we're leaving. Not until we've gone. And I've arranged it all. You've seen Jordan, haven't you? He's taking us to the airport and by this time tomorrow, we'll be stood on a beach, drinking cocktails.' A gentle smile lit up his face, 'Just imagine it, Lizzie. Sun, sea... it'll be perfect.'

I look from one side of the room to the other. Try not to look too excited as my eyes travel across the thousands of books that line the walls, the many that depict other countries, and deep inside I try to work out where we're going. 'You did say the word "married", didn't you?'

'Absolutely, just as soon as we can arrange it.' He takes my hands in his, holds me close, and for just a moment, I have the man I want. I have the love I've always wanted. And I consider just doing what he says and leaving with him. Until common sense kicks in and I begin to panic about the reality of what we're about to do.

'But I didn't pack. I don't even have a dress.' I pull myself out of his arms, begin to pace around the room. Feel the excitement diminish. 'Thomas. Every girl needs a wedding dress and I need my things and... and what about my dad, he'll be furious.' Biting down on my lip, I head toward the door. 'I can't just leave without telling him. I have to speak to him.' Lifting up my phone, I see the red battery symbol flash up on the screen. The phone is dead and ironically, at a moment I need it the most, it needs to be charged.

'Listen, I already spoke to him. He knows exactly what's happening and he's fine with it all.' With a swift movement, he reaches up, pulls me towards him. 'Now come on, have some fun with me.' Capturing my eyes with his, he holds out a clenched hand. Bites down on his bottom lip, then unclenches his fingers to show four small, white squares, each one printed with a red love heart. 'Stick a couple of these on your tongue, come for the ride. We'll take it together.' Tenderly, I feel his mouth move along my skin. He starts placing the kisses along my neck, then slowly moves to my mouth 'You always want to join in, but barely ever do... but tonight...' I open my eyes, to see him staring directly into mine. 'I want you to come with me.'

With trepidation, my whole body begins to shake. I don't like the feeling of being out of control and clearly remember the last time I took the drug, I only took the one, not two, and even with a small amount, the palpitations began. And after the initial fun, the vivid hallucinations had chased themselves around my mind for hours, along with the nausea that had left me to sleep on a bathroom floor, too terrified to move.

Picking the small square of paper up, I study it. 'Thomas...' I shake my head, press my lips tightly together. 'I don't think I can... I don't...' Constantly, I think of the times I've wanted to be like the others, the way I've always wanted to be a part of the crowd and I swallow repeatedly as Thomas places two of the squares on his tongue, then immediately his mouth is on mine, his tongue darts in and out of my mouth and with his fingers gently stroking my neck, I have no choice but to swallow.

46

ELIZABETH

Present Day - Monday Morning

'Oh Freya, I'll be sad to see you go.'

Sidestepping the kitchen counter, Elizabeth saw the way Freya hesitated, wouldn't quite look her in the eye and instead, she fussed Louisa, and even though it was a fruitless task, she continually tidied her pram blankets.

'And this little one.' Elizabeth looked towards Freya before also turning her attention to Louisa who with feet kicking around in the air was determined not to be covered up. 'You must be so proud of yourself, she's just adorable.' She paused, laughed, tried to understand why Freya was acting so strange, why the tension in the room had changed. 'Well, she's adorable when she isn't crying.'

'Oh, they all go through it. Some days are good, others not so. It's just a little exhausting when you're trying to cope on your own, and the friction that's been flying around this place for the last few days, well, it seriously didn't help matters. Did it?' Freya snapped, readjusted Louisa's blanket. 'Next time I see you, this one'll probably be driving a car and you, well you'll more than likely have a few of your own, don't you think?' With raised eyebrows, she took in a deep breath. 'Anyhow, it looks like you got what you always wanted, doesn't it?' She whispered. 'You went and got yourself attached to this house. Might not be with the original brother you went for, but I expect it'll all turn out in the wash. Now, won't it?'

Feeling the colour tinge her cheeks, Elizabeth felt the impact of the words, kept her eyes firmly on Alfie. He'd taken up residence in his old corner of the kitchen and now lay on a blanket that Cookie had provided.

Kneeling, Freya reached forward, gently ran a hand over Alfie's back. 'And you,' she tipped her head to one side and through glazed eyes, she dropped a single kiss on the top of his head. 'You be a good boy for Cookie, won't you?'

'Oh, he'll be fine,' Cookie said hopefully. She'd made herself a seat on the floor next to his bed and was handfeeding him small cubes of chicken that had been chopped up and placed in a tiny aluminium bowl. 'We'll build you back up. Won't we, Alfie?' She nodded determinedly and with her bottom lip trembling, she lifted up the corner of her apron and dabbed at her eyes.

'And darlings, we're off too.' Lucy strode into the kitchen, wearing her tight black leather trousers and high-heel boots. 'I have to get back to the office, but, mwah... mwah...' She leaned into Freya, kissed her on both cheeks. 'It's been so lovely to see you darling.' With a swish of her military-style jacket, she threw it over her shoulders. 'I just wish the weekend had been just a little bit more fun, but there you go. Maybe we should try and do it again.' She paused, thought about what she'd just said. 'Or maybe not. Now... has anyone seen William? I must say goodbye before I go.' She lifted a hand to her mouth, blew kisses around the room. 'And Timothy darling, could you be a love, help me out to the car?'

Feeling relieved that the others were leaving, Elizabeth stared out of the window where Bobby paced back and forth beside the greenhouse, a mobile phone pressed tightly to one ear. It was a sight that took her back to the night of the party, to the moment she'd bumped into him near the lake.

Excusing herself, Elizabeth quickly left the kitchen, moved down the passage and into the hallway where Henry and Patty were stacking cases one on top of the other. 'If you bring the car, I could wait here.' Patty lifted a handbag, threw it over her shoulder. 'Actually, forget it. I'll do it myself.' She strutted across the hallway, left Henry to guard the bags. 'I'll be just five minutes.'

'Right, well,' Elizabeth said. 'It looks like you were planning on staying for a lot longer than three days...' She gave him an awkward smile. 'I'm just off to pack myself, so...' With one finger pointing at the stairs, she did all she could to walk straight past, caught the sorrowful look behind Henry's eyes.

'Lizzie...'

Stopping in her tracks, Elizabeth took in a deep breath and felt herself bristle. William had been right; the memorial had been a bad idea. Nothing good had come out of having Thomas's friends here for the weekend.

'Look, I'm happy for you.' He pressed his lips tightly together. 'Just take it steady, okay.' He held out his arms, pulled her into an unnecessary hug.

Feeling more than uncomfortable, Elizabeth held her breath, waited for the moment to pass. Then felt Henry jump as Patty's face appeared in the doorway.

'Come on Henry, hurry up. You could have at least carried the bags down to the driveway.' She rolled her eyes, gave Elizabeth a smug, self-righteous smile. 'You just can't get a man to do what you want these days, can you?' She tipped her head to one side, laughed at her own joke. 'Well, apart from you. You seem to have William just drooling at your feet.'

'Patty...' Henry threw her a warning tone.

'What? Don't speak to me like that; you always said she was out to trap herself a Kirkwood and now she has. I'm only saying what everyone else is talking about. Why be so coy about it?' Overdramatically, she spun on the spot. 'Anyhow, let's go. Mummy's expecting us for dinner.'

Swallowing hard, Elizabeth angrily bit down on her tongue. Decided that it was easier to stay quiet rather than argue or fight her own corner. And without caring which step she stood on, or how many creaks the staircase made, she stamped up them all, let herself into Thomas's room.

Furiously, she travelled around the room at speed and with tears filling her eyes, she grabbed at her things and dropped them into her case. Each item was thrown with force as her temper accelerated. 'Why, why do they all have to be so nasty? Why can't I be happy too?' She cried out as she scooped makeup from the dressing table, threw it towards her case, cringed as it dropped from the bed, scattered itself around the floor, beside Ada's archaic trunk.

Puffing up her cheeks, she blew out slowly and noticed the way her fingers trembled with temper. 'They're not worth it.' Closing her eyes for a beat, she perched against the bed, did all she could to calm herself down, and while giving the room a last resentful look, she dropped her gaze to the trunk, stared accusingly at the out-dated Nokia phone that still lay on top.

47

ELIZABETH

Present Day - Monday Morning

With the phone in her hand, Elizabeth headed back towards the cottage, dodged the raindrops that had just begun to fall, and with a relief that she'd escaped the others, she pushed the front door open and slammed it behind her.

With her back against the door, she looked down at the phone, gave it a shake, and willed it to work. Suspiciously, she looked up and down the stairs, listened to the sounds of the house. It had a way of creaking all by itself, as though moving in the breeze. William still wasn't home, and feeling concerned, she checked her own phone, looked for a missed call and thought back to the previous day, to the time right after Jordan had been found, the way she'd made every attempt to call the Manor, to get the help they'd needed and the lack of signal that had thwarted all of their efforts.

Glancing at the clock, she decided to give it an hour. To wait for him to return. *He's a grown man, quite capable of looking after himself* she told herself and she knew it were true, but then twenty-four-hours ago, she'd have said the same about Jordan. And with that thought buzzing around in the back of her mind, she ran to the top of the stairs, peered out through the upstairs window, and checked the path that ran by the river.

Pacing slowly up and down the upper landing, she cast her eyes up to the artexed ceiling, to where a small square of wood was surrounded by a white architrave frame. It was the place where William had said the chargers were stored, but the door was high, one she couldn't easily reach or open and a very different kind of attic space than the one at the Manor.

Wandering back down the stairs, she felt defeated and padded into the kitchen. It was a small room but bigger than the one she had at home, surrounded by pine-coloured cabinets, built-in appliances, and a small but adequate cooker. Immediately, her hand went out to a small pine table, where her fingertips rubbed against its varnished surface before dropping down to its four wooden stools that were tucked neatly beneath.

Pulling out one of the stools, she sat down, drummed her fingers up and down on the table's surface, and tried to imagine making dinner for both her and William, a breakfast, brunch, or maybe even a midnight snack. 'Or maybe, a snack with a bottle of wine?' She reached forward, pulled a bottle from the rack, studied the label. 'Amarone Valpolicella Magnum 2018.' Nodding appreciatively, she pushed it back. 'Very nice. I wouldn't mind a glass or two of that, just as soon as William gets home.' Wishfully, she stared at her phone, jumped backwards as it bleeped.

Running late, hope you're making yourself at home. xx

As though taking his words as permission, Elizabeth jumped

up, grabbed hold of the bar stool, tested it for strength and with a fortitude she didn't know she had, she dragged it up the stairs where on tiptoes, she balanced on top, opened the loft hatch, and felt relieved to see a drop-down metal step ladder.

After much poking around, and shining the torch from her phone around in circles, she finally located the box she wanted. Lifting it slowly down each of the metal ladder steps, one at a time, she balanced it precariously before finally reaching the bottom and carrying it downstairs, where she dropped the box on the living room floor and pushed the contents from side to side. 'Nope, nope...'

She wasn't sure what secrets the phone might hold but knew for a fact that Ada wouldn't have kept it, not unless there was a reason to do so, and with that thought in mind, she lifted one cable out of the box after the other until finally, she found one that fit, and excitedly, she connected the phone to the mains, and watched the phone's screen, hoping for something to happen.

48

LIZZIE

Ten years before

Heading down to the lake, I dance in circles, feel the palpitations thrumming around inside my chest. Everything is happening at speed. With amusement, I feel as though I'm stood on a motorway, the cars flashing by me. For the first time in my life, I'm oblivious to it all; I don't care what's happening or how much danger I'm in. All I can think is that my life will change. We'll no longer be here. We'll no longer be told what to do or be surrounded by any of the others with their sharp tone or strong opinions.

Flopping onto the grass I feel the moisture soak through Ada's dress. I begin to giggle hysterically, know how annoyed she will be and then, with my arms held high above my head, I lie back and smile as Thomas lands heavily on the grass beside me. He's already peeling off the layers of his suit. The bow tie came off in the library, as did the cuff links and jacket. It's a look I find amusing and I kneel up behind him, lift his hands up and down by pulling on the long cuffs of his shirt sleeves while laughing hysterically. In my mind, he's a marionette and I'm using the cuffs as the strings, making his hands wobble around in the air.

'We're going in there.' He gives me a winsome smile, bats his eyelashes in an over exaggerated way and with shaking fingers, he pulls his hands free, begins to undo his shirt. Throwing it in the air, we both watch the way it floats down to where it lands haphazardly on a nearby bush. The first item of his clothing, that's quickly followed by the rest.

Even though I don't remember it happening, I'm naked. The dress has gone, and my underwear abandoned and suddenly I'm totally alone. Looking up, I sigh and, in an attempt, to amuse myself, I spin around in circles, my arms are held outwards, and I look up to look at the stars which are poking through a grey and overcast sky like tiny pin spot diamonds that I wish I could touch.

Staring intently, I realise that the sporadic sound of music can still be heard. Spotting the vocalist, I watch the way he walks to the doors, pokes his head through them and tries to gauge how many guests remain. Turning to the other two musicians, he seems to begin a debate. But after a few whispered words, they continue to play, even though the house has now emptied, and our last few remaining close friends are having parties of their own, none of which look as though they'll be ending at any time soon.

Slowly, I lower myself into the lake, swim though putrid-smelling water, make my way to its centre and through dazed, intoxicated eyes, I focus on the fire baskets. They're scattered around the gardens and excitedly I laugh as I see sparks shoot wildly upwards in colours of bright orange and red. I stare through the inferno of fire and imagine music bouncing towards me. It's animated. In the shape of quavers and crochets. Each one looks like the biggest of helium balloons. They're all different in size. And while laughing, I take wide-eyed pleasure in the eerie reflections of an overhanging willow. It reaches out and over the lake. Has long, spindly branches that droop downward until they touch the water to create a dangerous and boggy edge to the lake.

'Thomas... where are you?' I shout as loud as I can. I can't understand where he's gone, or why I'm alone. But quickly, I disregard the thought, throw my head backwards and immediately I feel the coldness of the water seep into my scalp, while all the time I'm watching bright, well strung tree lights. They're scattered around the garden but suddenly they begin to dim and as I watch it happen, a deep sadness overtakes my thoughts as one string after the other turns from dim, to dark.

Holding out cautious fingers, I reach for the old wooden diving platform but turn away as I spot partially naked bodies. They're lying between the reeds and moving past them I see Henry; he's naked and scrambling around on his hands and knees. I giggle at the sight. He reminds me of a baby orangutang, with his bare backside moving from side to side, shining up in the moonlight.

'Thomas, this isn't funny any more. You're scaring me.' The warmth I'd previously had has diminished. The feeling of being free and unrestrained has disappeared and now, all I feel is cold, scared, and alone.

Standing close to the edge of the lake, I turn in circles and squint in a frugal attempt to focus on the darkness. Slowly, as I hear familiar voices, I search the side of the lake. I'm fully expecting to see Thomas with his arms full of champagne and a wicker basket full to the brim of warm, floury bread, or leftover buffet.

While listening, I see the familiar shape of Lucy. She's naked and creeping around on tiptoes. Initially she has an arm held protectively across her breasts, until a look of mischief crosses her face and she sweeps a hand through her hair and tosses it seductively over her shoulder.

'Lucy,' I shout, 'have you seen Thomas? I... well, I seem to have lost him.' I ignore her nudity, kick my feet out behind me, float towards her and watch the way she spins around, shrugging her shoulders.

'Darling, isn't he with you? He's always with you. Isn't he?' Lucy's voice quivers as she shouts. She's obviously cold. 'Unless of course he's dancing with me.' She laughs out loud, but then stops. 'My clothes have gone... vamoose... disappeared.' Watching her, I see the way she begins to crawl on her hands and knees in search of clothes until she reaches beneath a bush, pulls out an old, damp shirt and gives it a suspicious sniff. 'My dress, the bright-red one. I left it here and it should still be here. God damn it.' Reluctantly, she pulls the damp shirt over her shoulders, turns back to the lake.

'Where's Jessica?' I begin to wonder if she's with Thomas.

'Oh, I don't know. I think she went to get food, oh... and champagne. We'd run out of champagne. All this sex, it makes you hungry darling, doesn't it?' Spinning on the spot, she lifts her face to the moonlight and for a moment, I appreciate the shape of her perfect body, and the way the shirt now drapes over her pert, naked breasts. And for a moment, I'm in a world of my own, a world where nothing matters and only the sound of Lucy laughing brings me back to the present. 'He probably thinks we'll end up walking back to the house, naked. Give old man Kirkwood an eye full. But personally, I doubt his ticker would take it.'

Laying back, I scull at the water. Disappointment sweeps over me, and I wonder if Thomas really did go back to the house, whether he's doing what he promised and collecting the bags, getting them ready for our great escape. It's a thought that makes my mind dance in time with the music. I'm swaying dreamily, looking up at stars that are suddenly so bright I can barely look at them and with a sudden rush of colour, they begin speeding towards me. It's my very own firework display. One hallucination too many.

Sighing, I move slowly towards the embankment and excitedly, I decide that I want to dance. And with wide-open eyes, I can imagine myself doing pirouettes around the lake, like the ballerina I wish I'd become.

Shivering, I climb out of the water and as though dancing through a mist, I move around on tiptoes, my body naked for all to see, and with my arms in the air, I dance enthusiastically, and even though I'm totally alone, I feel invincible, as though there's nothing I can't do.

49

ELIZABETH

Present Day - Monday Morning

Elizabeth listened to the voicemail, over and over. Then, cautiously, she read through each of the messages, saw the retorts, and through wide open eyes, she stared at the phone.

With her stomach twisting with disbelief, she swallowed hard, felt her mouth turn dry, and couldn't stop the palpitations that had begun inside. It was as though her heart was in a race of its own. Her eye began to twitch, her breathing accelerated, and her feet felt as though they'd been nailed to the floor. Even if she wanted to, she couldn't move. Couldn't react. Could barely breathe.

Watching the clock tick from minute to minute, she went over and over what she'd read. The voice she'd heard. 'How do I tell William; the phone was Ada's?'

The voicemail she'd heard had been damning. The tone she'd heard was serious and she was under no illusion that Ada had heard it too.

Reflectively, Elizabeth once again clicked play. Concentrated on the animosity. On the way the threat was delivered, considered all the reasons behind the words. *Just because they were said, it doesn't mean they were true.* Pacing, she wished that William would return but couldn't decide whether to tell him what she'd heard. She knew it could break him in two. That his whole life could change and everything he'd known before would be different.

With her mind in turmoil, she began to panic. Pushed the box of old remotes and leads back into the loft, moved the bar stool back where it came from in the kitchen. Everything looked as it had when William had left and just for effect, she flicked on the kettle, pulled two matching mugs from the cupboard, and waited patiently.

Standing there with her foot tapping on the floor, she began to concentrate on where the oversized kitchen clock hung on the back wall, its fingers bouncing into position as one tick after the other echoed around the room. The waiting had no end. The tension built inside her. And while thrumming her fingers against the table, she picked up a magazine, flicked her way through it but couldn't focus on a single image. With one eye firmly placed on the front door, the palpitations became worse than before.

'I'll destroy the phone or I'll damage the battery,' Elizabeth yelled. 'He'll never know the truth...' She knew it was the wrong thing to do. William deserved the truth. Glancing up the stairs, memories of the night before pinged through her mind. She felt a small, flickering smile cross her face and as she took in a deep intake of breath. She remembered the way William's hand had travelled across her, teased her, aroused her in a way she'd never known before. Until she remembered his words and felt them hit her with force, 'But there can't be any secrets. Not between us. Not if...'

It was a mantra. Something she knew she had to stick by and unable to bear the tension any longer, Elizabeth left the cottage and went in search of William.

Keeping as far away from the Manor as she possibly could, she found herself taking the route through the middle meadow where she found herself ducking behind the old oak tree and hiding behind it the moment she heard a noise.

Surreptitiously, she kept her eye on the front door and saw Timothy emerge. He walked purposely down the steps to hover around beside a Range Rover, his hand pensively rubbing at his beard, taking one last look at the house.

Feeling relieved she hadn't been seen, Elizabeth counted the seconds as Timothy climbed into the vehicle and drove towards those big, cast-iron gates. They were the same gates she'd driven through just three days before. Gates she knew she'd have to drive through again and with her hand resting on the phone, she tried to work out whether today would be her last day at the Manor, whether this phone and its messages would ruin everything.

Slumping back against the tree, she kept her eyes on the woods. It looked as though the police had left; their van was no longer parked near the monument. A small indication that life at the Manor might just return to their new normal. Whatever a new normal was meant to be.

'Lizzie, are you okay?'

The sound of Bobby's voice made her legs turn weak. Her hand went to the tree where frantically, she tried to hold onto the bark. 'Bobby, I... yes, I'm fine.' She tried to sound normal, tried to look him in the eye. But her breathing felt stilted. The weight once again pressed down on her shoulders and anxiously, she moved from foot to foot, wishing for William to emerge from the woods.

'Well, you don't look very fine.' Bobby gave her a look of

concern. 'Do I need to go get my wheelbarrow, give you a lift to the Manor, like I did Alfie?' He laughed at his own joke, pointed at the house. 'He's doing much better since Cookie took to hand feeding him small pieces of chicken. But then again, who wouldn't? He gets fed every twenty minutes he does and he's loving every minute.'

'Sorry, Bobby. I have to go.' She turned, began to move, heard the thud by her feet.

'Oh, wait on Lizzie. You dropped something.'

Frantically, her hand went to her pocket. She felt for the phone and with nausea turning her stomach, she felt her skin turn numb with fear. Praying that she wouldn't vomit, her eyes travelled from where the phone lay, up Bobby's wellingtons, and to where his face had drained of colour. 'Where did you get that?' he snapped with a voice full of emotion as he leaned over and picked the phone up.

Taking a step back, it became more than obvious that Bobby knew what the phone was, *whose* it was, and also what was on it. A painful silence filled the air and Elizabeth stared at the ground. 'Bobby...' her voice was barely a whisper, 'I'm sure there's an explanation, a reason why you said those things. Why you made that threat and...' She shook her head; still didn't want to believe what she'd heard, the threats Bobby had made. 'And I know Ada was difficult, but...' She stared at the phone, watched the way Bobby held it with shaking hands. 'Bobby, please tell me you didn't do it. Please tell me you didn't kill Thomas.' The words fell from her lips and in shock, she lifted a hand to her mouth, wished she could retract, take them back. Forget what she'd heard.

Vigorously, he shook his head. Turned the phone over in his hand and for a minute, she thought he'd slam it into the tree, get rid of the evidence. 'I should have known she'd keep this,' he growled. 'I should have known the truth would come out eventually.' He looked across the grounds, towards the woods. 'And my boy, my William. He'll be the one who has to pay.' A long, disturbing sob left his throat. 'None of this is his fault; he can't help who his parents were.'

'Bobby... does William know you're his father?'

Sinking down to sit on the floor, Bobby shook his head. 'Ada, she was the love of my life.' He sobbed. 'There was no one else for me. But this house, it took over her life. And a scandal, well that wouldn't have been allowed, would it?' He hesitated, looked down. 'And falling in love with a gardener, well, that would never have done.' He lifted a hand, wiped a tear away from his cheek. 'I was never enough, was I? Not when she had a husband, with a status.'

Thinking back, Elizabeth remembered the book, *Lady Chatterley's Lover*, the story of a woman falling in love with a gardener and the way it had been slashed, ruined, left in a hole in the floor. William had said that Thomas knew the truth, but the book showed how deeply he'd felt, how much he resented what had happened.

'Bobby. Do you want to hear the voicemails, what's on the phone?'

'No lass,' he said, 'I know what's on it. And no. To answer your question. I didn't kill Thomas.'

'But...' She went back to the voicemail, to the words he'd used. The definite threats he'd made against Thomas.

'I know how it sounds. I know what I said. But I couldn't have hurt him. No more than I could have hurt one of my own.' He passed the phone back to her. 'When James our first born died, it broke us both. And even though I still saw her on a daily basis, we drifted apart. Sometimes we didn't speak for weeks and then, then Thomas was born and... well.' He sighed, gave her a pensive smile. 'I could see how happy it made her. She was a mother. It was the one thing she'd always wanted to be and I... well, I did the right thing and kept out of her way. Then, as though my prayers had been answered, she came to me. It was a hot summer's night. A night when the weather was kind, warm, and fresh and the stars shone out in a cloudless sky.' Lifting a hand, he wiped a tear from his eye. 'It was the happiest night of my life and as a result, my William was born.' He nodded proudly. 'Most men would have taken off. Left her to play happy families with her husband. But I couldn't leave and from a distance, I watched my boy grow.'

'So, if the threat didn't mean anything, why did she keep it?'

Holding his hands out, palms up, he shrugged. 'I said what I did in the heat of the moment. I'd always resented the fact that James had died. That Thomas got everything and that my boy, my William was constantly pushed to one side. Bullied relentlessly. As a father, I wanted to jump in. To protect him from it all. But I had no rights. None at all.'

'It was you, wasn't it? The other night, following me through the woods?'

'Aye lass, that was me.'

'But why, and why did she keep the phone for all these years?'

He laughed nervously, 'It was so I'd never tell the truth of course. She knew how it sounded. Could have had me locked up for years, kept me out of the way, and I knew she'd do it. She'd been a barrister in her time, a good one. Making the evidence stick would have been easy for a woman like her.' He paused, pulled at a blade of grass, placed it between his teeth and chewed anxiously.

Seeing the tension building in Bobby's face, Elizabeth moved a hand to cover his. Held tightly to it. 'Would that have been such a bad thing? For the world to know you were William's father?' She sighed, still didn't want to believe his words had been true.

Once again, Bobby held his hand up and pointed to the Manor in a wand-like fashion, 'Because of this. This house. It meant so much more to her than I did, and she couldn't allow the truth to come out. The will, it would have been contested and Ada, she wouldn't have never risked losing the Manor. Not unless she had to.' He paused thoughtfully, 'My boy. He was dealt a bad card. Thomas made his life hell. But this was his home; as far as he was concerned, he was Dominic's son. So, why shouldn't he inherit it all? It might not have been his birthright, but he did deserve it. And in the end, I had to make sure that happened. Didn't I?'

50

LIZZIE

Ten years before

The silence is far too much. Panic overtakes my mind. I hear a strange yowling noise coming from the other side of the lake. And quickly, I make my way around its edge, hide in the bushes, and almost stumble over two people who are deep in the thrusts of lovemaking, totally oblivious to the fact I'm there.

Without waiting to see who it was, I stagger past. Feel the nausea overtake my mind and without a moment to spare, I feel the acid hit the back of my throat, and the food I'd eaten earlier that day, expels itself from me. Crouching, and with both hands holding onto the floor, I wait for the spasms to pass. Eventually, I turn to see a naked Thomas leaning against the willow and with a warmth rising through me, I sit down on the grass, admire his perfectly chiselled chest, his strong, muscular legs, the way his hand goes to an arousal that even in a moonlight sky is more than noticeable.

With a smile, he reaches behind the tree and then unexpectedly, I hear the soft, gentle giggle, Freya's unmistakeable Irish accent. Naïvely, I feel happy that I've finally found them both and stand up to skip towards them. I'm about to shout out, to tell them I'm there, but feel confused as Freya drops the last of her clothes to the floor. She dances sensuously in front of Thomas, beckons him with a finger, then turns in circles with her arms outstretched, throws her head back in an unrestrained laughter.

It's a sight that makes me close my eyes. It's a sight I don't want to witness and I shake my head vigorously, hope that my vision is just another one of the hallucinations, another part of my subconscious I've chosen to see. Counting to ten, I dare myself to open my eyes, stare back in the direction of the tree. Holding my breath, I watch as Freya straddles his body and begins to rock back and forth as his mouth drops sensuously to her breast.

Stopping in my tracks, I use the tree to hide me. I can't watch what's happening, don't want to believe it's true.

Darling, Thomas has done the rounds with everyone here. More than once. And mark my words, he'll most probably take another round with those who'll let him before he settles down and chooses a wife.

I shrink to the floor, curl up in a ball and with my eyes tightly closed, I hold my hands over my ears, as though by doing so I won't hear the words that bounce back and forth in my memory.

Waking up from a drug-induced darkness, I realise that the last of the beautiful, coloured lights that surrounded the garden are flickering and as I watch, each of the strings go out. I cast my gaze around the shadows to where Thomas still sits, although now he's quiet, still, and all alone. The only sound is that of heavy, determined footsteps. They're approaching where Thomas sits, and I look up to see Bobby striding towards the lake.

51

ELIZABETH

Present Day - Monday Morning

'You were there. I saw you.' Elizabeth jumped up in panic. Looked from the Manor to the lake. Could suddenly see images that tormented her mind. 'That night, I remember you being there...' She furrowed her brow, her breathing accelerated, and defensively, she held both hands outright, wished for a weapon. 'I saw you, you were walking towards the lake, towards the tree where Thomas was found.' Her eyes flickered as rapidly as her mind as she stared into his eyes, looking for answers.

'Then you'll know. It isn't what you're thinking.'

Lifting her hands to her head, she raked them through her hair. 'I... I don't know what to think. I saw him. I saw Thomas, he was right over there.' She pointed to the willow, 'He'd been with Freya, they were... they were.' She spun on the spot. Looked for William. For someone to help. But the grounds were silent and other than smoke bellowing out of a single chimney, the Manor looked almost at peace.

'Lizzie, I swear to God, it wasn't me. I didn't kill him.' Standing up, Bobby turned to the tree, and slammed his hand against it. 'But I do know who did...'

52

LIZZIE

Ten years before

With my eyes tightly closed, I sit on the floor, hold my head in my hands. The drugs are still whirling around inside me, I'm seeing things I shouldn't see, things that can't be real. Things I don't want to see and slowly, I move back towards the lake until I'm sitting on the embankment where I sit and stare at the low hanging willow.

The lovemaking has obviously finished, or maybe it didn't happen at all. I drop my feet back into the water, where I kick them back and forth. The splashing causes a distraction and with a smile I start to believe I'm mistaken. That the vision had been just another crazy hallucination. One my mind had created just like it had the fireworks, the music notes, or the balloons that had floated towards me.

'It didn't happen.' I whisper the words over and over as a long, guttural noise fills the air and fearfully my eyes shoot to the willow, to where I see not one, but two people stood beneath it and as a million scenarios flick through my mind. I wish for an end to this night, for the hallucinations to calm and for a deep cataleptic sleep to overtake my body.

Reluctantly, I lean backwards against the embankment, peer through the branches of the tree, and see Bobby stood there, but he's moving around quickly and has hold of a woman.

She's raging out of control, lashing out at Thomas. It's a tangle of arms and legs, of uncontrollable, thundering anger. An anger Bobby is trying to stop. Then, as a weapon is grabbed from her hand, I see it thrown into a fire basket and automatically, I feel myself move backwards as a sporadic flurry of sparks erupts from within, and a violent, incapacitating shivering begins to overtake me.

'Lucy... did you see that?' Again, I search the embankment. I wait for a response that doesn't come and I soon realise that Lucy has gone, that the band has stopped playing, and the only sound that now penetrates my mind is that of the water perpetually moving around me.

53

ELIZABETH

Present Day - Monday Morning

'Bobby, who was the woman?' Moving backwards, Elizabeth took one step at a time and even though she wanted to run, she didn't know which way to go, where the safety would be, and from somewhere deep inside, she heard herself scream as Bobby grabbed her by the shoulders, looked into her eyes.

'Lizzie, you have to believe me. She didn't mean to do it. She...' He looked up, searched the sky for an answer. 'She'd found drugs. In the library. Was as high as a kite. And I tried to stop her, tried to calm her down. But...' he paused, furrowed his brow as though the memory flashed back. 'It gave her a strength I'd never seen. A strength too powerful for anyone to stop.' He hesitated, swallowed. 'She was just a child. Didn't know what she were doing.'

'Who, Bobby? Who didn't know?'

With the images still racing around in her mind. Elizabeth screwed up her eyes, she could clearly see now what she'd blocked out before, the way Bobby had grabbed hold of the woman, tried to restrain her and with a scream that could have shattered glass, she saw Anna's face lit up by the moonlight.

'Anna... it was Anna.' Closing her eyes, Elizabeth felt ten years of emotion build up inside. Her whole body began to shake, and with a loud, piercing cry, she fell to her knees, felt the sobbing begin.

'Lizzie, please... she was just a child.'

Bobby's voice broke through her emotions and with short, exhausted breaths, she looked at him through tear-filled eyes. 'Bobby, it's a secret too many and we don't have a choice,' she sobbed. 'We have to tell William, the police, we can't keep this to ourselves.'

Nodding, he stood up, began to pace, wrung his hands nervously together. 'Lizzie... tell them it was me. She was just a child... still is one in many ways and I just know she wouldn't survive in prison. It'd kill her... and...'

Elizabeth placed her hands over her ears and wanted nothing more than to block out his words. With images of the last three days flashing up and into her mind, she thought of Ada. Of William. Of how all this would affect him. 'Bobby, we can't do that. Not now she killed Ada too.' She turned to the house. Pointed to the patio. 'Surely... you want justice for the woman you loved?'

Thoughtfully, Bobby looked up at the sky, nodded slowly. 'You're right... Ada does deserve justice. But Lizzie... Anna didn't kill Ada.' He went quiet, stared at the lake, at the memorial beyond. 'I did.'

54

ELIZABETH

Present Day - Monday Morning

It was a confession that Elizabeth had never expected hearing and one she certainly didn't believe. Every inch of her body reacted, and she felt a sharp, indescribable pain tear through her. Her stomach turned and an explosion in her mind asked a million unanswered questions.

Panicking, she scrambled like a sprinter off the blocks. Could feel the ground sway uneasily beneath her feet. And disorientated, she grabbed at the air. At the grass. At anything she could hold onto.

Screaming for William, she dragged her phone from her pocket, held it tightly in her hand, wished for it to dial itself, for it to bring her some help and when she went to stab at the screen, she saw the old Nokia looking back at her. Angrily, she threw it to one side, saw it bounce between the roses, where she stared at it for far too long. Tearing herself away, she once again set off towards the house. She jumped into the air, looked over her shoulder and towards the woods, tried to see if the police were still there, if she could attract their attention, or whether she could scream loud enough that for once in her life, she'd get help at a time when she needed it the most.

Tripping, she stumbled towards the house, could almost touch the stone mullion windows and then, as though a thunderbolt had hit her, she stopped. Realised that Anna would be inside. That the one person she should be running away from, she'd inadvertently run towards. A thought that made Elizabeth freeze, and now she didn't know what she should do, or where she should go.

'Lizzie... wait...' Bobby's wheezing, breathless voice yelled out behind her. His cap had been removed, tossed to one side. His mud-covered wellingtons clumsily thudded through the flowerbeds. 'Lizzie... for your own sake, please, I'm begging you, don't go in there.'

'For my sake, why the hell is it for my sake?' she questioned, kept her back against the wall. Her breathing quickened. She looked from left to right, tried to work out which way she should run and as she grabbed at breath, she held a protective hand out towards him. 'You're mad. Seriously, you're as mad as a bloody hatter and I don't believe you killed Ada... it all... you're just protecting her.'

'Lizzie...'

'No...' It was a shout that came from within her, a deep-seated fear. He'd been a man she'd always considered to be a friend. Someone she'd have previously trusted with her life. 'Why would you hurt her? I... I just don't think you would... for years, you did everything she asked.' She flicked her head to one side, slid her feet backwards. One step at a time.

'You're right. I did love her. But once I realised what she'd asked my boy to do. I hated her with every bone in my body.' Bobby fell to his knees, held his head in his hands and Elizabeth saw the way his whole body heaved with emotion. With his eyes full of tears, Bobby's face contorted, full of remorse. 'If he didn't do what she asked, she was going to expose him...' He stopped, dropped his shoulders. Looked at the floor. 'If he'd done what she asked, he'd have gone to prison. It was a double-edged sword; whatever he did, he'd have lost the Manor. He couldn't win.'

Blinking the tears away, Elizabeth felt her mouth go dry and instinctively, she clenched her fists, ready to fight. 'But she'd have lost it too and...' Disbelievingly, she took a step back, stared at the house. 'She loved this house and I... I just can't imagine her doing that.' Squinting as though she were trying to see the Manor through different eyes, she went over and over Ada's words.

Thomas, he would have never let this house become a hotel. But William, he has a mind of his own. He's very different to the rest of us and God only knows how, he's in charge now. He's changed everything.

With his hands gripped prayer-like, Bobby knelt before her, gave out a long, loud, distressing growl. 'Can't you see it? She was dying. She didn't care any more. All she cared about was Thomas. The fact that he was a Kirkwood and above all else, she wanted revenge for his death. She wanted his killer to pay with her life.'

Retreating, she waved a hand in the air. Could immediately see Ada's face, the uncharacteristic way she'd smiled, welcomed her in. The wide-open arms. It was an image imprinted on her mind, as was the way William had turned on her, the way he'd told her to leave.

Now do as I ask. Get in your God damn car and go. Before you to become a pawn in her God damn games.

They were words she hadn't fully understood and while shuffling her feet slowly backwards, she held her breath, reached out for the Manor, saw the look on Bobby's face, the questioning way his eyes searched hers.

'Bobby. Who did Ada think killed Thomas?'

Closing his eyes, he struggled with the words. Stared at the floor. 'Lizzie, she thought it was you.'

'What?'

Shaking her head from side to side, Elizabeth could barely believe what she heard. That through all that had happened, Ada had still believed her to be the one, the person who'd brought murder and scandal to this family. 'But it wasn't me, I didn't kill him...' She tried to dispel the accusation, wanted to scream it out loud.

'Lizzie, this whole weekend was built on revenge. She wanted you to pay for what she thought you'd done. She told William to kill you, to bury you deep in the woods.' Bobby whispered sadly. 'But William, he couldn't do it... he wouldn't have done it.'

'But what if he had?' Elizabeth felt the tears once again scald her cheeks, and with the sleeve of her arm, she defiantly wiped them away.

'Oh Lizzie, you are naïve. Even a blind man would be able to see how much William loves you. He's always loved you. Surely, you can see that too?'

55

ELIZABETH

Present Day - Monday Morning

With the words hitting her like a thunderbolt, Elizabeth quickened her pace, turned back and forth, and with one eye on Bobby, the other on the house, she knew she couldn't listen to him any more, and had to escape. Turning at speed, her feet went from beneath her, she hit the ground at an alarming rate and felt the pain as the gravel pierced her skin. Everything happened at speed, every part of her hurt. She couldn't move, couldn't stand, saw the back door open and from somewhere inside the house, she heard Anna's voice came through the mist that now surrounded her mind, 'You bastard, you told her.'

Terrified, Elizabeth clawed at the ground, felt the roughness of a grate beneath her fingers, the sound of water gushing down a drain, a loud, piercing screech that came from within the house.

Seeing a pair of feet emerge, Elizabeth blinked frantically. Went to push herself up, saw the way Anna stepped forward, pointed a knife at Bobby. 'You said you'd never tell. You promised me, you gave your word.' She thrust the knife through the air. Took a swipe at his face.

'Anna. I swear to you, I didn't tell her.' Bobby's voice was full of fear, his hands shook relentlessly. 'But that night, she was there. Our Lizzie, she was sat by the lake. She saw what happened, and... and... she's on your side. Aren't you, Lizzie?'

Nodding frantically, Elizabeth took a step forward. 'Please, Anna. Put the knife down.'

'What the hell...' Appearing in the doorway, Cookie her hand held to her chest and screamed as she took in the gravity of what was happening.

'Cookie, no...' Elizabeth yelled. 'Go inside, phone the police.' Holding both hands up, palms out she jumped to her feet, took a step towards Anna. 'Anna, listen to me. We have to phone them. We have to tell them what really happened. I'll stand up for you. I'll tell them what I saw. That you didn't know what you were doing.' She paused, caught the look in Cookie's eye, the obvious confusion she felt. 'We'll speak up for you, won't we Cookie?'

'They won't believe you. Not now. Not after I put the drugs in her whisky.' Anna thrust the knife forward again, forced Bobby to walk backwards, where he now stood in the entrance to the old greenhouse. 'They were supposed to make her happy, make her nice, more tolerable and now, now I've ruined it all. I killed her too.'

'Anna, it wasn't you that killed her. It was me. I killed Ada. Now give me the knife.' Bobby nervously whispered, and held out a hand.

'I don't believe you and I don't have to do anything you say, do you hear me?' She paused, took another step forwards. 'I've listened to you for years and look where it got me.' Once again, she thrust the knife forward. Laughed as Bobby jumped back in terror, caught his back on the old wooden frame, heard the whole green-house creak under the pressure.

Looking up, Elizabeth swallowed hard. She could see fine sawdust falling from the roof, from between the panels that precariously held onto the last remaining sheets of glass and instinctively, she took another step forward, held one hand out to Anna, saw the way she shook her head.

'Lizzie. Don't come any closer, it... it isn't safe.' Bobby shouted the words, kept his eyes firmly fixed on the way Anna waved the knife around before him. 'It doesn't have to end this way, Anna. You need to trust me. I'll help you. Like I did before.' He nodded, 'We'll all help you.'

As though hypnotised by the words, Anna looked down at the knife, then back at Bobby. Tipped her head to one side, began to laugh uncontrollably. Then as quickly as she began, she stopped. Her bottom lip trembled; her gaze became fixed, detached from reality. 'I won't go to prison, Bobby. I... I just can't.'

'Anna, no one blames you,' Elizabeth shouted the lie. Felt her legs weaken, and with every ounce of strength she had left, she held onto the stone mullion windowsill, used it to hold herself upright. 'I took the drugs too. I know how you felt, I know how they affected you.' Fearfully, Elizabeth watched as Bobby reversed into one weakened panel after the other. More dust dropped from the roof; the sound of cracking began.

'Alfie... here boy.' William's voice could be heard bellowing in the distance and with a newfound terror, she looked at the scene before her, didn't know what to think or how to act. All she did know was that William was about to walk into his very own nightmare and with her eyes fixed on Bobby's, she knew he was terrified too.

'Anna, it's William. He's coming...' She had to think quickly. Held her gaze. 'And right now, it's just the four of us. We can keep the secret; between us, we can protect you.' Elizabeth couldn't decide if it were a lie or not, but right now, it didn't matter. All she wanted was for Anna to drop the knife and for them both to come out of the greenhouse. For the whole nightmare to be over.

Holding her breath, Elizabeth glanced to one side. Saw Cookie sidling towards her with eyes full of tears and held out her hand. Took Cookie's hand in her own, then closed her eyes for a beat as Alfie dropped over the step behind her, looked cautiously on.

'Alfie, here boy...' William's voice echoed through the grounds. It was enough to make Alfie take a step forward, and with his tail wagging and his body practically bending in two, Elizabeth caught her breath, and stared at Bobby, who slowly shook his head, before fearfully turning towards her.

'Look after my boy and tell him... tell him how much I loved him.' His words were slow, painful, and then as though charging like a bull, he ran at a central post. Pushed it as hard as he could. It was enough to make the whole structure tremble. A loud, thunderous noise filled the air. Both wood and glass exploded simultaneously, and while clinging to Cookie, Elizabeth heard a shrill, indignant scream fill the air before there was nothing but silence.

56

ELIZABETH

Present Day – Six Months Later

Moving around the kitchen, William spread his hands lovingly across the stainless-steel worktops, swiped them from side to side. 'Can you believe it's ours?' He held a set of keys up in the air, threw her a broad, affectionate smile. 'The kitchen alone is sick.' He whispered, 'Not to mention the golf course attached. I can't wait to get out there, take on a few greens.'

'Well, there's nothing stopping you once you get a gardener, otherwise you'll end up having to mow it all yourself.' Realising what she'd just said, she dropped a box next to his hands on the counter, gave him an apologetic look. 'I'm so sorry. I just...' Still finding it difficult to believe that both Bobby and Anna had been killed, she held a hand up to her mouth, closed her eyes, could still see the exact moment when the dust had settled to reveal two life-less bodies. It had been a sight that had tormented her dreams, along with the howl she'd heard erupt from William's lips and the strange eeriness that had immediately surrounded the hotel just a few moments later.

'For what it's worth,' William pulled her into his arms, dropped a kiss lightly on her lips, 'I think you were right. The Manor was cursed.' Lifting a hand, he held it out, palm up. 'But this is a new start, living here, don't you think?'

Sighing, Elizabeth pointed to the door, to the van that stood outside. 'What I think is that there's still plenty of boxes where this one came from.' She laughed, blew out through puffed up cheeks, then smiled as one of the delivery men plonked another box next to hers.

Slowly, William reached out, allowed his fingers to graze the box, then with a smile, he tore it open. 'Where should we hang this?' Reaching into the box, he pulled the Lowry from within and practically danced around the room, holding it up against each wall in turn. 'This picture, it depicts a normal life, with normal people, going about their everyday business,' he said wistfully, before standing it upright on top of one of the units, where it leaned against the wall. 'I want to see this every single day.' He shook his head, turned to look at her. 'I won't hide it in a corridor, not like I did before.' He paused, reached out to touch her hand. 'I was ashamed of who I was. But now...' He pulled her into an affectionate hold, dropped a kiss on her forehead. 'Now, we can be proud...' He surveyed the room, 'Look at what we have.'

'No, not there. Put that in the dining room.' Cookie's voice suddenly filled the room.

Amused, both Elizabeth and William walked towards the hallway where they saw her stood on the bottom step, barking orders at the removal men. 'No. Don't take them in the house. They're tools. Do they look as though they belong in there? Now take them outside. Put them in the barn.'

'By standing on the stairs,' Elizabeth said to William, with her

shoulder nudging his, 'she thinks she looks taller and more impos-
ing.' They both laughed, and just for a moment, they stood and
watched her and felt pleased with her decision to come with them,
where she'd promised to help Elizabeth with the recruitment and
housekeeping.

'I'll have the linen upstairs, and that box of crockery, that wants
to go in the kitchen.' Cookie shouted with the authority and precision of a sergeant major. 'And don't you go putting it in the wrong
room,' she said. 'We've marked the boxes carefully, there shouldn't
be any mistakes.'

'I'd best go and help before the removal men put their tools
down and go on strike.' Elizabeth gave William a loving smile,
pressed her mouth gently against his. 'Oh. When you get a minute
chef, go and start arranging your kitchen and while you're in there,
stick the kettle on.' Winking, she took her place on the step beside
Cookie. Watched as piece after piece of antique furniture was
slowly lifted in through the front door and into the hallway.

'Ah, the chaise longue.' She pointed to the newly upholstered
settee, remembered the days she used to lie on it in the attic and
the delight she'd felt when they'd found it along with the rocking
chair, the baby's crib, and a number of other items that had all
been piled up in a spare room at Bobby's house, where he'd obviously stashed it rather than taking it to a skip, as Ada had
demanded.

Elizabeth carefully allowed her fingertips to graze each item as
it was carried past. Each piece depicted a time before everything
had gone wrong. A time when her only real worry had been her
charity top purchases and whether or not she'd worn the right
dress to fit in with the crowd.

As the last piece of furniture was carried in through the door,
Elizabeth heard the honk of a horn, the growl of tyres on the

gravel, and looked out to see a second furniture van pull up outside the neighbouring cottages.

With her eyes full of tears, she watched her father climb out of the van, his eyes bright and full of wonder as for the very first time, he laid eyes on the two cottages, one of which he was about to move into. 'Your Aunt Peggy,' he said, 'she's on her way too.'

Elizabeth nodded, pulled her dad into her arms. 'I'm pleased you're here. From now on, we'll all be together. It's what I wanted for such a very long time.' Glancing up at the hotel, she studied its architecture. She didn't think for a moment it held any of the secrets that had been buried within the walls of Kirkwood Manor. But what she did know was that she'd got what she'd always wanted. She'd caught herself a Kirkwood and although it had been a long time coming, her whole family was going to be together. They were going to live in houses that were surrounded by fields and trees... and even though her plan had taken ten years more than she'd ever imagined, she'd now got everything she'd always wanted.

57

LIZZIE

Ten Years Before

In the knowledge that Thomas had pushed the drug into my mouth, that I'd had no choice but to swallow. I realise that once again, he's taken control. He's made me do something he knows I don't want to do. It's a feeling that makes me boil inside and while loathing every movement he makes; it takes all of my effort to smile in his direction. I know what's to come and with my lips pressed tightly together in a terrifying manner, I watch the way he begins to undress. Provocatively, his bow tie is thrown at his mother's desk, along with his cuff links and jacket and for a moment, I revel in the hilarity of how the cuffs on his shirt have doubled in size, how they're now hanging much lower than his hands. Giving him the appearance of a baby orangutang, waiting to play.

'I need the loo.' He presses his lips firmly to mine, smiles. 'I could be a while.'

Him leaving the room gives me the time I need. I want to find the truth before my mind has been overtaken by the drugs, and quickly, I begin to check the bags, the ones he's packed for us both and without hesitation, I pull back the zipper, take the passports from inside, and while nervously looking over my shoulder, I flick through the pages. First, I see Thomas's stern-looking face looking right back. 'He's telling the truth.' I whisper the words disbelievingly; and while nodding and smiling, I flick open the second passport and even though I have no idea how he'd have got hold of my passport. I'm fully expecting to see my plain-looking face, looking back. But instead, it's William's face that's within and suddenly, I realise that Thomas has lied. I've been deceived and no matter how much I wanted it to be true, there will be no beach, no wedding, and certainly no happy ever after.

It's a pain I simply can't bear and as I roll my head around on my shoulders, I can feel the drug taking effect. Slowly, I'm moving through mist. I'm desperate to escape the world I'm currently in. And although I'd been dreading what the drugs would do, now, I hope for it to happen soon, for it to take over my mind and I wonder what hallucination I'll see first. How strong it will be. Whether I'll be flying like before or running away and falling into a fast-flowing river, one I can't seem to escape.

Unusually, I'm amused by the thought of my own demise and while waiting for Thomas to return, I turn to the door to see Anna, stood there peering in.

'Sorry Miss. I was looking for William and well, I saw you in here, wondered if you were okay?'

She'd obviously seen the way I was dancing alone, swaying my arms from side to side and with sadness, I catch sight of the girl she is. She's a girl deeply in love with a man she can't have and ironically, I can see that we're very alike, apart from the fact that I've been allowed to take just a few steps in these shoes, in a life where people have en suites, grounds to walk in, and lakes of their own. It's a lifestyle I like and unlike Anna, who's been shunned by them all, especially by Thomas, who's made it a mission to keep her and William apart.

Beckoning her into the room, I push the door closed behind her and with a mischievous grin, I pull her into a hold. 'Oh Anna, I'm so sorry Thomas is so cruel to you, and to William. You really don't deserve it.' I pause, think. 'You'd make a wonderful couple,' I add for effect, take a step back, and keep hold of her shoulders. 'If only Thomas wasn't around to stop you.' I'm still reeling. Still hating him for what he's done, for the lies he's told and for the dreams he's shattered.

'But Miss...'

I hold a finger to my lips, 'Shush. Anna, it's all going to be okay. I promise. William, he's confided in me. He's told me what you have to do.' I nod, make sure her eyes are fixed on mine. 'He wants you to take these.' I place the remaining five blotters into her hand, 'Put them on your tongue and let them dissolve.' I nod, take one of them from her. Pop it onto my tongue, show the way it's done. I look through the window, directly at the lake. 'He wants you to meet him, down by the lake... in an hour. There's talk of everyone going for a swim.'

I watch the way she grins excitedly and wait until the blotters are firmly placed on her tongue. Then, with a squeeze of her hand, I give her my most genuine smile. 'You'd love to be a part of it all, wouldn't you?' I quickly realise that the passports are still on the desk, and I push them back into the bag in the hope she doesn't notice. 'Thomas, he keeps you and William apart,' I take her hand in mine, 'and he won't stop. You do know that, don't you?' I watch the way she shakes her head, the tormented look that takes over her eyes. 'He's cruel. Nasty and there isn't a single one of his friends that wouldn't want him gone.' I think of all the lies he's told, all the deceitful promises he made and while reeling inside, I use a finger to draw a line across my throat and look up to make sure she understands. 'And personally, it wouldn't surprise me if one of these days he gets exactly what he deserves.'

Right now, I know that Anna hates him just as much as I do. I know I've said enough, and I walk out of the room to leave her with her thoughts... in the knowledge that the drugs and the hallucinations will help her do the rest...

ACKNOWLEDGMENTS

This book has been a difficult one to write and has delved into a world surrounded by drugs and hedonism, of which I knew little about. However, saying that, I have to admit the research has been eye-opening. I would like to thank family members who are employed in professional capacities: my cousin Paul Thomson who is a qualified Clinical Pharmacist and his wonderful partner, Cheryl Donnor, who is a drug and alcohol recovery worker. They have both given me information on drugs over the year and the knowledge I needed to complete this story. Without them, I literally couldn't have completed this story and I'll be eternally grateful.

Each year, hundreds of authors donate books to raise money for Children in Need and I'm proud to say that in 2022, a fabulous £24,061 was raised for the charity. I'd therefore like to say a huge thank you to Ashley Clayton, for the generous donation made to Children in Need, in exchange for a signed copy of my book, The Serial Killers Girl. It's a wonderful charity, one that I'm proud to support and your donation was more than appreciated.

Many thanks to Owston Hall Golf Club, where my promotional videos were filmed. The hotel is set in ancient parkland, and home to Robin Hood Golf Course where my husband, Haydn and his golf buddy Simon play on a regular basis and where myself and Simon's wife, Julie love to sit and watch, while devouring the afternoon teas that are served in the conservatory that overlooks the golf course.

As always, I would like to thank my amazing husband, Haydn for his love and support. He's my absolute rock and I have absolutely no idea what I'd do without him. xx

To the fantastic team at Intec who I work with on a daily basis. I'd like to thank you for keeping me going, for all the hard work you do and for all the laughs we have and the tears we share. You're all amazing. Stuart, Joanne. Haydn, Johnny, Rachel, Janine, Paul, James, Ollie, Mike, and another Paul. Same name, equally as wonderful as the first.

I'd also like to thank friends and family who all keep me going all the time, the support you give me on a daily basis is amazing. Thank you. Therefore, special thanks to Annemarie Brear, Kathy Kilner, Jayne and Alan Stacey, Stuart and Joanne Thompson, Jean Fullerton, Jenny Woodall, Milly Johnson, Chrissie Bradshaw, Amanda James, Mel Hewitt, Jane Lovering, Jane Lacey Crane, Lizzie Lamb, Adrienne Vaughan, and last but definitely not least, the wonderful, Rachel Dove.

To all the team at Boldwood Books: I couldn't do this without you and I literally pinch myself every single day with appreciation that I get to work with the best publisher ever and I'm so proud to be with a company named Publisher of the Year at the RNA Awards in 2021 and Independent Publisher of the Year at the Independent Publishing Awards in 2022. You really do get it right. All of the time.

And last but definitely not least, as always to my fabulous editor Emily Ruston. Emily is just the best: she keeps me on track, helps me to add the sparkle to the story, and knows exactly what each of them needs to give the perfect level of tension.

The Weekend was a concept we came up with together over lunch and I have Emily to thank for the brainstorming session, the original idea we came up with, and the concept behind it. Thank you x

ABOUT THE AUTHOR

L. H. Stacey is the bestselling psychological suspense author of over seven novels. Alongside her writing she is a full-time sales director for an office furniture company and has been a nurse, an emergency first response instructor and a PADI Staff Instructor. She lives near Doncaster with her husband.

Sign up to L. H. Stacey's mailing list for news, competitions and updates on future books.

Visit Lynda's website: http://www.lyndastacey.co.uk/

Follow Lynda on social media:

 facebook.com/LHStaceyauthor

 twitter.com/Lyndastacey

 instagram.com/lynda.stacey

 bookbub.com/authors/lynda-stacey

ALSO BY L. H. STACEY

THE

Murder

LIST

THE MURDER LIST IS A NEWSLETTER DEDICATED TO SPINE-CHILLING FICTION AND GRIPPING PAGE-TURNERS!

SIGN UP TO MAKE SURE YOU'RE ON OUR HIT LIST FOR EXCLUSIVE DEALS, AUTHOR CONTENT, AND COMPETITIONS.

SIGN UP TO OUR NEWSLETTER

BIT.LY/THEMURDERLISTNEWS

Boldwood

Boldwood Books is an award-winning fiction publishing company seeking out the best stories from around the world.

Find out more at www.boldwoodbooks.com

Join our reader community for brilliant books, competitions and offers!

Follow us
@BoldwoodBooks
@TheBoldBookClub

Sign up to our weekly
deals newsletter

https://bit.ly/BoldwoodBNewsletter